I0654538

Our Haunted World

OUR HAUNTED WORLD

Ghost Stories from Around the Globe

Sixteen New and Haunting Stories
from the Americas to Asia

WHITLOCK PUBLISHING
ALFRED, NY

Our Haunted World first published in 2013.

Whitlock Publishing
P.O. Box 472
Alfred, NY 14802

Editorial matter © Allen Grove
"Pestfurlong Hill" © Neil Williams
"The Dancing Water" © Donna Burgess
"Ghost Fleet © Shawn Proctor
"The Church of the Open Sky" © Stephen Gaskell
"Shona" © Dave Siddall
"Three Steps" © Melissa L. Webb
"The Hermits of Hahajima" © Mark Lee Pearson
"House of Dreams" © Michael Sebastian
"Night of the Wild Hunt" © Eliza Granville
"Ghost in the Rear-View" © Jeff Kozzi
"On Shadowed Ground" © Kevin McClintock
"The High Priest's Cat" © Christine Lucas
"Reckoning" © C. Dennis Moore
"Talk To Me" © Jamie K. Schmidt
"The Woman of Chitral" © Sarah Islam
"The Angel in the Trees" © Dan O'Brien

ISBN 10: 0-9770956-8-1
ISBN 13: 978-0-9770956-8-1

This book was set in Dante on 55# acid-free paper that
meets ANSI standards for archival quality.

Printed in the United States of America.

CONTENTS

Preface

The world is a scary place.

When we put out the call for submissions for this book, we did not want the same old predictable tales set in the same old familiar haunted houses. Sure we were looking for stories that would raise the hair on our necks, but we also wanted works that had a strong sense of place. We got what we wished for. Wonderfully horrifying stories poured in from around the globe. The result is *Our Haunted World*, a collection of sixteen stories that take us to some of the most haunted places on earth.

Several works are grounded in history—the radioactive devastation of Chernobyl in Donna Burgess's "The Dancing Water," a German concentration camp in Kevin McClintock's "On Shadowed Ground," and Japan's war-ravaged landscape in Mark Lee Pearson's "The Hermits of Hahajima." The collection opens with a young girl unearthing a box of bones as England's past collides with the present in Neil Williams's "Pestfurlong Hill."

Other stories draw on mythology. Eliza Granville's "Night of the Wild Hunt" is inspired by the terrors of the Wild Hunt, a

European myth about an army of ghostly hunters who ravage the land at the head of a malicious storm. The very sight of the hunt brings death or misfortune to its witnesses. Christine Lucas's "The High Priest's Cat" is anchored in the ancient Egyptian belief that cats were guardians of the underworld, and that spirits and evil creatures could be driven away by a cat's presence.

This collection of tales will take you from the surf of Bali to the mountains of Pakistan, from coast to coast in the United States, across the ocean, and throughout Europe. So get ready to travel the globe. Don't expect the best accommodations, for this won't be a comfortable journey. You'll find nightmares at every destination. Still, when all is over, you'll be glad you took the trip. And don't worry. We won't tell anyone if you sleep with the lights on.

* * *

The production of this collection—from story selection to editing to book design—is the result of the efforts of Professor Allen Grove and many of his talented students at Alfred University: Katie Baildon, Julia Baird, Melanie Baker, Megan Brzustowicz, Sandy Burnley, Megan Caggianelli, Máire Cosgrove, Allex Kirkland, Rachel McCune, Jessica Marello, Geoffrey Nassimos, Ginger Pierce, Jaclyn Rath, Amanda Schaible, Amy Stallard, and Jaime Wyzykowski.

Pestfurlong Hill

by Neil Williams

What nature meant by such a useless production 'tis hard to imagine, but the land is entirely to waste.

DANIEL DEFOE COMMENTING ON THE LAND AT HOLCROFT AND PESTFURLONG AS HE PASSED BY ON THE ROAD TO MANCHESTER IN 1724.

"LOOK DADDY, we've found pirate treasure."

Andrew looked up at the soil-encrusted object being brandished in front of him. He wiped the sweat from his forehead with the back of the gardening glove.

"It looks like an old tea caddy. Be careful you don't cut yourself. It looks rusty."

"A caddy? What's a caddy?"

Flora held the container in her hands as if it were the Holy Grail as her father tried to explain what it was. She was a vision in shades of pink from her flowery Wellingtons up to the salmon cap with a flap on the back. Only the out-sized green gardening gloves spoilt the ensemble. Behind trailed her friend Milly under a wide brimmed sun hat; she too was unsuitably dressed for a day digging up the garden.

"It doesn't sound like tea." Milly gave it a shake like she was mixing a cocktail; the contents rattled. "Maybe it's gold coins."

"I don't think so. We're a bit too far inland for pirate treasure."

"I can't open it. Daddy can you do it?" Again she thrust the tin at him.

"I'll have a look in a minute. Anyway, I thought you were supposed to be helping me dig up the weeds, not looking for buried treasure."

She didn't answer; both girls were now running back up the garden towards the house.

"Hey, don't run with that trowel."

They weren't listening. He watched them go shaking his head in resignation then returned his attention to the tree stump he was attempting to dig out. He leaned on the handle of the mattock and fanned himself with the brim of his hat. It was too hot for this kind of work. He raised his head and closed his eyes, trying to feel some coolness in the slight breeze that rustled through the trees on the steep bank beyond the fence. There was the buzzing of insects, the far away bark of a dog and the laughter of children. It was an idyllic summer's day. For a brief moment he felt like he'd revisited his own childhood, when the sun had burned hotter and the sky had been a deeper blue than any he'd experienced since.

He and Jill had decided to split their work holidays for that year to look after Flora over the long summer break. He'd cover the first half of the break and Jill the latter. A crossover in the middle would allow for a few days away somewhere. In previous years they'd relied on grandparents to look after Flora, but now that she was older she wanted to stay at home and be near her friends. Also expecting their parents to look after such an active six-year-old for eight hours a day was a bit too much to ask at their age. But most importantly it presented him with the opportunity to finally sort out the garden. He'd spent years half-heartedly trying to keep it in check; weeds and brambles had slowly and insidiously claimed it as their own. Now he'd finally charged himself with the task of sorting it out. They'd both agreed on a plan for the garden; there would be a green house in the far corner, a vegetable patch at the bottom and a patio.

Flora was less of a bother than he'd feared. She had spent most of her time playing with her friend Milly from across the road. Milly's mother was usually at home, so the two girls would frequently go over there to play. He gave them a certain degree of freedom on condition that they always told him were they were going. They'd start off most mornings with him in the garden before disappearing into the house to watch television. He'd put up an old tent as a shelter for them, and they were most frequently found in there when the sun was at its highest.

He swung the mattock into the dry brown earth around the stump and clawed it back exposing the cool black soil beneath. Worms, their pale bodies glistening, coiled in the exposed trench. He hefted the weight over his head again and took another swing. Again it sank deep into the inviting earth. The blade caught on something hard as he dragged it out. With all his weight on the handle he pushed up the blade. A brick came along with it. Another one. Wherever he dug in the garden he always encountered bricks; he was starting to amass quite a collection. Crouching down into the trench he lifted the brick out and tossed it to one side. As he was about to stand a shadow passed over him.

"Don't stand too close dear; it's not safe."

The shadow moved away.

"Flora?"

There was no reply. He looked behind him; the garden was deserted.

Andrew straightened up and called again. Still no answer. He dropped his gloves on the stump and walked up the garden towards the house. As he approached the tent he caught sight of a slight movement within. He slowly bent down onto one knee and reached for the flap that hung loosely over the entrance.

"Flora, are you..." he called again. As he pulled back the flap, two pale faces popped through the aperture.

"Boo!" they both shouted in unison. He tottered back genuinely startled as the two children lay giggling in the mouth of the tent. "Did we scare you?"

"Just a bit," he said recovering his composure.

He looked back down the garden. There was no way they could have cleared that distance without him seeing or hearing them.

"Who were you talking to?" Flora climbed out of the tent; she shaded her eyes with her hands as she followed her father's gaze.

"I thought I was talking to you."

"Oh. Then who was the lady?"

"Lady?"

Flora rolled her eyes and gave him her finest look of contempt.

"We saw the lady when we peeped from the tent; we thought it must be Mary."

"Why would Mary, and that's Mrs. Watson to you, be in our garden?"

"She could have jumped over the fence, like this." She jumped towards him arms wheeling. "I think Mrs. Watson's fence jumping days are a long way behind her. There was no one else in the garden; just me."

Flora regarded him suspiciously for a moment before darting back into the tent and retrieving the battered tin. She and Milly then ran giggling into the house.

"Go and wash your hands. I'm going to do lunch now," he called after them. He turned and surveyed the garden once more before following them inside.

He stacked the plates on the draining board and looked out into the garden while the water gurgled out of the sink. Flora and Milly had taken up residence in the tent again and he could hear their chatter through the open kitchen window. His gaze travelled out past the old tree stump with the abandoned mattock leaning against it to the gentle rise of the hill beyond the fence. The hill itself was not particularly high, but the surrounding terrain on the other three sides was featureless farm and mossland. From the top you could see across the emptiness to Alderley Edge or Manchester and beyond to the Pennines that reared up like a cat's back. Distant church spires and the towering stacks of old disused mills seemed to tear through the patchwork of greens and browns like rusted nails. At dusk the lights of the city would shimmer beneath the darkening sky; before them the electric blue dome of The Trafford Centre shone like a beacon calling the faithful to shop.

"Hello my name's Flora. What's yours?" The voice from the tent drew him back from his thoughts. He didn't catch everything being said over the sound of the draining water.

Flora said something like, "Hello Jenny, this is my friend Milly."

Someone cried out and Milly burst out of the tent eyes flooded with tears. She stumbled through the opening, throwing the flap aside and ran across the lawn towards the house. As the flap of the tent fell back Andrew caught a glimpse of Flora inside. But it didn't look like Flora even taking into account the saturated red and yellow hues that bathed the interior. The figure crouched at the back of the tent seemed much taller, older too. The hair looked darker and lacked Flora's cascade of curls.

He barely had chance to take in what he'd seen when Milly darted sobbing past the open kitchen door.

"Milly, wait!" he turned and started after her, then hesitated momentarily. Flora was still in the tent; the flap now obscuring the entrance.

"Flora!" he called back as the tent was thrown open again. This time it was unmistakably Flora who pouted glumly through the opening, a questioning "what did I do?" look on her face. He left her there and gave chase after Milly.

"Are you coming out of there?"

Andrew was back at the mouth of the tent. He'd just returned from seeing Milly safely back home.

"It's a good job Milly's mum was in. What on earth were you doing?"

Flora raised her head and stared back at him bristling with defiance. "It wasn't my fault; it was Jenny."

"Who the fu… hell is Jenny?" he tried to keep a check on his anger.

Flora glowered at him silently for a moment. Her eyes looked black in the unnatural light, but he could still sense the cogs of her mind turning.

"The lady from the garden."

"What lady…?" he suddenly recalled what she'd said earlier. And that fleeting glimpse of the girl who wasn't Flora crouching in the tent. A single bead of sweat crawled icily between his shoulder blades and down the curve of his spine. Had he really seen someone else? It seemed so implausible now, just a trick of the light.

"Jenny wanted to play, but Milly said she couldn't."

He glanced around the tent; Flora was quite alone.

"Did you and Milly fall out?"

"She didn't like Jenny." Flora shrugged her shoulders.

"And where's Jenny now?"

Flora didn't answer; she just pushed her lower lip out.

"Is she real? Did Milly see her?" Andrew tried to probe further; Flora shook her head.

"She might be a bit invisible," she ventured a cautious response and returned to whatever it was she was playing with in the tent.

"But you can see her?"

"Well of course I can. She's my friend now." The tone was almost sarcastic.

"An imaginary friend?" Andrew tried to read her expression as she nodded a silent reply. "But I thought Fluff was your imaginary friend?"

"It's Ruff actually," she rolled her eyes as she corrected him. The name changed depending on her mood. "Anyway, he's just my pretend friend; he's not real."

"But an imaginary friend is?" It had never occurred to him that there was a hierarchy to all this.

"I think you should go and apologise to Milly for scaring her; that wasn't a nice thing to do."

"But I didn't. It was Jenny." Flora looked indignant as if she had other more important things to be doing.

"There's only you in here Flora, doing your daft voices. We'll both go over to see how Milly is in a while." He rose and started to back out of the tent. He noticed the open tea caddy at her knees. "I see you got the lid off. Was there any treasure?"

Flora shook her head and looked down into the container. "Just old bones; dinosaur bones I think?"

"Dinosaur bones, really? That must have been one very old tin and a very small dinosaur," said Andrew still withdrawing. "What are you going to do with them?"

"I'm just counting them at the moment. Will you help me?" She squinted up at him as he stepped back into the sunlight.

"I can't right now. I need to finish what I was doing in the garden."

"But I haven't got anyone to play with now." She adopted her finest sullen expression.

"Well, you should have thought of that before you frightened Milly. Anyway, I thought that you had Jenny to play with now?"

"Don't be silly daddy; Jenny can't possibly help me."

He was already strolling back down the garden. "Oh really, and why ever not?"

"Because Jenny hasn't got any hands."

Andrew was still wrestling with the tree stump. He'd dug a trench around it, practically undermined the thing and still it wouldn't come out. He laid down the mattock and tried to manhandle the tree from the soil. It moved quite freely and he twisted and turned it as if he were trying to extract a giant's tooth. He cursed through a mask of grime and sweat as finally the remaining root that had stubbornly anchored the stump to the soil snapped. He tumbled on his back cradling the misshapen block of wood as he tried to regain his breath. He gazed up at the limitless blue embroidered with the trails of aircraft that flashed silver in the afternoon sun. He felt he might almost fall into it.

"It's a fine thing I'm not a betting woman; I'd ha' put good money on the tree winning that." Andrew tilted his head up in the direction of the voice. An elderly woman was leaning over the fence, one elbow resting upon it.

"Hi Mary; doing a spot of gardening?" He smiled at the woman who looked upside down from were he lay. How long had she been there? He felt slightly embarrassed at the thought of her calmly watching while he had been heaping abuse and threats on the inanimate stump.

"I do hope Jill's not home; I'd hate for her to catch you two like that." He looked down at the stump he was still clutching to his chest. He pushed the thing away and got to his feet brushing the soil from his clothes.

"Lovely weather we're having," he said lamely. "I'm finally getting down to sorting the garden out. It's hard work though."

"It is. You need to keep on top of it."

"I keep digging up loads of bricks." Andrew pointed to the stack at the foot of the garden. "Do you have the same problem?"

"We used to when we first moved in here. They'll be from the factory."

She might have left the comment at that, but she saw the question forming on Andrew's lips.

"The Royal Ordnance Factory. This used to be farmland until the outbreak of the war. They built the factory to make the ammunition here."

"Right here?" He pointed to the ground at his feet.

"All over. The site covered hundreds of acres. A few of the bunkers are still standing; all filled in, mind. But almost all of it was demolished. Most of the rubble went into making the mounds and the hill here." She nodded at the profusion of green beyond the panelled fence.

"There was no hill before?"

"Like I said, it was farmland."

Andrew was aware of the old U.S. Airbase at nearby Burtonwood; a few of the enormous aircraft hangars still remained.

"They built it to be near the base, I imagine."

"That might have been one reason, though Elsie always said that they picked the spot because it was so isolated. Hard to imagine now, I know. And usually quite misty at night, so that's why the factory was built here. It was usually hidden beneath mist or cloud. Just as hard to see it in the daytime too, so the Germans never found it and it escaped the bombers. You should take a walk up the hill some evening and watch the mist rising up."

"Hello Mrs. Watson." Flora appeared from the house having heard voices and being afraid of missing anything. She sucked noisily at a carton of juice with a straw.

"Oh hello dear; please call me Mary," she replied. Andrew caught Flora's sideways glance of disdain as she neared them. "Are you enjoying your holidays?"

Flora nodded by way of a response.

"Flora, go and put some shoes on if you're staying out here," said Andrew looking down at her feet. She stopped abruptly and returned to the house.

"I bet she's a handful," said Mary.

"She certainly is," he replied, watching her retreat.

After a few moments silence, Mary said, "You know Elsie, my oldest sister, used to work at the factory. Those that weren't working the land ended up here. There were thousands of young girls here, brought in from all over the country. A lot of Irish girls were brought over here too. It was hard work and dangerous too, with all those explosives."

"You never worked there?"

"How old do I look?" she glared at him. "No, I was just a little girl. Elsie worked as a secretary, thank God. So she wasn't exposed to the most dangerous work. Some of the girls, especially those working on the detonators, suffered terrible injuries; deaths even. It was volatile stuff; handle it the wrong way and bang! No more fingers, or worse."

"She just has a very active imagination; you know what she's like?"

Jill settled into the sofa beside Andrew cradling a large glass of red. Flora had finally gone to sleep. The singing and protests that she wasn't at all tired had finally ebbed away to nothing.

"She put the fear of god in Milly and had me going for a bit." Andrew felt weary from all that digging and pulling. He was going to hurt tomorrow.

"Kids invent stuff like that. Look, she claims she's got a monkey, who's also her baby brother, who sleeps on the top bunk of her bed. She refuses to accept that she doesn't even have a bunk bed."

Andrew had heard it all before.

"I think he's actually supposed to be an ape; he doesn't have a tail."

"The only good thing about it is she's stopped jumping on her bed," she carried on ignoring his comment. "She's afraid she'll bump her head."

"Today wasn't like that though; it was more real. I thought I saw..." he trailed off as he tried to conjure into his mind the figure in the tent but it eluded him.

"I think I can see where she gets it from."

Jill gave him a look.

"Well it doesn't seem quite so strange in the cold light of..." he glanced out at the darkening sky. "Night."

"Anyway, they'll have forgotten all about it by tomorrow and will be best of friends again."

"I suppose you're right," Andrew replied. He let his head tip back and stared up at the ceiling as his thoughts turned to redecorating. Almost immediately he sat up again. "Damn."

"What's the matter now?"

"I forgot to put the bin out."

It was much cooler outside. Even with so many windows open the house still clung to the heat of the day. He carefully guided the large plastic bin past the two cars and righted it, handle turned out, at the end of the drive. He stayed there a moment, savouring the refreshing coolness of the evening breeze on his skin. The street lights had just come on and the circling insects bobbed and weaved like a myriad of tiny satellites. Above him the brightest stars already studded the dimming sky; to the west the moon drifted above the rooftops, pale as a painted backdrop. He looked down the road towards the quiet cul-de-sac at its end. He could see the opening to the narrow path continued discreetly between the furthest houses and linked up to the main trail that snaked lazily through the trees up to the summit of the hill. He remembered what Mary had said about the rising evening mist; here the approaching dark seemed all hard edges and sharp lights.

He stole along the pavement to the path, suddenly conscious that all he had on his feet were a pair of tattered slippers. Where the path joined its larger parent he paused and looked up the gradual slope of the hill. Descending from the top was a man walking a dog, the animal straining at the length of a retractable lead, its nose pointed down at the ground. It darted this way then that across the path catching the scent of numerous others. As they approached, both looked up at him as if a man alone at such a time and place was a cause for suspicion. He was half tempted to start calling out, pretending that he was out walking a dog that had run off.

Once on the main trail, he became aware of the roar of the motorway. It was a sound always present, but the trees and the raised ground around them reduced it to a low hum that he barely even noticed it anymore.

He looked back down the main path. The dog and its master had passed through the narrow gate and were now little more than silhouettes in the greying light. A little further up the hill the path forked, the right hand route skirting around the hill before rejoining the main path at the summit. Andrew took the most direct path. A haze was already rising up from the fields surrounding the hill as he reached the top. In the distance the city lights shimmered under a cobalt sky, and to his left the motorway stretched away pulsing with that same vitality. A few straggling crows flapped across the empty fields, their discordant cries echoing across the landscape. The mist was thickening to an opaque white and seemed to be pooling in the shallowest places. It seemed to flow like water; rough furrows in the soil could not contain it for long; hedgerows were soon overwhelmed. Only when it reached the foot of the hill did it seem to flounder and rise no further.

Andrew was suddenly aware of how dark it had become. The sky still retained some trace of daylight, but the ground was now couched in blackness. It was also a lot cooler; the rising mist seemed to have sucked up the remnants of the day's heat. He rubbed some heat back into his bare arms as he turned and descended from the hill. It had been barely ten minutes since he'd stepped outside and he felt as if he were returning from a different world to the one he'd walked out into. The only constant was the drone of the traffic and the slap of his slippers on the gravel path; the birdsong that had accompanied him up the hill was silent now. He set off in the direction of the street lights that flickered tantalisingly through the trees.

As he returned to where the two paths intersected, he became aware of another figure standing on the lower path. Someone else out walking a dog, he reasoned. He strode on with barely a glance in their direction. But he noticed two things: firstly, he could see no dog and if anyone was here to admire the view, they were on the wrong side of the hill. It was only when he had gone some distance and was within sight of the road that he glanced back. Nobody was there. Keep to the path...he thought to himself, quickening his pace...and beware the full moon. A decidedly gibbous moon waxed sickly overhead as he hurried home.

"There you are. I wondered where you'd got to." Jill drained the remaining wine from her glass and passed it to him as he entered the room.

"Get me another while you're up. There's a love."

Had something caused him to wake? He raised his head from the pillow and checked the time. The room was reduced to a palette of dark greys tumbling into blackness. The display on the alarm clock was the only colour; the numbers glowed like a branding iron. It was a little past three in the morning, still dark outside and still so warm. The dawn chorus wouldn't start for another couple of hours. He turned his pillow over and pressed his face down into its coolness. Then he heard it, a voice, a whisper; words spoken in a low conspiratorial tone. He rolled onto his back and stared sightlessly up into the shadows trying to hear more. He held his breath and imagined reaching out with just the one sense. He could hear the faraway drone of the motorway and Jill's soft breathing beside him; but it was the beat of his own heart that distracted him the most. It was definitely Flora's voice that tugged at very periphery of his hearing; it seemed to tinkle like a faraway wind chime touched by the gentlest of breezes. She was talking in her sleep again. Should he get up and check she was all right, or should he wait a while? Maybe she'd settle by herself. If he got up now he knew it would take him hours to get back to sleep again. He slowly let his eyes close.

Another voice had joined Flora's, a slightly deeper voice. He dreamt of sunlight and brightly coloured fabric rippling in a light breeze. His eyes snapped open; he must have drifted off. Another voice, indistinct but definitely a woman's voice. Jill must have gone in to check on her. He listened to the sounds of the voices from Flora's room. Flora must have woken up; they appeared to be having a conversation. Happy to let Jill deal with her, he turned over to the empty side of the bed.

It wasn't empty. Jill was still asleep beside him.

He slowly swung his legs to the floor and stood up. Each creak of the bedsprings, the squeak of a loose floorboard as he tiptoed to the door, seemed like a klaxon in the stillness. Jill didn't stir once. He grabbed the dressing gown from the back of the door. As he pulled it over his naked shoulders, he stepped out onto the landing. Everything seemed quiet now. He stole over to Flora's door. Silence. From within the room came the faint orange glow of the night light. He stepped up to the door, pausing for a second to listen. He slowly let the door swing open.

Flora was sitting up in bed facing towards the window. He couldn't tell if she was awake or not. He entered the room. The light bathed everything in a deep amber glow. From auburn shadows the impassive eyes of numerous soft toys glinted. He crouched down and gently placed his hands on her shoulders.

"Come on now, lie down. That's a good girl," he gently directed her back onto the pillow and pulled the duvet over her. He picked up her bear that had fallen from the bed and pressed it into her arms. She instinctively hugged it.

"Daddy, is it morning yet?" Her eyes half opened.

"It's still very early; you go back to sleep now." He brushed a curl of hair from her face. "You've been dreaming. I thought I heard you talking."

"I want to play outside."

"You can't go out now. It's much too dark. Come on, go back to sleep."

"Jenny is waiting for me."

"Jenny?" The crouched figure bathed in hues of red and yellow rose afresh in his mind.

As did the voice. He'd frequently woken to hear Flora chatting away to herself. Was he really sure that this was any different? A slight breeze rippled across the curtain. He froze momentarily as if expecting them to part. He waited a moment before rising, but nothing entered the room save for the distant hiss of traffic. He cautiously pulled back the curtain and looked down into the garden and across to the impervious black silhouette of the tree fringed hill beyond; to the spot where the path circled the hill. In the shadows thrown out by the jostling branches it would be easy to conjure some waiting figure. He firmly closed the window and turned back to his sleeping daughter.

"Oh Flora," he whispered to himself and smiled, "what does go on in that head of yours?"

He kneeled down by the bed and started to cover her. She had turned onto her side but still hugged the teddy. Her left hand made a tiny fist at the back of the toy's neck. It was as he was laying the duvet over her he noticed something pale in her grasp. At first he took it to be a crumpled tissue and very gingerly reached out to take it from her. He took hold of the object with his fingertips where it protruded slightly from her hand. But it wasn't soft like he anticipated; it felt hard and oddly waxy. In the uncertain light it was difficult to see it clearly. It was as he was manoeuvring himself for a closer inspection that something touched his shoulder.

"Daddy screamed like a girl!" laughed Flora repeating what Jill had just said, showing a mouthful of breakfast.

"Just eat your toast." Andrew was starting to get a little tired of the jokes at his expense.

"Scaredy cat, scaredy cat!" Flora continued.

"Look what you've started," he said to Jill as he gestured to their daughter perched on a chair by the kitchen table, legs swinging merrily.

Jill put an arm around his shoulders in mock comfort.

"You were rather shrill. I'm surprised you didn't wake up the whole street."

"You nearly gave me a heart attack, sneaking up on me like that. It's not funny," he protested, but he could see he was outnumbered.

Andrew didn't see too much of Flora that day. Jill was right, as usual. She had gone over to play with Milly after waving her mother off to work, and the two of them had spent most of the day haring around Milly's garden. Flora would pop back every now and then just to make sure she wasn't missing out on anything before disappearing again. Andrew spent another day in the garden adding to his brick collection and continuing his education on the history of the area by his neighbour. Flora hadn't mentioned anything about the previous day, and Andrew knew better than to raise the matter again. Alone in the garden, Andrew felt more vulnerable and was constantly watchful. Mary's occasional appearances over the garden fence were, when not making him jump, welcome distractions. The tent stayed up but the door remained securely zipped up. He didn't once consider looking in there.

What is it with kids, thought Andrew. They complain they're tired and can barely keep their eyes open when you need them awake, and they'll practically fall asleep in a plate of spaghetti. But as soon as you get them near a bed, sleep is the furthest thought from their minds.

"Go to sleep Flora," Andrew called up the stairs and waited.

"But I'm not tired," came the reply. He started the ascent.

"Come on Flora, you should have been asleep hours ago." He reached the top of the stairs and peered into Flora's bedroom. He could see the back of her head over the end panel of the bed.

"What are you doing? It's too dark to be reading; you'll hurt your eyes."

"I'm not reading; I'm doing a puzzle." She didn't turn round.

"Well I don't care what you're doing; I want it put away and you asleep now." He stepped into the room, his foot kicking something that went clattering across the floor. "And what have I told you about leaving stuff on the floor?"

Flora turned and looked at her father. In the fading daylight that leaked through gaps in the curtains, her eyes looked almost black, pupils fully dilated. He reached past her intent on clearing away the objects on the bed. Flora threw herself forward covering them with her hands. "I'm not finished yet." She started to scream as he pulled her back, an arm about her waist. He reached down and grabbed a handful of the pieces that Flora was trying to protect. He immediately let Flora fall back onto the bed and recoiled as he recognised what he held. He rubbed a thumb against the hard waxy surface. He knew what it was. Flora had gripped one of them tightly last night. But it wasn't this that sent the shockwave of revulsion through him as he tumbled back. On the bed before the sobbing Flora were two small groups of the objects so white that they seemed to shine against the lilac sheets. The nearest was now scattered and incomplete. The other, there was no mistaking it, was a collection of bones that had been carefully placed back together.

A human hand. Delicate fingers splayed outwards

Andrew reached back and tugged open the curtain. What little daylight remained spilled through the narrow gap and gave substance to the arrangement of bones. Jill had just entered the room, wondering what all the commotion was. She found Flora sobbing in protest as Andrew scooped up the rest of the bones from the bed. He picked up the tin from where he'd inadvertently kicked it and dropped the bones into it. He secured the lid and sighed in relief as if he'd just imprisoned some malevolent genie.

"What on earth is going on?" said Jill trying to make sense of what was happening. Flora was still crying reaching for the tin that Andrew was keeping a safe distance from her grasp

"I'll explain in a minute. Flora, go to sleep."

Flora flung herself back onto her bed, her sobs waning. Jill, not sure what else to do, went to close the curtain. "That's weird."

Andrew turned his attention from Flora to find Jill staring out of the window. "What is?"

There was a trace of nervousness in his voice that couldn't be hidden.

"There's somebody out there looking directly at the house." She caught Andrew's look of concern and added, "It's probably nothing really; it's just a girl."

"A girl?" Andrew approached the window; behind him Flora had stopped her sobbing also distracted by her mother's comment. Andrew peered through the gap in the curtains. The figure wasn't as immediately evident as he had expected. He scanned the line of trees beyond the panel fence for several seconds before his eye was caught by the shape of a grey-clad figure, a shadow almost, expelled into the failing light from shadows far darker. He instantly knew the face, but it was now pale and expressionless, stripped of all summer warmth and colour. Eyes appeared to be empty voids under the black tendrils of hair. The arms hung loosely down, the hands not visible. Ordinarily he might have thought them tucked away in pockets, but he knew better. "You can really see her?" he asked. It came out as barely a whisper.

"Well of course I can see her." She turned her attention to Andrew. "What's wrong?"

"I've seen her before," he replied.

"Who is it?" said Flora. She was out of bed again and trying to see what was happening.

Jill looked back to where the figure was standing. There was no one there. Andrew, who hadn't taken his eyes off the girl, watched as she evaporated into the shadows.

"Where did she go?" said Jill searching the hillside.

Something in the garden below caught Andrew's eye. He looked down, moving closer to the window until his forehead touched the chill glass.

The girl was standing in the garden.

Even taking into account the approach of night, the girl seemed to have been drained of any trace of colour, her skin like white marble in the dark grey ill-fitting overalls. The thick black hair with its untidy fringe crowded around a pale thin-lipped face. The eyes were almost hidden in shadow. Any light that fell upon them was not reflected back.

Jill saw her too and visibly jumped. She raised her hand to her mouth to stifle the scream that was poised there.

"Can I see?" chanted Flora repeatedly like it was a mantra, while trying to elbow her way through to the window.

"How could she get...?" Jill started to speak, weighing up the distance from hill to garden, trying to make sense of the girl's sudden reappearance.

"Is it Jenny?" Flora asked rather too brightly. She was now jumping up trying to see past her parents.

"Be quiet Flora," said her father, his voice echoing none of her cheeriness.

Jill looked dumbfounded as she searched both husband and daughter's expressions for some clue as to what was going on. She looked back at the girl who now seemed a few paces closer, though Jill hadn't seen her move. She fumbled for her husband's hand as the figure slowly raised both arms towards them as if pleading.

27

Both arms ended at the wrists in torn blackened stumps.

"Oh God!" sobbed Jill stepping back from the girl's gaze. She instinctively gathered Flora into her arms.

"It's my friend Jenny," said Flora.

"She isn't your friend," replied Andrew. He also started to back away from the window feeling the full glare fall on him. He still held the tea caddy. He gripped it tighter now. "I'm sorry Flora, but she can't ever be your friend."

"What's wrong with her hands?" Jill was struggling to make sense of it. There was now a look of genuine fear in her eyes. "Oh my God, what is she?"

Andrew put an arm around her, kissed her, and guided her away from the window. "Get Flora back into bed and stay with her. I'll be right back."

"You can't go out there! Shouldn't we call someone?" Jill held on to Flora who had started to cry again.

"Who are we going to call?" he winced as he said it.

"But what does she want?"

"I think I know what she wants."

He disappeared downstairs. She was about to call him back up when she heard the front door shut.

It wasn't until he'd reached the diverging footpaths that Andrew stopped. The ever-present hum of the traffic and the call of songbirds were the only sounds. The sky remained bright, but the sun had dropped below the horizon. The hill was now a patchwork of shadows. A gentle breeze rippled through the leaves and their movement jostled for attention on all sides. There was no sign of the girl. He peered down the slope of the hill to where she had been standing. The undergrowth was intact; no one had forced a path through it. Ducking under the branches he had a clear view of the house. He could see the slightly parted curtain at Flora's window and the faint trace of a light within. As soon as he reached the hill he started to harbour doubts about his course of action. What had he left Jill to face? He put the tea caddy under his arm and slid his phone from a pocket. It seemed to take an age before he got an answer. Even with the house in sight, Jill and Flora still seemed a world away.

"Are you okay? No, I'm fine." He took another look around. "No, I can't see anyone. I'm coming back now."

He looked down at the illuminated phone in his hand. Already the bright display had attracted numerous insects. He put the phone away and held the tin up for closer inspection. He hadn't paid it much attention when Flora had first shown him the tin. It was a small and rectangular container; at the top was a hinged lid held shut with a hook. Almost all the enamel decoration that had once adorned the tin was gone.

He thought about the contents and recalled what Mary had told him of the factory. A tragic accident with a detonator and a young girl left dead or dying. The pieces of her shattered hands scooped up into the nearest available container to be forgotten or lost.

"Jenny," he said quietly. He felt an overwhelming sadness wash over him. He turned the tin over and the contents rattled. It sounded much louder than he expected. He glanced around, aware that something had changed.

The birds had stopped singing.

Andrew ran up the path to the top of the hill. He felt less vulnerable there. Here he had clear ground all about him and could see anyone approaching. Below the hill, the empty fields bled a low mist. Andrew turned back to face the path and very gently turned the tin in his hands. Again its contents rattled. "Come out to play Jenny," he thought to himself. He scanned the trees looking for any movement that wasn't part of nature.

"I know you're here. I have something that belongs to you."
He raised the tin up and gave it another shake. The whole hill
seemed to be holding its breath, but still nothing revealed itself.

"Well, if you want these you'll have to find them yourself."
Andrew turned away and unclasped the lid of the tin. He test-
ed the weight of it, wondering how far across the field he could
throw it before it scattered the contents like seeds.

"You need to find somebody else to play with," he said and
swung his arm back. Just as he prepared to throw, he looked
behind him at the container in his hand—and into the face of
the girl standing directly behind him.

He found Jill waiting for him on the stairs when he returned. Her eyes were ringed with red. She held a crumpled
tissue in one hand, the phone in the other. As soon as she saw
Andrew enter, she rushed down to him full of questions. He
folded his arms about her.

"Is she asleep?"

She nodded as Andrew released her and placed a hand on
the balustrade.

"I'll just go and check on her," he said as he mounted the
stairs.

Flora lay asleep on her side facing the window. Her right
arm was hooked around the neck of her favourite bear. Andrew softly entered the room and closed the curtain before
crouching down by his daughter. He brushed away the curls
that had fallen across her face and waited for her to settle when
she stirred slightly. Her left hand remained free, the palm facing
upwards. He gently placed his index finger onto the open hand;
tiny fingers encircled it and instinctively tightened their grip.

The Dancing Water

by Donna Burgess

A S A MAN GROWS OLDER, the fragments of memory, long buried with time are again uncovered, just like the day Anton's grandfather gave him the tiny vial of Dancing Water. Grandfather had been a keeper of bees, among other things, on a small swatch of land not too far from the banks of the Volga River. Anton had followed him to the hives, as he always did on spring visits, his open hands fanning the waist high wild rye that grew all around the farm, the screened hat that Grandfather had shoved at him pulled too far down on his head.

At a distance, the hives themselves appeared like a half-dozen bureau cabinets plopped down among the grasses and scrubs of the field. Anton approached, ever apprehensive and afraid of being stung. Of course, Grandfather was never afraid. Anton did not think the old man had ever been stung by his bees, which were of course of better quality and nature than the plain old wild variety bugs that flitted around on Grandmother's flowers back around the other side of the house. Out there Grandfather went, face and head bare, hands uncovered. The bees rose from the boxes in great, black buzzing clouds.

Grandfather allowed them to light on the backs of his gnarled hands and the worn-out skin of his face and ears.

They crawled along Anton's oversized beekeeper's hat, their electric hum like the purr of a cat, and he held his breath, his sweaty fists clenched at his sides.

"Never shoo at them. Don't panic," Grandfather said. "Don't flail about like a silly little girl."

Perhaps the bees sensed the old man's gentleness. Was it possible that a simple insect could be more perceptive than a human?

Later, when he led Anton to the shed, it was nearly dusk. Anton was nearly thirteen, but that did not stop Grandfather from playing pretend, the same as they had when Anton was small. Anton often imagined Grandfather was only a boy himself, wrapped in the withered shell of an old man.

Anton's twin sister, Elena, was inside the house with Grandmother. Anton had asked if he should go and ask her to come and play. She was usually the princess, queen or fairy to his knight or swordsman.

Over the many summers with Grandfather, they had acted out the tales of the fearsome Baba Yaga, the witch with the iron grin and a taste for children lost in the forest, and the legendary knight Ilya Muromets. During those wonderful times of pretend, Grandfather's rough voice could take on the lilt of royalty or the growl of an ogre. When Anton closed his eyes, he fully expected to find Prince Vladmir or Koshchey, the evil tsar of the netherworld, standing before him when he opened them again.

"Not today, boy," Grandfather said. "Today's game is for you only."

Anton had decided when he was very small the shed was a magical place, where Grandfather made things of wood and sometimes metal or even fire or liquid. The smell of sweet hay, the old mare's coat, and petrol created an odor that was not exactly pleasant, but certainly memorable.

Shelves lined one wall and on top of those shelves were jars so thickly covered in dust and cobwebs it was impossible to see what was inside. Grandfather told Anton once that some housed fairies during the cold months. Anton had taken his word for it and never bothered to check for himself. Along another wall stood a huge secretary that contained one hundred tiny drawers. Within each drawer lay some strange treasure—coins with devilish images embossed on each side, teeth and trinkets of all sorts made of amber and bone.

One drawer had a lock. Grandfather removed from his pocket the key (which dangled on a ring with a dozen or more others just like it) and unlocked this special drawer. From within he extracted a vial attached to a long cord of leather.

The sun slanted sharply through the gapped-toothed rafters of the shed roof, creating sinister shadows across Grandfather's kind face. He passed the tiny glass bottle to Anton and hesitantly, the boy took it.

Inside, a viscous dark blue liquid swirled and seethed as if amid a miniature cyclone. The glass itself felt strangely warm against his fingers, as if it were a living thing.

"This is for you and your sister only," Grandfather said. "The elixir of life—it will heal any ailment. When death is at your door, this will stop it from entering." He smiled and the lines around his eyes deepened into gashes, but the light had changed and he was only Grandfather, not a wicked troll. "Who knows, boy? Perhaps it will make you live forever. It's the blood of Peter Pan, maybe?"

Grandfather went on, "I purchased it from a Balkan gypsy when I was but a boy in the army. He said it had once belonged to St. Germain, a nobleman of uncertain origin." He winked. "A dabbler in the occult was what he was. Claimed to be several thousand years old. St. Germain the deathless, he was known."

More play, but Anton held the vial up to the yellow rail of light that spilled in and played along. "A witch? Or warlock, maybe?" he suggested.

Grandfather shrugged. "Perhaps. Legend has it he was banished from St. Petersburg in the Revolution of 1762." He nodded toward the vial between Anton's fingers. "But that, he left behind."

He leaned closer to Anton's face, the taint of vodka on his breath. "Do not lose," he instructed gravely. "And do not waste."

Once home, Anton shared the story with Elena in the soft lamp glow of their new apartment home—one of many that housed the workers of the Chernobyl plant. Elena held the vial to the light, entranced by the swirling blue liquid. Out in the living room, Mother was still unpacking and chattering excitedly to Father, who was just getting ready to go to work for the night.

Sixteen stories up, Anton's bedroom window supplied a clear view of the newly completed Pripyat Ferris Wheel. Through the window of her bedroom, Elena could see the Towers of Chernobyl, glowing like strange lighthouses on some out of the way planet at the edge of the universe. She claimed it gave her nightmares, but Mother and Father paid little attention.

On clear nights, they picked up BBC World Service on the little transistor radio—father had shown them how to pick it up although the government often jammed the signal. That was what they listened to then—news—but they liked the sound of spoken English. It did not always come in clearly, but Radio Moscow grew old quickly and the Heavy Metal cassettes were not allowed late at night.

Elena laughed, playing along. "Then we must hide this! It's far too valuable to leave lying around."

Giggling, they carved a small opening in the new plaster wall behind Anton's bed and placed the vial inside. Then to be safe, Anton moved his poster of the Scorpions from his closet door to cover the hole.

The accident occurred not long after that night with the Dancing Water. News did not immediately come over the radio or the television. Instead, it came by telephone. Father called—something he never did while at work.

It was after one a.m. on April 26. Elena and Anton had stolen out like they often did once they thought Mother was asleep. Standing in the shadows outside the apartments with another teenage brother and sister from the complex, they passed a cigarette back and forth and danced to some tinny-sounding pop song on the transistor that Anton had tucked into the pocket of his trousers.

Holding her gigantic belly with both hands as if she were keeping the baby in place, Mother appeared in the open hallway, having become frantic to find Elena's and Anton's rooms empty.

Elena stubbed out the cigarette on the brick wall and dropped the butt behind a shrub. Mother was so relieved to find them, she did not scold. Instead, she took their hands in hers and together they turned toward the plant, her face as flat and white as the moon above.

"Your father called," she said. "An accident. I don't know anything else."

They could not see flames, but smoke billowed up, shiny, pale and beautiful against the inky night sky. It blew toward Pripyat and licked their damp brows with a poisonous kiss.

Across the courtyard, Anton saw a thin, rather sickly man watching them. His face was as sallow and drawn as a wraith. Anton shivered. He was so familiar, someone Anton had known all his life, yet could not place. He chewed his lip, confounded. The man did not move, did not watch the sky, only Anton and his family. He bit his lip, also, mimicking, almost mocking.

"Mother, do you know that man?" he asked.

Mother glanced at the stranger and shook her head quickly. "Don't look at him," she whispered.

Her eyes glazed over, shiny with tears as she squeezed Anton's hand too hard. "We should get indoors," she said, after a moment. Then she rubbed her bulging belly through her white nightgown. Perhaps she was wondering what she had done to the baby. Perhaps she was wondering what the wind had done to them all.

In less than two days they were away from the wonderful new apartment and away from the place created as a home for workers of the plant. In a rush to evacuate, they were not allowed to carry anything more than the clothes they wore. They gave up all because all they had was contaminated.

They were told they would be able to return in a few days. One thousand buses came and took them all away. The city of roses grew small in the rear window and Anton and his family never went back.

The Dancing Water was forgotten. For over twenty-five years, the last drops of St. Germain's precious elixir sat behind the leather-clad ass of a washed-up heavy metal singer. Anton said nothing of it, even as he watched his father and his mother die, rotting from the inside out because of poison rain. Grandfather had told him—for him and Elena only.

* * *

Dreams played out, miniature lives behind the shade of the eyelids. Nearly a quarter century since Grandfather and the bees—Anton had forgotten about the Dancing Water until

Elena mentioned it. She wore the perfume of death now, and in the light of her hospital room, she appeared like Mother's ghost rather than Elena, Anton's sweet and feminine alter ego. The pink scarf tied on her bald head created the illusion of transparency in her skin. Beneath her eyes were purple smudges, like errant makeup. The giggling teenage girl who had helped Anton hideaway the vial was gone.

"In the end, the poison will claim us all. In the end, we all pay, one way or another," she told Anton. She gripped his hand as if she was trying to hold on to this world. "Bring me the Dancing Water."

Anton frowned and leaned closer. "What? I don't have it."

His sister shook her head slowly. "Get it," she rasped.

"It's not real, Elena."

Elena allowed her cool hand to slip from his grasp. "Maybe none of this is real."

* * *

Memories are more relentless things than even ghosts. And more haunting. Anton's memories were constant; he carried the mark of them on the palm of his hand in the shape of his younger brother's uneven teethmarks.

After Mother's death, they were sent away, the three of them—Anton, Elena and the baby, Boris, named for their father. They had no one left—the grandparents were too elderly and too poor to take them in and Mother was proof that a woman could die of grief. And what did she have after Father died? The accident had occurred in late April, 1986. Cloned by the poison in their blood and their obligation to their employer, 600 men, called liquidators, had been sent in to clean up. As they boarded the bus for the last time, Anton and Elena could not pick their father from the crowd of men in white suits and surgical masks.

By August, Father and twenty-eight others were dead of radiation sickness. Mother had the baby inside her to worry over.

When the baby came out all wrong, she had nothing else.

Not long after, Anton, Elena and little Boris found themselves left to the design of the government so they were sent to an orphanage. It was called an orphanage, but the sign read Minsk Asylum. Elena was sent away to live in the girls' dorms and Anton saw her only at meals and prayer.

As Boris grew, Anton became his protector from the other boys and from the nurses whose patience had been worn thin. The time passed like sludge along a drying creek. At four, Boris was scarcely bigger than a toddler. Because of his exposure to radiation, his ailments were many. He was an ugly little thing with a mouthful of misaligned teeth and eyes that seemed to work independently of each other when he was tired.

He bit his fingers sometimes until they bled. His legs flayed out at the knees, misshapen, folded back beneath his bony torso, moving only in wild spasms. He pulled himself along the dirty linoleum of the asylum floors with arms overly muscled from constant use. He shrieked at the sight of Anton. He shrieked at the sight of everyone. He did not speak, save for calls for a mother only he could see. His language was a series of grunts and gasps only he knew.

The nurses held his face tightly enough to leave marks and spooned congealing oatmeal into his gaping mouth and then left him writhing on the floor in the corridor all day. He was not alone—there were many like Boris inside the walls of Minsk. When the meltdown occurred, everyone thought there was safety inside the wombs. They would come out normal; they would come out fine. Some magical thing. The boys of Chernobyl.

The sounds of the asylum had long ceased to startle him, but Anton would still jump awake, his mind filled with dread of the coming day. He lay there, on the lumpy mattress, sweat like a cold, wet blanket against his skin. The rooms grew so cold over night, he could see his own breaths puffing up from his face toward the water-stained ceiling above. He would shift his gaze then to the finger-smudged glass, up to the waning moon's dull reflection, and would wonder if Boris felt anything at all. Did he know? Was there any awareness inside that deformed, screaming body?

Finally, when the child started screeching for Mother early one morning, instead of lying there and staring at the moon, Anton got up and crept in the darkness to the children's ward. It was only weeks until Anton and Elena's eighteenth birthdays. When that day came, the asylum would turn them out to find their own way—work or more school. Boris would be left with no one but nurses who hated being there.

The heavy ammonia stink of urine and dirty diapers filled the ward. Anton clamped his hand over Boris' mouth to quiet him and found the flat of his palm just wide enough to cover his nose as well. He stared down into the muddy, stagnate pools of his brother's eyes. In that murky reflection, he saw himself, twin images, his own mouth a small round opening that he breathed through to endure the stink of the room, his eyes distant, determined as he smothered the boy with his hands.

How Boris had struggled, the wretched creature, biting and grunting. But sometimes the right thing is the cruelest thing. He left jagged teethmarks on Anton's palm that the nurse noticed the next morning. Anton told her he had gotten into a fight with another boy. She never mentioned it again. But in her eyes, Anton thought he saw something that might have been relief.

As his brother cooled, the stench growing even worse, Anton prayed he would not go to hell for this. But maybe he was already in hell. He slipped down the thick darkness of the corridor to his own bed before the nurse made her nightly rounds.

Boris' ashes were spread on a field outside the orphanage where poppies bloomed wild and orange as the sun. He was quickly forgotten to almost everyone but his brother and sister.

So many years later when Anton was on the slippery slope of dreams, he still heard Boris shrieking for Mother. He imagined the poison seeping into the womb, penetrating the walls of Mother's body and converging on the fetus that would become his brother.

God was either a tyrant or a comedian, decided Anton, to allow Boris to escape the creeping death with his ugliness.

Anton tried to reason to himself that if a man has a good heart, he would be haunted by the terrible things he did. He carried the burden of Boris, Mother and Father on his back like a stone. Elena, perhaps, could exorcise those demons. He had only to bring back the Dancing Water, after all. It was hers, as it was his. Grandfather had said that.

But...What if?

★ ★ ★

Anton rode his motorcycle north. He stopped at a small grocery about 90 kilometers away from the city, likely his last opportunity for uncontaminated food, water and fuel, and overheard talk of an egg by the side of the road. Most would not choose to travel farther than the egg. Anton had not heard of it before, but in the parking area, he stopped a decrepit farmer climbing from a Mack flatbed overtaken in rust and asked. The old man explained that the egg had been brought back from Germany. "It represents life."

The symbolism meant nothing to neither of them.

"All I know is that it is the point where civilization ends and the road to Chernobyl begins." Lower, he added, "The ground there is sullied now. Nothing good will ever live there again."

Grandfather told Anton once that Chernobyl meant wormwood in Ukrainian language. In religious study, he encountered that word again and again in the Book of Revelations. It scared the hell out of him, how Chernobyl was bound to the end of the world. To some degree, it was true—it had been the end of *that* world.

Closing in on Pripyat, the land became a wonderland made from nightmares. Empty villages, abandoned farms and deserted towns lined the two-lane blacktop. Anton rode as fast as the little bike would carry him, his essentials in a pack strapped to his back, the sky the color of bone at the horizon. There were no cars, but occasionally he encountered a bus carrying tourists into the desolation zone. Cement barricades blocked certain roads, but with the bike, he skirted those easily. Finally, he stopped for a pee and standing along the shoulder of the empty roadway, he marveled at the silence. No chirping birds, no rustle of four-legged things. No soft drone of motors. Just the wet splatter of his piss wetting poison earth, his breathing and the steady, rapid thud of his pulse in his ears.

At least that was how it was for a sublime, uninterrupted moment. Then there was something—not so much as a noise, but a sense. A *presence.* Anton glanced up as he zipped his jeans and realized a wolf was staring at him.

He froze and stared at the creature. The creature stared back, unmoving, its maul in a wide, perpetual grin. Then it turned and flitted away into the woods, gorgeous and gray, a thing untouched by man.

Or so he thought, until he realized the wolf had a second, perfect head protruding the left shoulder. Even as it loped away, that second head craned back, watching Anton, fangs exposed in a grin that was the twin of the other.

The sharp, acidic stink of wild urine filled the air, and for a moment Anton wondered if it belonged to the mutant wolf or to himself.

★ ★ ★

He reached a credential control point sometime before dusk. From there, he could see the sloping rooftop of his old schoolhouse. An armed guard stepped forward, asked why he was there.

"I want to go to my old home," Anton told him, unsure of what else to say.

The guard shook his head and pointed his rifle back the way Anton had come. Anton considered bickering, but what was the point? Besides, did he really want to argue with a man carrying a rifle?

As he turned his back, the guard called out, "We all come home eventually."

Anton ignored him and sped away.

When he was out of the soldier's sight, he pulled to a stop. Removing his cellular phone from his pack, he thumbed Elena's number and placed the phone to his ear. Nothing. He tried again, and again silence. He had come this far. What good was returning empty handed?

He decided to wait until dark.

★ ★ ★

Under the cover of trees a kilometer from the control point, Anton ditched the bike and walked along the empty road in the darkness. There were no sounds, save for his footsteps crunching along the old pavement. He listened for a rustle of movement in the woods after seeing the strange, mutated wolf earlier. He had heard tales of wild boars and packs of wolves that had overtaken the area. They had free reign now, and for that he was somewhat envious. To live an existence without the intrusion of man—perhaps the accident had been indeed an unexpected gift to at least some living things.

The air turned cooler and he wished he had worn a heavier jacket. He removed his gloves from his coat pockets and pulled them on. Snow lay on the ground like litter where the trees had not blocked its descent to the poisoned earth. He wondered if it would snow again.

The sky had become gray with low clouds as he entered the city. His breath steamed in front of his face and his eyes watered from the cold. He stayed close to the buildings, ready to vanish inside if anyone—guard or tourist group—came along.

Anton knew he should have gone straight to his old home, but the ghost town teased old memories to the surface. Things he had long forgotten he relived. The secondary school he attended loomed ahead, cast in deep shadow. The front door hung open like a beaconing gesture.

Come inside, Anton. We have missed you here.

Sometime after the accident, during Bible study at the orphanage, the headmaster read to them from Matthew, *"Let no one on the roof of his house go down to take anything out of the house. Let no one in the field go back to get his cloak. How dreadful it will be in those days for pregnant women and nursing mothers!"*

Anton recalled the strange feeling he had gotten, hearing that scripture. Now he wondered if April 1986 was really the prophesy the old teacher had read to them.

Apprehensively he entered the long corridor. It was only slightly warmer there, but still a relief from the gray dusk. Strewn papers carpeted the floor. On the walls, good work was still tacked on display. School spirit banners. Calendars that had not seen another day since April 27, 1986.

The air stank of damp mold and decaying books and wood. The paint had peeled from the walls like old skin, revealing even more decrepit flesh beneath. Here and there lay gasmasks. He was not sure why. Things such as that were a blur. Talk of the shiny smoke clouds had circulated the school—everyone knew. But the dangers were minimal, they were assured. The government had whitewashed the deaths. But the government could do such things. Even in democracy, rulers did so with a fist of iron. They were simply more discreet about it.

Lies were painted in the colors of the flag and that was the same for all countries, not only the Soviet Union.

Anton stepped through the door to the science lab. He had argued with Elena that morning over something that he could not remember. Two hours later, he held her hand in his as they boarded a bus to drive away from the life they knew.

He kicked a broken globe to a corner of the lab, and it laid there, a world split in half.

The creak and echoing screech of old wood made him jump. He looked around, back to the door. Nothing.

The slow, metallic cry of piano notes rang out, horribly out of key. It was not so much a song, but rather the touch of one who did not know music. Anton stood motionless for a moment, listening, his breath caught in his lungs.

After a few minutes, the notes stopped.

He left the school as the world took on the bruised look of falling night. The Ferris wheel towered, its spokes etched in black ink against the powdery sky. Rain began pattering down, soft as a girl's sigh. He picked up his pace. What terrible things would the rain do to him? Eat holes through his skin where it fell?

Shortly, a set of headlights sliced through the blanket of night, the rumble of the engine almost welcome in the deathly silence. Anton moved into the shadows of the buildings and watched it pass, packed with tourists, a worm with a full belly. As darkness grew, the buildings became nothing more than vague shapes, smudges against a paler horizon.

Anton neared the amusement park, not quite finished twenty-five years ago and never enjoyed. He wanted to use his flashlight, but was afraid of drawing attention. He stumbled from time to time on the broken pavement where weeds and spindly baby birch saplings had pushed through. The moon provided only dim illumination. Shapes moved in the corner of his eye. Was it the limbs wavering in the wind or something else?

He moved quickly. The skeletal girders and outstretched arms of the rides made him uneasy, as if he were sneaking by giant spiders waiting for their prey. He sighed, boot heels crunching along, but something stopped him. It sounded like the coo of a small child. He stopped a moment and listened. There it was again. Despite the cold, sweat rolled in oily rivulets along his neck, under his jacket. The sound grew, as if the approaching. After a brief moment, another voice joined.

Then another. Anton squeezed his eyes closed, his breath seeping between his clenched teeth. He pressed his palms to his ears, muffling the noise, but not killing it completely. When he removed them, it sounded as though a crowd had joined him. Laughter, calls for mother, delighted screaming. A calliope started, tinny and strangely off-key.

Anton opened his eyes and looked around. There were people everywhere. The ghost town was now inhabited by so many. The amusement park was teeming with life, but how could it be?

Something was very wrong. In the darkness, they rushed around, climbed onto dark rides, cried out in delight on a Tilt-a-Whirl that did not spin, a Ferris wheel that did not turn.

A small girl in a summer dress, inappropriate for the colder weather, fluttered by like a fragile moth. Anton grabbed her arm.

"What are you people doing here?" he asked.

As the girl turned her small face to his, the moonlight caught her features. Her flesh had peeled away from her cheeks and nose, revealing the delicate bone beneath, stark against the darkness. Anton gasped and let go.

"This is where we go when the world ends," she answered, her voice too airy and rough for such a small child.

She rushed to a stooped over man twenty yards ahead and took his hand. As they moved away, she glanced over her shoulder at Anton, who wiped his hand furiously on the seat of his pants, as though part of her had come off on him.

He sprinted toward his old apartment building, passed the cavern of the Pripyat Café, his boots slipping in the remains of snow that lay heaviest in the places the sunshine never touched. He turned and looked back once he was away.

Nothing. The strange crowd had vanished and the world was again sinister and empty. He jogged across the cracked roads and the weed-infested lawns and courtyards. Big gymnasiums with hockey rinks and swimming pools, shopping centers, hotels and hospitals, all looted and many covered with chilling graffiti paintings of shadowy children. People had lived there, once upon a time.

He wondered if his home had been looted as well. Perhaps the Dancing Water had been discovered. It may be gone.

He recognized the Taganka apartment building by the distinctive hammer and sickle emblem that sat atop the twenty stories. Just as he approached the building, a guard truck rumbled by training a wide, blinding spotlight along all the entrances, scanning for looters who may have slipped into the city undetected. Anton fled the light like an insect. Skirting around the back of the building, he found himself standing in the little courtyard where he and his sweet twin had danced with two other teenagers in a rain of poison twenty-five years earlier.

The grass was still sparse here in the piss-colored moonlight. He stood for a moment regarding the desolation of his old home. Only after he heard a voice did he realize that a boy was staring very intently at him.

The boy whispered, "Mother, do you know that man?"

The mother shot a quick look his way, placed her hand to her mouth, as if in horror and shook her head. "Don't look at him."

The wretched familiarity of the moment made Anton's belly clench and the tiny hairs in the back of his arms prickle. He turned and headed for the back entrance of the apartment building.

The door had been pried away and hung loosely on one rusted hinge. He pushed it aside and went in, the gloom swallowing him.

In the cavern of the building, Anton was able to switch on his flashlight without worrying about being spotted by the guards, as there were few windows in the lobby and none in the stairwell. His feet and his harsh breathing competed in the otherwise silent corridor. A rotting hay-filled doll with chaotic hair and one half-closed eye lay on the landing of the second floor. He pushed it aside with his toe.

Once on his floor, he moved slowly along the yellow stream the flashlight cut through the blackness. Things scurried in the shadows, but he did not turn the light toward the sounds—he would just as soon not know what was secretly watching him. However, the thought of the mutated wolf popped into this mind and he wondered despairingly what the rats might be like.

When he reached the door to his old home, he saw that it had been jimmied open and stood ajar. Even after so long, he felt violated. Many of their old belongings—books, papers, photos—were scattered on the floor. He would take those now. Mother's favorite lamp, an atrocious blue and white thing, lay in pieces.

Anton fled to his old bedroom. That room was very much has he had left it, but still his heart leapt against the confines of his chest as if it wanted to escape. With shaking hands, he ripped away the Scorpions poster and shoved his hand into the cave of the wall, unmindful suddenly of spiders or even double-headed rats.

There was a frantic moment when he was positive the vial was gone, but after some frantic groping, his fingers wrapped around the cold glass. He pulled it from the plaster, his hand and the vial shrouded in sticky cobweb. Trembling, he held it before the flashlight.

Inside the dusty glass, the Dancing Water swirled, rotating as ceaselessly as the earth's path around the sun.

Wiping his hand on the leg of his jeans, as he had when he had touched the hand of the ghostly little girl, he collapsed on his bed. A plume of dust sprang from the covers and settled upon him. He held the vial before his eyes again, shining the light on it. He laughed. He had it. Now he could go home.

But what would he tell Elena? In the cool darkness, he thought of the doctor's visits. The Chernobyl death—it waited for all who had breathed the poisoned air. It was just a matter of time. Lingering, like a serpent in the grass.

Anton imagined it, the cancer, like a sinister mass, seething, cells migrating, dividing, multiplying, a spiderweb of illness woven through the soft, wrinkled fibers of his flesh. He would die as Elena was dying, eaten from the inside out, saving the brain and the heart for last because the disease was a hateful thing. The Buddhists called it Karma, but every faith carries a similar concept—getting what one deserved. If Elena would not be spared, there would be little chance for him.

Gripping the vial savagely in his fist, Anton looked around, feeling for a moment as though someone had seen inside his heart. He shivered, hung the precious elixir around his neck and stretched out on the bed. The trek to this apartment had taken more out of him than he expected. He would rest a bit before returning to his bike.

He dreamed of the doubled-headed wolf who had visited him outside the city. It spoke to him with the voice of his grandfather. "She becomes one with the night and weaves the darkness into her hair."

★ ★ ★

The shrieking woke him and he lay a moment, the cold seeping in through the broken window, wondering if he were back in the Minsk Asylum. Tears had dried on his face and made his skin feel too tight around his eyes. Instinctively he checked his throat for the vial of Dancing Water and sat up, rubbing his eyes. Dreams were many things and maybe these had been harbingers. In his heart, he knew Elena was gone. The wolf had so much as told him.

Outside, it was still night, but he must have slept for several hours. The shrieking pierced the quiet once again. Perhaps he was still in the trenches of the nightmares, he reasoned. He bit the inside of his cheek hard enough to bring the taint of salty blood, and squeezed his eyes closed.

This never worked, he had only recently discovered. When he opened them again, nothing had changed. The sickeningly familiar stink of urine and soiled diapers flooded the air and the sliding, fumbling sound of something moving, awkward and halting, grew closer to the open door of his bedroom.

Anton stared toward the door as Boris slithered passed, moving along with overly muscular arms, dragging his dead lower half behind, leaving a trail of something glinting wet in the gloom.

He contemplated for a moment if he wanted to follow. Did he really want to see? Did he really want to know?

The little transistor radio hissed to life from the spot on his nightstand where it had stood for the last quarter century. *An accident has occurred at the Chernobyl Nuclear Power Plant. One of the atomic reactors has been damaged. Aid will be given to those affected and a committee of government inquiry has been set up.*

He jumped. Snatching up the little receiver, he flung it against the wall. It crashed in a minor explosion, but the announcement continued, although more faint than before. He fled the room before he could hear anymore.

In the hallway, Boris' slugstrail ended after only a few feet, as if he had been swept away by an unseen hand.

Slowly, Anton moved back toward the living room. Shadows writhed on the wall and he thought he heard a voice, murmuring. Not an unhappy sound, but something familiar yet buried by layers of time.

Elena moved from the cloak of shadow to allow him to see her clearly. Her skin glowed, nearly transparent. Even in the poor lighting, her veins and blood vessels shown through her flesh like a roadmap, revealing rivers and estuaries.

"Elena?" he whispered, his mouth parched.

"I've been waiting for you to realize," she said, her voice as thin as the cold air.

"What are you doing—"

Elena put up a skeletal hand and shook her head. "It doesn't matter now." She moved to the broken out window. "Look."

Anton joined her, the cold wind blowing in, immediately numbing his cheeks and chin. In the pale night people milled around below, some talking, some singing, others laughing. Their sounds floated up slowly to meet his ear. Beyond, the Ferris wheel lights flashed to life, brilliant against the velvety horizon.

"We all come home eventually, Anton," she said.

★ ★ ★

Just inside the line of trees stood a motorcycle, left abandoned, by the look of it. The old man pulled over, squinting against the early morning sun. He had errands to run, things to do, a broken tractor engine to repair, but all of that could wait. He thought he recognized that bike. He climbed from the cab of the rusted Mack truck, his knees creaking too loudly in the silence of the country. He pulled his tattered coat tighter around his throat and stepped carefully down the sloping shoulder. Old bones were brittle and even more so in the cold—he could not afford a fall. The wolves were many out here.

Only yards from the road, he spotted the man, or what was left of him. His throat had been torn away. The pooling blood had frozen in the cold of the night.

The old man approached slowly, mindful of other sounds. It was a sad thing, this man. So young. But many even younger than this one had suffered worse ends. At least this death was quick.

Suddenly the soft crush of leaves underfoot, not his. He stopped, waited, his old heart fluttering like a wounded bird.

From the trees, a wolf stepped forth. It turned first the upper head, and then the lower head and regarded the old man almost knowingly with two sets of eyes.

The old man wet his lips and retreated a step.

The wolf, a wretched thing created from the poison air and water of the region, moved to young man's ruined body. Lowering one muzzle, it lapped at the frozen blood as the other head curiously watched the old man.

After a few moments, the creature trotted back into the cover of the woods and vanished.

Ghost Fleet

by Shawn Proctor

I AM A GHOST.

I am haunted.

I stoop down to draw the lines and numbers in chalk on the ocean liner's stained deck. Then I throw the stone on the hopscotch board and begin. One square, two squares, three, then I stumble. Again, I pick up the stone.

Beyond the corroded bow, a tugboat drags the ship through the Indian Ocean. Gripping the railing, I feel the metal's connection to me. We are linked. Then I turn to where my sister Diana used to wait for her turn to play hopscotch, but she is not there. She has been gone for so long.

As a ten-year-old boy in 1947, I first climbed the gangway onto the ocean liner just behind my parents and Diana. She and I watched silently as the 600-foot ship passed through the San Francisco Bay, away from Alcatraz and the Golden Gate, away from Angel Island. We entered an ocean that shimmered, clear as crystal. We tasted sea air, felt pure salt dry on our lips.

Aboard the ship, Diana and I were told not to be heard or seen. Sometimes we watched water break over the hull, the blue turning to foam. It was like a dream, with the bow cutting wake and pushing us outward and outward.

Bored, we devised games for ourselves: tag on the lower decks, hide-and-go-seek in the dining halls. After four days at sea, she and I began playing hopscotch on the main deck. We drew a court near the bow in chalk we had filched from the dining hall hostess. As the youngest, I went first, tossing my stone and jumping square to square until I reached the final box. But when I tried to turn, I lost my balance and slipped, smearing the line.

Diana was twelve and reached the end each time. She glanced at me and pretended she was about to fall. Her hands drew ovals as she teetered. Then she returned, gracefully retrieving the stone along the way.

"There," she laughed. "Your turn. Your turn."

We were not supposed to play on the ship. We were not to draw on the deck or pocket chalk. Often a grim steward interrupted our game. He would loom over us and gasp upon finding the markings.

"This is unacceptable! Look at this mess," he scolded and shook his finger at us. "Where is your mother? Father?" Then mopping away our board, he said to himself, "Spoiled brats. They must make their parents' hair gray."

I have a secret: I wanted to win. More than anything, I wanted to surprise Diana by finishing the hopscotch board and handing her the stone, giving her that smile. No matter the steward. No matter the trouble.

So long after dark I stole from my family's cabin and drew the board on the deck by the full moon's light. The chalk hissed as I worked. Then I tossed the stone and began. One, two, three, and all of the way to the turn.

Over and again I tried, knowing the longer I stayed away from my sleeping family the more I risked discovery. My mind bubbled with fear. Minutes passed; breath crackled in my throat. On the empty deck, I could hear the knocking of my foot on the wood and the sea winds howling in my ears. But I would still lose my balance each time I spun around to finish.

On my last try I tossed the stone near the end and began once more. I leaped over the box with the stone and landed at the turnaround square. This time I remained upright and began to jump back. As I reached down to pick up the stone and finish, I heard a voice and froze. It was the steward's familiar growl as he sang to himself the song "Don't Explain." I knew that without my parents or sister nearby he would be bolder, angrier. He might even thrash me. I ran. The bow seemed far away as I hurtled through the darkness, the stars streaking overhead.

"What's this? I don't believe this," the steward shouted. "They played more games!"

I could not resist; I glanced over my shoulder, thinking I would see his eyes, a searing red like coal in the nighttime. But it was as if he had vanished. Then I felt a heavy collision, my head ringing, teeth throbbing. Blackness. Then the pain stopped, and my face and chest felt cold. What scared me even more was that I could see my own body—my torso, arms, and head—in my vision, as if I was separated. My form, which had collided with the railing, pitched overboard and tumbled toward the water. I watched as my body fell. I fell. My bare feet vanished into shadow, and my body was gone.

I did not understand. If I had fallen, what of me was left?

At first, I wanted to believe this was a dream, that I had been concussed. I stumbled back and looked at my hands The deck showed through the translucent palms. The flesh had become like a rush of fog, trailing vapor with each motion.

Then I saw the steward again, standing where I had fallen. Shadow ringed his eyes as he looked at my blood on the rail and swung around to the chalked boxes. He scanned the deck and rubbed his lower lip. Grunting, the steward began washing away my hopscotch board, the chalk lines I had made. With bucket in hand, the steward walked to the bow. He scrubbed the railing, blood turning the rag pink. He spit as if he had a foul taste in his mouth, then dumped the soiled water into the ocean. "Brats," he whispered.

In the morning, Diana and my parents began looking in familiar places for me. Soon, their steps were driven by panic. Then the crew searched the whole ship, but it was already too late.

Haunted, I watched Diana sitting on the deck, covering her face in her elbow. She whispered, incanted, and traced the hint of the chalk squares with her finger. Two days later my family left.

Pollution and oil leak from the doomed ocean liner. Like crumbs, asbestos fibers and rust flakes mark our passage. We motor along shipping channels as a beach crests on the smoke-traced horizon. We near our end.

I could not follow my family when they left. Forces tethered me to the ship where I beheld the world from afar: the ports at Southampton, New York, and Liverpool. I sailed through the Panama Canal and around the Cape of Good Hope.

I watched couples walk the deck late at night and listened to confessions a man could only reveal to an ocean, black as velvet. Yet every girl who came to the bow, to see as I once did, only reminded me of Diana, still looking for me. I could not forget how her freckled nose crinkled and bright sun reflected in her eyes when she smiled.

Decades passed and the ship became outdated, dwarfed by newer ocean liners. We booked fewer passages as rust ringed the metal portholes, and red and black paint cracked from the keel plates.

Finally, the ship was dragged into a backwater dock near Baltimore. There, we saw row upon row of vessels, all dormant. Barnacles crusted their undersides. We remained with that fleet for years, hearing only brackish tide water patting against the hulls.

One gray morning, ship workers came to us. Everything of value—all of the brass and gold—was stripped. They left only a husk. Then I saw from the deck a handful of grimy tugboats pull us out into the Atlantic, past the breakers and through international waters. Next, a large, ocean-going tug relieved them and took the ship further away. The captain turned off the tug's locator beacon. To other ships, we became invisible.

Even now as the tug pulls us toward our destination, I see Diana, always out of the corner of my eye, flitting down a hallway. But when I turn to look there is nothing.

A hollow voice on the tug's radio calls, asking for our location and status. No answer. We continue toward the ship-breaking yard in India. There, workers will set upon us with blowtorches and hacksaws. They will gut the ocean liner for scrap, yet the vessel's poisons will linger on. The toxins, once spilled, will infect the sea for generations.

Our fate lies together.

Until that day, when we finally crash onto the beach, I will continue tracing squares on the deck. I toss the stone. The game goes on. One, two, three, and down until our end.

The Church of the Open Sky

by Stephen Gaskell

"Game on, Cory!"

My brother, Ty, didn't wait for a reply. He just turned his board and paddled away. Beyond him, under postcard blue skies the sea looked like a featureless plain.

What could he see?

And then I saw it. A huge swell that had formed hundreds of miles off the Balinese coast was finally reaching its destination.

"Damn!" I stopped straddling my board and chased after him with furious strokes. It was like he had fucking radar. Maybe he felt the currents in his toes, or could hear the ocean rumble. Whatever it was, he was always first.

And I was always behind.

The smell of board wax, ritualistically applied a couple of hours earlier, mingled with the odors of salt water and sweat as I watched the swell hurtle in. As it crossed the continental shelf it slowed up and resolved itself into a set of six or seven waves. The third one was the prize. Super-clean, it was one of those perfect waves which comes only once a session. If at all.

Ahead, I saw Ty adjusting his line to meet it, his powerful tanned arms slipping in and out of the water with barely a splash. My own stroke was choppy and messed up. I had the advantage of youth and could beat him at arm-wrestling these days, but without finesse, that extra strength meant nothing in the water.

He was going to get the wave.

Sunlight glinted off his back as he swivelled about, readying himself. His propeller arms started up again and he raced towards me. His expression was a mixture of reverence and focus, but as he passed he took a moment to give me one of his crazy grins like all he cared about was the rush.

I made it over the crest and watched him disappear as the wave broke with a tremendous crash. If I had more balls I might've screwed etiquette and dropped in right in front of him. If I had more balls I wouldn't always be second-best.

I pictured him cocooned in the tube having the ride of his life, while the judges on the beach looked on with amazement. Even the monkeys overlooking Uluwatu from the cliffs screeched with delight in my imagination. Perfect scores all round.

I punched the water. The sun's rays bristled on my shoulders and neck. The next wave was lame. And the one after that too. The last one of the set was different though. Not as clean as the one Ty had caught, but gnarlier. And bigger. It was heavy-duty in fact.

In other circumstances I would've left it, but here, pumped-up and craving to prove myself, I couldn't. I twisted about and began paddling before I lost the nerve. The warm offshore breeze carried hints of the palm trees.

When the wave catches you it's like being between the jaws of an enormous, angry monster. You just gotta make sure it doesn't swallow you up. Behind me, I felt it closing in, re-arranging itself and rising up like a cobra about to strike. It hissed as the water was sucked upwards. I began to climb.

Five feet.

Make your move too early and the wave will break on you. Ten.

Too late and you'll tumble and be slammed twice as hard. Fifteen.

Time. I grabbed the rails and sprang up as fluidly as I could. The lip fizzed just behind my head. Model entry, I thought, stoked, as I flashed down the solid half-pipe and sea-spray licked at my face. The monster roared, infuriated. Adrenaline coursed through my veins. A one hundred percent natural high. I carved up and down the wave, the sea floor so near I could see tropical fish hiding in the reef.

On the shore ant-like people were clapping or waving. Ty was surrounded by a cluster of girls in skimpy bikinis. I felt a big smile grow on my face; they'd be swarming around me in a minute. Ty broke away from the girls and walked up the beach, board under his arm. Pride flared in my chest. He couldn't stand to see me win.

And then I fell. Everything went into soundless slow-mo. The nose ploughed into the water flipping the tail upwards and catapulting me forward. The people on the beach looked like statues. In the crystal-clear water I saw a purple jellyfish nestled between the coral.

Impact.

The sound and fury came back, noise like standing under a jumbo jet at takeoff. I tumbled round and round so fast I lost sense of up and down. Fierce pain burned my torso from hip to shoulder. I felt the leash yank on my ankle so hard it snapped. Burning lungs. Panic like the time Ty held me underwater in the swimming baths.

Air. I needed air.

I thrashed, desperate.

Never fight the ocean. I heard my brother whisper. *You'll never win.*

I relaxed. As I came to rest near the sea bed, I watched the churning motion of the wave recede, regained my bearings. I was about to kick off, when a shimmer of coloured light to the side caught my eye. I turned my head expecting to the glimmer of scale or fin, but something else coalesced out of the gloom. My blood ran cold. The ethereal form of a young man glided close. He looked Balinese. A ragged scar ran up from his jaw to temple.

I closed my eyes, telling myself I was hallucinating.

Then I blacked out.

* * *

"Stand back! Gimme some space!"

Sun in my eyes. Wet sand underneath. Fire down my side. Sea water came up my throat and I coughed reflexively.

"Cory! Jesus, Cory. You scared the shit outta me." My brother cradled me in his arms. His heart pumped hard through his sopping rash vest. I wanted to say something funny, but I was too weak and my lungs were still filled. All I could do was splutter sea water down his back.

Now, not only is my brother better at everything I do, he's a fucking lifesaver too. Shit. Couldn't someone else have rescued me?

I collapsed back flat on the sand. Someone sterilized my gash, causing me to cry out in pain. It wasn't all bad. There were some beautiful girls cooing in sympathy and leaning right over me. "Is he okay? He was under for ages," one of them said.

"We Compsons got big lungs. Right, Cory?" Ty said.

I nodded, wincing.

"So why'd you take on that wave, brah?"

I didn't want to get into any motivational analysis so I ignored the question. "Thanks…" I croaked, "…thanks for saving my butt, Ty."

"Don't thank me, I just pulled you out from the shoreline. How you got washed in so fast is a miracle." He gripped my shoulder and looked at me hard. "Why that wave, Cory?"

A numbness was spreading from my side. I peered down. The wound was wide and deep and the colour of red chilies.

"Did I beat you, Ty?" I said softly.

"Did you beat me?" he whispered. His eyes were wide, disbelieving. He raised his voice. "Did you beat me?" Some surfers staring at the waves out of respect or false nonchalance turned around and looked at us. "Are you serious? How many times, Cory? How many fucking times?" He clenched my jaw so I couldn't look away. "This isn't about you and me. It's not about you and anybody else. It's about you. You alone. Nobody else. If you want to beat something, beat the ocean. Just make sure you do it every time."

He let go and walked away. He was right. I know that now. But back then I was still a kid and I had to live every day in the shadow of Ty Compson—surf legend, rock star, buccaneer— and it killed me.

A long shadow loomed over me. A lanky dude with a tangle of red hair and a wild beard crouched down. "Ty's pissed 'cause he cares," he said.

I grunted. I didn't feel like having a Kodak moment with some weirdo.

He looked at my gash and sucked in air. "Nasty cut. Don't worry, we'll get it fixed up faster than you can say magical surfing Mecca." He grinned. "You, me, and your brah are going on an adventure."

★ ★ ★

The dude's name was Bob Laverty. I'd heard his name mentioned on the beaches of Kuta and Uluwatu. He was Sir

Francis Drake of the surfing world. Instead of combing islands searching for Spanish gold, Bob hunted for unknown surf spots where perfect waves peeled off in exotic settings.

And he'd just spied some sweet loot while flying in from Jakarta. He told me he'd gasped "wow!" so loudly the guy next to him had woken up with a start and the air-hostess had run down the aisle to see if everything was okay. Well, we all said "wow!" more than we should have in those days. Bob brushed off his outburst with an inane remark about the clouds.

That was how careful Bob was about keeping new spots low profile. You see, word was getting out about Bali. Soon hundreds of guys would be landing at the island's airport and heading straight for the beach and the line-up. Bob wanted to get off the beaten track and find those hidden barrels of gold before anybody else.

I was totally up for it. Bob was a Californian who'd bailed on an executive position in his father's business and had an American dream enthusiasm which was infectious. Even Ty's reservations about the straits, the malaria, the communists, and the jungle, couldn't put us off the mission.

We were doing this.

Our route was going to be fully guerilla. Ferry to Java and then overland to the spot.

We hired three Suzuki 80's with the fattest wheels we could find and set out from Kuta with the morning dew still fresh on the greenery. With boards hung at our sides and camping gear backpacked well over our heads, we were ridiculously overloaded.

Bob led. With his snarl of flaming hair and rolled-up British Admiralty sea chart poking out the top of his pack, he looked like a Viking adventurer. Ty and I followed, goofy grins plastered across our faces.

Volcano tops rose majestically out of the mist. We traversed hills terraced with stepped paddy fields, the only sounds our growling engines. I felt like Marco Polo boldly approaching terra incognito.

At a small village where hikers began their ascent of Gunung Agung we stopped for coffee and scrambled eggs. As I went up to pay, a worn photograph tacked to the bamboo wall stopped me cold.

It was a close-up of a young local man with a boisterous head of hair. He wore a wide smile which revealed a set of gap-ridden teeth. On his cheek was a deep scar from eye to jaw. He looked completely at ease with the world.

The woman who'd served us breakfast held out her hand for the money. I counted out a few bills, hands shaking. "Who is that?" I asked, pointing at the photo as she checked the notes.

A sorrowful look passed over her face before she answered. "That's Thanh, my beautiful boy. He die last year."

I had to ask the next question. "How did he die?"

"He die surfing Uluwatu."

★ ★ ★

All the way down to Gilamanuk the woman's words spun around my head. Did I really see a ghost in the water? Or was it a trick of a desperate mind? Maybe I'd seen Thanh's photo before, at one of his old hangouts—a beach bar or a board-shaper's outfit in Kuta. The only thing I knew was that there was a connection between this expedition and what had happened in the water.

Whatever the truth, I needed to get to the bottom of it. There could be no turning back.

★ ★ ★

On Java we made good time gunning along the broken roads.

The last village before the spot was called Grajagan. We found a couple of fishermen to take us over the lagoon to the coastal beach. We ripped over the hard-packed sand with the red sun dipping below the tree line of the jungle and a mild breeze carrying hints of timber and soil.

A flock of flamingos crashed skyward as we passed, and our spirits soared with them. For a while I forgot about Thanh, forgot about living in Ty's shadow, forgot about everything except the moment.

It was bliss.

Eventually the sand gave way to loose, broken coral. Even the fat tires of the Suzuki's couldn't cut the surface and we had to ditch the bikes in the jungle. We knew we were close from the sea spray carried on the wind. We set out on foot energized, but when we stepped back onto the beach we sank to our shins in soft sand.

"Holy shit!" Ty said, staggering backwards.

We stood at the edge of the jungle and scanned the beach for a route across. The glittering quicksand stretched ahead as far as the eye could see.

"This stuff is a death trap," Bob said, rolling grains of the fine sand between thumb and forefinger. "What now?"

"We cut through the jungle," I said, staring into its dark interior. The air was alive with the clamor of insects and birds and monkeys.

"Are you nuts?" Ty asked.

"We can't back out now," I said. "We're so close I can hear the surf. Listen."

I couldn't hear jack, but we all pricked our ears anyway. Something important was going to happen at the spot. I had to get there. Even if they'd backed out then, I think I'd have gone on alone.

"You're so full of bull," Ty said, but instead of heading for the bikes he pulled out a machete from his pack and walked into the jungle.

He always had to be first.

★ ★ ★

We trekked for over an hour in single-file, only pausing for Ty to hack away vines or brush that blocked our way. Mosquitoes buzzed around and bit us incessantly. Creepers snagged our feet and our strength faded in step with the dying light. We moved in silence, not because we were trying to hide, but because of a reverence for the place.

Several times I felt the eyes of animals on me.

Barely able to see one another in the darkness, we groped our way to the edge of the jungle and collapsed, exhausted.

★ ★ ★

"Get up."

I woke up with a heavy feeling, my body aching from head to toe. Somebody was shaking my shoulder.

"Rise and shine, dudes! Looks like we died and went to heaven." I opened my gummy eyes to see an upside-down Bob swinging his head from side to side. Even upside-down and with his wild beard I could still see the enormous grin on his face.

I flipped onto my feet and ran to the beach. He was right. The surf was magical. The waves looked like they were cut from glass. Flawless tubes which ran and ran and ran.

I tipped my head back and screamed.

We'd found another shrine to the church of the open sky and it was time to worship. Bob joined me, draping an arm over my shoulder. "I'm naming it G-Land," he said. "I think it fits."

G-Land. It had a good ring to it. "Let's go play," I said and ran back up the beach. Ty was still cocooned in his sleeping bag, but he was wriggling about inside. "Surf's up, Ty. Come on."

It was funny. Out in the middle of nowhere with nobody else around, I felt none of the choking feelings of rivalry. I just wanted to share the experience. Nothing more.

He groaned and began another bout of furious motion.

"You okay, brah?" I said, crouching down.

He sat up, writhed his way out of the bag and kicked it away. Every inch of his body was peppered in mosquito bites. Where he'd scratched, his nails had left long gouges of red raw flesh.

"Jesus!" Bob said.

I gaped dumbly at my brother. Bob and I'd been bitten too, but nothing like this. Ty began rifling through his pack, scattering rash vests and tinned food and camping gear.

"You need treatment, brah," I said, mesmerized by the scarlet streaks like war paint on his back.

"Surf's good?" he asked, pocketing a bottle of lotion in the back of his shorts.

"Cory's right," said Bob. "Malaria ain't a picnic. You need to see a doctor."

"Did you see any hospitals on the way?" Ty replied, delving his arm into the pack as if it were a grab bag.

"We can go back—"

"Here it is!" Ty rattled a bottle of pills like a maraca and clicked off the cap. "Larium. We shoulda taken 'em before but better late than never, right?" He poured a small mound of black and white capsules into his palm and offered them around. I took one.

"Take another one for luck, Cory."

What harm could it do? We were behind on our dosage plan after all. I took another one. Bob took two as well.

"Looks like I get seconds," Ty said. He popped his hand up to his mouth, jerked his head back, and swallowed the pills.

"How many was that?" I'd counted at least five.

"Enough to beat the crap outta any malaria in the bloodstream," Ty said, unzipping his board bag. "Now, let's catch some waves."

I shook my head. And he was supposed to be the sensible one.

* * *

We surfed as if G-Land was a theme park and we had unlimited rides for one day only. It wasn't so far from the truth. Limited supplies meant our stay would be three days max. It was such a pure experience even Ty seemed to forget about the fire licking his body.

First, there was the focus.

No lifeguards, no helicopter rescue, no familiarity with the reef. Just the three of us and nature unleashed. Razor sharp coral, powerful rips out to the ocean proper, prowling sharks, and impact zones so violent wiping-out didn't bear thinking about.

Then, there was the rush.

Skimming along inside a whispering almond barrel, pristine rainforest on the shoreline and the spines of sea urchins swaying below, you were cut loose from everything.

Apotheosis of a surfer.

Eventually, with a crescent moon rising in the purple skies we paddled in. It was low tide and we splashed over the exposed reef, pulling off our vests and warming our chests in the waning sun.

We walked in silence, the only sound faint burrs and chirrups from the distant jungle. My body felt drained but at peace. A million mosquitoes wouldn't wake me tonight.

"Fuck!"

A couple of yards ahead Bob toppled to the ground clutching his foot. A steady rivulet of blood ran from a long clean slice along his sole.

"Let me see," Ty said.

"Careful," Bob gasped, nodding at a section of sunset coloured coral.

It took two looks to see what he was indicating as it was so well camouflaged. A stonefish. Dead. Its lidless eye like a black marble pressed into its wart-like skin. Grooved spines protruded from its fins.

"This fucker's poisonous, isn't it?" Bob said, shaking.

Ty carefully picked up the bloated fish and studied it. "Deadly," he replied, running a finger along tips of the spines. "Lucky for you none of the glands popped. It's just a cut."

I could see the relief wash over Bob. "Nine hours surfing a deadly reef and I get downed on the shoreline. Epic."

We wrapped a vest tight around Bob's foot and helped him limp back as he hung an arm on each of our shoulders.

We looked like three guys at the end of a bar crawl.

★ ★ ★

"You guys carry on tomorrow," Bob said. His face looked serene in the flickering light of the fire.

"You sure?" I turned over my twig-skewered frankfurter that fizzled in the flames.

"Sure. It's no biggie. I got to ride G-Land. That's the main thing. The rest is all part of the adventure."

"Amen to that," I said, and bit eagerly into my dog.

"We'll give you a good show," Ty said. "Won't we, Cory?"

There was something about his voice which was odd. Maybe the cadence was wrong or he was slurring his words slightly. Or maybe it was just the tone.

"Yeah, it'll be a good show," I said without heart. Maybe the bites were irritating him again.

The brush crackled in the fire and we ate beans and corn, knocking our forks against the sides of the cans. Above, the night sky was luminous from a million constellations.

After a while, Bob said, "You know what a virgin spot means, don't you?"

I shrugged my shoulders.

"There's an old myth about—"

"Is this more of your spiritual crap, Bob?" Ty said.

I didn't know what'd gotten into my brother. He never talked to anyone like that. I met Bob's eyes over the flames. My own incomprehension was mirrored on his face.

"I'm going to bed." Ty got up, swayed and left. From the darkness we heard the sound of retching.

"It's the Larium," Bob said. "I checked the bottle. Possible side effects include nausea, dizziness... and personality change. I felt funny myself when we came out of the water. Probably why I stepped on that fish. I was hoping I was the only one. You okay?"

"A mild headache, that's all. We gotta stop him from taking more pills."

"Already covered that base," Bob said, rattling the medicine in his hand. "We gotta stop him from going in the water, too."

"Right," I said, "I'll get up first light and hide his board."

We cleared up the rubbish and doused the fire, the stones hissing like snakes.

"What was the myth?" I asked as we made our way up the beach, Bob hopping along, leaning on my arm.

"The myth is this. It is said that ghosts linger in the seas. In bays, in ports, in harbors, in deserted coves and in the gentle waters of tourist beaches. These apparitions are the spirits of dead men. Any man who dies in virgin waters where none have died before, whatever his station in life, will be trapped on this Earth and will haunt those waters for eternity." His voice dropped to a whisper. "And it's a safe bet nobody's been lost here yet." He suddenly pinched my side and yelled: "So don't go dying out there tomorrow!"

I didn't react in the slightest.

All I could think of was nearly drowning at Uluwatu and seeing Thanh.

Could it be true?

* * *

I was alone in the jungle.

The odd star could be seen through the canopy as I scrambled through the undergrowth. A chorus of frogs croaked in unseen places.

I was running from something.

Something fleet and deadly.

Ferns brushed my shins. The forest smelt of a spring day after rain. Fresh. Anticipating.

Ahead, through a last bank of trees, I saw moonlight reflecting on the calm sea. White surf lapped at the shore.

I'd nearly made it. The beach offered sanctuary.

Behind me, the beast panted with smooth breaths.

And then I tripped. I spun head-over-heels onto the ground. As I flipped myself up I saw that I was an animal myself. An animal with a velvet black hide.

A panther.

I twisted around and tensed, expecting to be attacked

any moment.

A pair of eyes, tar-black pupils inside a halo of the palest green, hung in the air. The shape of the beast gradually became clear as we both waited.

It was a panther too.

A panther ready to pounce like myself.

My calves burned. Something flashed in the panther's eyes. I leapt.

We snarled in unison. Wild, primitive cries. And then I knew what I'd recognized in those eyes.

★ ★ ★

"Cory! Cory!"

Through the sleeping bag I felt a hand tugging at my foot.

I opened my eyes. Bob was leaning into the tent. A faint breeze blew in carrying the smell of the ocean.

"Your brother's gone out."

I rubbed my face, reality and dreams still blurring.

"Ty's gone out to surf. Look!" Bob moved aside. Through the hazy early morning air I saw a figure in the water. It was Ty. He was caught inside, duck-diving the breaking waves. He wasn't getting anywhere.

"He's still all fucked up on those pills," Bob said. "I tried to stop him. You gotta get him out of the water, Cory."

I kicked off the sleeping bag and scrabbled out of the tent. G-Land was different at this time of day. Everything was stark. Focused. The sand felt rough between my toes and the sky was flat. Beyond Ty, who was still struggling in the wash, the surf was all choppy.

I grabbed my board, dashed down to the shore, and launched myself into the water, not even bothering to fasten the leash. The waves lapped over the board, chilling me.

Ahead, Ty had pushed through the breaking waves and was straddling his board outback. All I could see was his broad back, his gaze fixed on the horizon. I powered on, dipping deep beneath the surface with each passing break. "Hey, brah!" I shouted when Ty was in earshot.

He turned his head. His neck was taut and flush. "You tryin' to join my dawn patrol, Cory?" he said menacingly. He looked exhausted. His face worn and scuffed like the sandpaper we used to smooth the boards.

I had to play this right. "I was hoping. Jack shit rollin' in though. Think I'm going to paddle in and get some breakfast. How about you?"

Ty was a hog when it came to food, and I could tell my words were making him hungry. He checked the horizon again. Nothing was happening.

"Okay, let's eat," he said, "I'll race you. Last one back to camp's a Mommy's boy."

It was a jibe from our childhood. He always said it when I ran crying to Mom after he beat me at a game or in a fight. The taunt still worked. I felt the wounded pride tightening in my chest. A mashed up wave broke and Ty started paddling. He had the panther eyes. Goading. Sneering.

I pointed the board at the beach and paddled hard.

We caught the same frothy nothing and pumped our boards like bellows. I had to win. The rough waters churned against the bottom of the board. Balancing was hard.

And then we touched boards and I was falling.

Into the chilly waters. Darkness. Spinning like being in one of those astronaut training gyroscopes they have at fairgrounds or student balls. Dizziness. I was in a bad spot, the turbulence keeping me pinned down, while my lungs screamed for air.

Finally I came up, leaping out the water like a salmon. I felt light. Liberated. That was way too close and way too stupid.

On the shoreline I saw my board being washed down the beach. With its lime green leash trailing behind it looked like an escaped dog. Ty was lying face down on the beach. He coughed up some seawater and rolled over. And then I saw Bob hobbling down the beach, his crutch a branch of gnarled wood.

He passed my brother and splashed into the water.

I waded towards him.

"Where you going, Bob?" I called.

He didn't reply. Just kept slogging on, bearing down on me like a freight train. His face looked desperate.

"What's the matter?" I said.

He was right up close, the waterline halfway up his chest. An awful gasping sob left his lips.

And then he passed me by, not five feet away.

I spun around. Effortlessly.

And saw my lifeless body face down in the water.

* * *

They did what they could to revive me, hauling my body to the beach and giving me mouth-to-mouth, but it was too late. In the afternoon they performed a simple service and then buried me in a small glade near the edge of the jungle.

I tried everything I could think of to make contact, to let them know my essence was still alive, to let Ty know it wasn't his fault, but they remained oblivious to my presence.

The next day they packed up in silence and left.

Over the following days, I learnt that I was tied to this place. That if I strayed too far from the locus of my death I would begin to fade away. The thought of complete death terrified me and I always turned back.

G-Land was my kingdom.

About a month later, Ty returned. In that single month he'd changed a lot. His skin had lost its shine and his build was thinner. He never smiled. There was a restlessness about him and I often found him gazing out at the water.

He cleared a section of jungle and built a hut which was to become the first of many. News of G-Land got out and new surfers arrived. Ty Compson's surf camp grew.

I found that the worlds of the living and the dead sometimes touched so that by day I could be a guardian to troubled surfers. By night I would join them around the campfire and listen to their stories.

One day Ty experienced a bad wipeout. I glided over to him, impervious to the vicious undertow that was pulling him deeper. He was pale and his lips had a blue tinge.

I placed my hand against his face, the ball of my thumb resting against his jaw line and the tips of my fingers against the side of his brow.

He opened his eyes, startled.

"I'm still here, brah," I mouthed, "and it wasn't your fault."

Years sloughed off his face. He smiled.

I took his hand and pulled him upwards.

Shona

by Dave Siddall

EVERYONE SAID JOHN BLACK WAS A BAD MAN. But no one knew how bad until that summer when a girl went missing. And though there was never any proof, never any evidence linking him to the girl, people talked. Black vanished. Later, when his bloated, violated body washed up on the cold sea shore, those same people agreed: it was a fitting end to such a bad man.

The girl, it has to be said, was never found.

I had heard the story before, and when my colleagues discovered the location of my transfer, I heard it many times over. Looking out of the train window, the story played again in my mind, and I wondered how one person could do such a thing to another.

Settling back in my seat, I yawned and closed my eyes. Lulled by the carriage's gentle motion, I had begun to doze when a sudden lurch jolted me awake. I stretched my arms and gazed once more out of the window. A flat sea sulked beneath an endless grey sky. I passed a hand across my eyes and looked over the carriage. I shared it with just one other person. She sat opposite and two rows up. Pretty with cropped blond hair, she was young enough to still be at school and must have gotten on at one of the many small stations while I had been dozing. A silver cross hung around her neck and when she saw me looking, she stared back. I coughed. "Going far?"

"All the way," she said and stuck her tongue between her lips. She was chewing gum and blew a small pink bubble. It burst and she sucked it back into her mouth.

"I'm going to Greyscar."

Her eyes widened. "Greyscar."

"D'you know it?"

"Not much to know about Greyscar, mate."

"D'you live there?"

She snorted. "You don't live in Greyscar—you just exist." She turned her head away from me and looked out of the window.

I left her alone and let my mind drift with the carriage's sway. A minute passed.

"Why you going then?"

I looked back at the girl. "Work," I said. "I've been transferred from my depot."

She shook her head. "You must have pissed off someone bad to end up in Greyscar."

"I volunteered."

Her mouth dropped in mock horror. "You've got problems. Either that or you're running away from something."

Maybe a flash of truth crossed my face, for an eyebrow arched. "Girlfriend troubles eh?"

"No."

She stopped chewing and licked her lips. "Something else then?"

I opened my mouth, then just as quickly closed it. Heat flushed my cheeks and I turned back to the window. Lost in the glass, the ghost of my reflection stared back: thin, pale, a shadow of the man I once was.

The girl coughed. Maybe she saw a remnant of the hurt that had crossed my face for her voice softened. "How long you here for then?"

"Six," I shrugged, "maybe eight weeks."

She cocked an eyebrow. "You may never get out alive."

We held each other's eyes. A moment later we burst into laughter. "Come on," I said, "It can't be that bad?"

"Oh, it is." Her face clouded as something dark passed in front of her. She drew in and pulled her legs beneath her. "It'll wrap itself around you, get under your skin and before you know, you'll wonder what happened to your life."

She was so sad, so sure of herself, but a decade and more had passed since I had experienced the same teenage angst, hopes, dreams and the unrealistic expectations of youth. I looked at myself in the window. Had anything really changed?

The train began to slow and Greyscar's long, low platform slid past the window. The girl had risen and stood by the doors. As the train shuddered to a stop, they clattered open and she stepped down and away. Grabbing my bag, I quickly followed. It was dusk. A row of Victorian style lamps cast their dismal cones of light upon the platform. Already the girl was halfway along the footbridge.

"Hey," I shouted. "What's your name?"

She stopped walking and looked down. "Shona." As she said it, a mist closed around her, and she was gone.

Fastening my coat, I followed her over the bridge. I stopped and looked at the town. Whoever it was had named Greyscar well: an ugly slash of habitation between the fells and wild Irish Sea. I took it all in, then set off walking.

Opposite the station was a row of pebble-dashed terraces. I crossed and followed the road towards the town centre. On either side tall, stone-built houses glowered upon me. Nothing stirred. I put my head down and walked quickly, my heavy boots resounding off the cracked pavement. Sloping upwards, the road eventually opened into a central square. I took a moment to look around: the war memorial with its faded wreaths, the pot-holed road and shop fronts with single yellow lights giving the whole a seedy, sinister aspect. Greyscar wore its decay like a medal. On the far side was the Barley Mow, its bay windows bulging like greedy eyes. As I pushed open the door, a dozen faces turned from the TV. Stale beer and the lingering tang of old tobacco impregnated the walls. I slipped past half a dozen ragged tables and put my holdall on the floor by the bar.

"Mrs. McAvoy?" A sparse, frigid woman looked up from behind the counter. Any warmth she had once possessed had long since leached into the grim surroundings. "I'm Matt West." Nothing flickered in her dull eyes. "We spoke on the phone—about a room?"

Understanding lightened her features. She shook her head. "Sorry." She put the glass she had been drying beneath the counter. "I was miles away." Turning to a board behind her, she reached for a white fobbed key. There were spaces for six. The others remained in place. "A few weeks you said?"

I glanced along the bar—every face was turned towards mine. Even the pasty-faced kid playing the games machine in the corner paused with a coin in the slot. "It may be longer," I said. An air of expectancy wafted around the bar. "I'm working down the yard." I jerked a thumb in the railway's general direction. "While the regular man's on sick leave."

"That'll be Bob." An old man with a thin face and jug ears waved his pint glass in the air. "He goes to Carlisle tomorrow to get his hernia done." He shook his head. "Can't drive a train with a hernia."

A collective grunt of understanding circled the bar and they went back to their beer and TV.

The key was pushed into my hand. "Thanks."

"Call me Brenda," she said and followed it with a smile that did little to soften her features. She jerked her chin to indicate a thick-set man sitting on a stool at the far end of the bar. "That's Dougie."

Momentarily curious, he lifted his bloated face, stared, then quickly returned his soggy-eyed gaze to the newspaper in front of him. A glass of whisky sat near his right hand. He lifted it to his mouth then wiped the thin whiskers of his beard. For a moment more Brenda stared at her husband. Then she took a deep breath and straightened herself. "Shall I show you the room?"

I picked up my bag, but before I could follow her through to the parlour a voice pulled me back.

"Get 'im a pint. Can't walk into a pub on a Sunday without havin' a pint." It was the boy from the slot machine. Tired of the game, he was looking for better sport. He walked with deliberate slowness and placed his empty glass on the counter beside me. "Go on," he said. "Have a pint." His eyes never left my face. "You've gotta' have a pint on a Sunday."

Everyone watched. It was a defining moment: would I take a drink and join the company, or would I sneak to my room and lock myself away? I dropped my bag. "I'll take a beer," I said and pointed to the boy's empty glass. "Get him one too." The boy said nothing; he didn't even thank me. But as he reached for his fresh pint of lager, I saw his mouth curl into something other than just a grin.

* * *

Silence smothered the world. It was five a.m. I had the streets to myself, but even as I closed the Barley Mow's door, I felt the same oppressive weight hanging over the town that had dogged me since arriving. I breathed deeply and set off towards the yard.

My mouth tasted foul. One drink had led to another. In the Barley Mow the night had ebbed and flowed—Brenda served, Dougie drank. He moved only once from his seat at the counter. A barrel needed changing and he fumbled with the key on his belt before sloping off to the parlour and the locked door of the cellar. I guessed that was his domain.

I did as was expected: answered the questions of the curious and stood my round at the bar. Soon my novelty waned and talk went back to the new season and Whitehaven's prospects in the Championship. The atmosphere was marred only once.

"John Black," I said. "I believe he used to..." Like a paused motion picture, sound and movement ceased. Every face was staring at me.

Brenda came from behind the bar. "We don't talk about him," she said leaning into me. "We don't even mention his name." She turned her back and moved amongst the tables collecting empty glasses.

I waited until talk trickled back to normality and then sought sanctuary in another beer. But I sensed a change. Isolated at the end of the bar, once more I was an outsider. The brief moment of fellowship was gone—perhaps forever. The slack-jawed kid did little to hide his amusement. Enjoying my unease, he sat with a sly grin on his face and even now, the morning after, his thin, unsavoury face was the one that remained in my conscious.

The shunting yard was a little to the north of Greyscar station. I made my way past the signal box to the cabin and booked on with the clerk. Then I picked my way across the tracks to the engine. It had rained during the night, and a half moon's reflective light glistened off the slick rails. I connected the batteries, turned the key and waited until the engine settled into a steady throb before making my way back.

I paused in the doorway and looked in. The small windowless cabin was set with plastic chairs and formica tables. A dozen dirty mugs littered their tops. The warmth was suffused with the stale stench of men at work. A heady aroma of packaged food and wet clothes drying by the electric fire completed the brew. Les Griffin was there. He waited until I poured myself a mug of tea then folded his newspaper. "Finish that and we'll make a start."

It was Les's job to prepare the trains for departure. I would work under his instructions, and for the next few weeks our partnership would either flourish or fail. Both of us knew the score. Some never reached a rapport while others knew their partners so well it made the work easy.

I took a sip and put the mug down. "Start now if you like?"

"Plenty of time lad."

We had met a few weeks before when I had visited the yard to see the workings and learn the layout. "Much on," I said.

He consulted the train list on the table. "A Carlisle trip, two ore for Workington and a ballast for night working at St. Bees." He slurped his tea and eyed me over the rim of his glasses. We'd see.

But I knew my work and Les's hand-signals were clear and precise. We made short work of the wagons stabled in the yard overnight, and as dawn broke the familiar sounds and smells of a working freight yard filled my world. By ten we had the bulk of the work finished and were in the cabin waiting the return of the Carlisle trip. In the corner, a game of 'three card brag' was played out by a pair of waiting train crews.

I sat opposite Les and stirred sugar into my tea. Behind him, the clerk had folded the cover of a paperback novel back on itself and was silently reading.

I yawned.

"Late night was it?" Les munched a sandwich. I shrugged. "Believe you're stopping at the Barley Mow?"

I looked up and nodded.

He smiled and ran his tongue round the inside of his lip. "You'll find some characters in there, lad."

"I've noticed." I felt myself frowning. "Boy about eighteen. He's got this way of looking at you." I jabbed two fingers in front of my eyes.

Les nodded. "Joel Graves. He can be an awkward little so-and-so." He stopped eating. "Why, what's he done?"

"Nothing," I said. "Not yet."

"He was a good trail-bike rider, scrambling and such. He even had an invite to try speedway with 'Belle Vue' but broke his ankle larking about on a mate's Honda." John shrugged. "Now he thinks the world owes him a favour." He shrugged and went back to his sandwich and newspaper. A slice of to-mato landed on the print and he flicked it away with the back of his hand.

"Is there anybody you don't know about?"

"Like?"

"John Black?"

He raised his head and looked at me through half closed eyes. Behind him, the clerk shifted in his seat. "Now why would you want to know about him?"

"I've heard the story, and when I mentioned his name in the Barley Mow, I thought I was going to get lynched."

Les ran a finger under his nose. "It's still raw to a lot of people. The girl and what happened after."

"You mean his suicide?"

Les pursed his lips. "Aye, that's what they say isn't it." He looked down at the table. "You've only heard a story and sto-ries get stretched and distorted." He lowered his voice. "John wasn't such a bad bloke, you know." He pulled a face. "A bit odd perhaps." He put a hand beneath his chin and wiggled his fingers. "Had this great black beard and come winter or summer, always wore a trench-coat. But you expect that with an off-comer."

"Off-comer?"

"Aye, come from somewhere else."

"You knew him then?"

"Course I did," and he jerked a thumb over his shoulder. "He were box man."

I sat back. So John Black was the signalman at Greyscar. I wanted to hear more but Les laid a hand on my wrist. "Just remember," he said, "There's more than one side to every story."

"Sure," I said. There were things I wanted to know, things I wanted to understand, but his reluctance to continue was clear. Taking the hint, I looked at my watch. I pushed the chair back. "I'll see if the trip's wired through yet."

Les nodded and bowed his head back over the paper. As I left the room I heard the booking clerk. "What was that all about?"

"Lad's got a lot on his mind."

"Yeah?"

"Don't you know?"

Standing on the other side, I looked through the crack in the door and saw the clerk shake his head.

Les folded the paper. "There were this incident on the main line a few months back…"

I walked outside. I should have known the story would follow. I stumbled my way to the engine, climbed into the cab and there, hidden from the world, I buried my face in my hands.

★ ★ ★

My shift finished at two. Going back to the Barley Mow had little appeal, so I made my way to the bottom end of the shunting yard and jumped the wall. I found myself on top of the sea defences. Across the Solway Firth I could see the hills and mountains of Scotland. Hazy in the afternoon light, they shimmered in the distance. The taste of the sea was on my tongue: salt, seaweed and something else, bitter and not altogether pleasant. I spat on the ground.

The sea defences were a set of stone steps leading to a shale beach. It made a neat path and I followed it for a mile or so when I saw a girl sitting near the beach. I carried on, moving down a step at regular intervals until I stood next to her. "Hi."

Shona never moved. She had pulled her skirt over her knees and was staring at the sea breaking against wooden groynes and rolling over the shore. A series of purple bruises ran along the inside of her leg. More were on her wrists. "Shouldn't you be at school?"

"Who d'you think you are—me mam?"

Not wanting to argue, I lifted my hands defensively. Like the last time, she was chewing gum.

Shona lay back and stared at the sky. I sat beside her and followed her gaze. A blur of white soared high above. "I think I should have liked to have been a seagull."

"Any reason?"

"Freedom," she said. Then beneath her breath so I almost didn't hear added, "There's no one to stop you little bird, no one to clip your wings."

I looked down at her. "You'll get your chance Shona. You'll fly. You've got all the time in the world."

"You think?" She shook her head. "I'm stuck here forever." She sat up and looked at me. "And so will you if you're not careful."

"There are worse places."

A shiver ran through her and she shook her head. "Bad things happen here. Things you wouldn't believe."

I felt she was on the verge of telling me something—something dark and secret. "D'you want to talk?"

"No."

"If someone's hurting you…?"

"You don't understand. But if you stay here long enough you will." She hugged her knees for comfort, and just for a moment there seemed so much sadness inside her that it would all come spewing out. But it passed and Shona moved back into the light.

"So, how d'you like our little town?"

"It's okay," I stammered.

"And the locals?"

"They're—okay too."

Her lips parted and her eyes widened. She held the pose then burst into laughter. "You're weird."

"I shall fit right in then."

We were quiet for a while as I stared out to sea savouring the cold air. Eventually Shona asked, "Why did you come here?"

"I'm covering for a guy having surgery."

"I mean here." She jabbed the step with a finger.

"It was as good a place as any."

She ran a hand through her hair. "Don't say if you don't want to. But don't lie to me."

I opened my mouth, then felt a familiar protest in my guts. I looked at the ground. "I needed a hole to crawl into."

She snorted. "A hole is right."

I didn't laugh. It was hard, but in the end I just said it. "I killed a boy." I waited for some reaction, for shock and revilement, for her to get up and walk away. She didn't. She just sat there so I stammered on. "I was on the main line slowing down for a station and as I turned the corner he was sitting cross-legged in the four foot between the rails. I applied the emergency brake but it was too late. Just before we hit, he looked up and smiled." A wave of nausea passed through me. I shook my head. "What makes someone do such a thing?"

Shona pulled a hand free of her cardigan and placed it in mine. It was small and cold, but at that moment it was the warmest thing in creation. "Was it hard telling me?" she said.

I nodded. "Yes, but you would have heard soon enough. I've learned there are some things you can't keep secret."

"But you chose to tell me. That's a start."

"A start?"

"Yeah. You keep too many things inside. One day you'll burst and everything will come tumbling out."

I looked down, moved the shale around with my foot.

"Did you see anyone?"

"Like?"

"A counsellor."

"No."

"Why not?"

I opened my mouth then just as quickly closed it. "You ask too many questions."

"If you don't ask, you don't know. Shit!" She scrambled to her feet and looked back towards the town.

I followed her gaze. In the distance I could see a figure coming our way.

"Don't say I was here. Don't say you saw me—ever." Before I could reply she ran down to the beach. I looked back. It wasn't long before I recognised the hunched figure of Joel Graves. He wore a baseball cap and grey camouflaged jacket. He walked with his hands dug deep in its pockets. As he passed, his eyes swivelled left and right. He said nothing, but he had seen—I was sure of it. And as he walked into the distance, I had a bad feeling that one day, some day, he would let the world know.

* * *

The Barley Mow had its usual mix of idlers and wasters. Brenda was serving and Joel Graves sat on his stool slotting money into the games machine. He had removed his jacket and folded it over a chair, but his baseball cap remained in place. His eyes scarcely moved from the flashing lights. Brenda watched as I made my way towards the back parlour and the stairs leading to my room. "Can I get you anything, Matt?"

I shook my head. "Maybe later."

I climbed the stairs and lay on my bed looking out of the window. At five o'clock I went down and ate. At six I went back to my room.

The pattern continued. I worked, slept and took long walks by the sea. Day followed day with metronome repetition. The locals remained aloof. I guessed by now they all knew about the boy's death. So I kept myself to myself, going into the bar for an occasional beer but leaving the whisky until I was alone and could drink from the bottle in my room. Only Shona showed an interest. She was a regular on many of my walks, appearing after I had left the confines of the town and disappearing before I returned. I guess she didn't want to be seen in my company, and I was happy to oblige. I began to take her company for granted. In her frail demeanour I saw something of myself. In me, I think she saw a worthy cause. And so the days passed.

It was my third week in Greyscar when a girl went missing.

I was in the Barley Mow looking at a series of framed, black and white photographs showing the town as it once was. Dougie was behind the counter helping himself to a whisky when Brenda bustled in from the kitchen. She placed a steaming plate of pie and mash on my table, then walked away. I sat down and called her back. Wiping hands on apron, she stood by the table. Her mind was elsewhere, the lines on her forehead furrowed to a V. "Any salt and pepper?"

She waved an apology. "Sorry Matt, I'm a bit distracted today."

"Oh?"

"A girl's missing, see."

My chest tightened. "A girl?"

"She never came home from school."

"What's her name?"

"Sarah Cowap."

I breathed a sigh of relief and picked up the knife and fork. "I'm sure she'll be fine." I used the fork to smooth mash into the gravy. "She's probably gone to meet friends. You know what girls are like."

"Aye," she said, "I do. And that's what they said fifteen year back when another girl went missing." She turned abruptly and went to the kitchen. I watched her go. As she passed the bar, I saw Dougie. Our eyes met. For once he seemed more alive, more attuned to the situation. I turned away but his eyes continued to burn the back of my neck. After a few minutes I pushed the plate away. I had lost my appetite.

* * *

The next morning a sharp wind blew from the north. I pulled the door of the Barley Mow shut and walked the empty streets to the yard. I hadn't slept well. Something nagged at my conscious: a thought, an idea, the spirit of John Black perhaps? Whatever it was, it rolled in my head all night.

I checked the engine, then went to the cabin.

The atmosphere was charged, the air almost crackling: no early morning banter, no offer of tea, nobody talking. Even

Les confined his conversation to the job in hand. Mid-morning found me sitting alone on the engine and nursing a mug of tea. Even if not openly hostile, a cold war had begun and I couldn't understand why. The reason became clear when I returned to the Barley Mow. They were waiting for me as I closed the door.

"Mathew West?" A police sergeant and constable stood at the bar. The room fell silent.

"That's me," I said.

The sergeant nodded. "I'm Jones. I'd like a word."

"What about?"

"A missing girl."

Brenda was behind the counter running a cloth around its edge. "Is this the girl you mentioned last night?"

Brenda opened her mouth but before she could reply, Jones broke in. "Know anything about it?"

"Only what Brenda told me." Jones pulled himself away from the bar and gestured to the parlour. He stood to one side and held the door open. As I took a step forward, a voice followed me.

"I seen him with a girl." Joel Graves swivelled round on his stool by the games machine. "A young girl." Sergeant Jones let the door fall shut in my face.

He looked at Graves. "What girl?"

He shrugged. "Just a girl."

There was a stir, a murmur from those whose days revolved around beer and the Racing Post. "Where was this?"

Graves sipped his beer and put a finger to his lips as if he were thinking. "On the beach."

Jones looked at me. "Well?"

I shrugged.

"Was it Sarah Cowap?"

"No."

"So who was she?"

"Not Sarah Cowap."

His face soured. "I haven't time for this." He grabbed my arm. "Bevan." He called the constable. "Take Mr. West into the lounge and see that he doesn't move." He held out his hand. "Keys."

"What?"

"Work keys. Locker and such."

I pulled them from my pocket. "I suppose you want my room key as well?" At that moment Brenda found a spot on the counter that required serious concentration. She rubbed harder with the cloth.

"Aren't you supposed to have a warrant or something?" Jones snatched the keys from my hand. "I guess not." As Bevan pushed me through the door and into the parlour, he looked me over one more time.

"Bevan," he said, jabbing a finger in the constable's chest. "Don't let him out of your sight." The door closed behind me. And as it did, I just had a chance to see Joel Graves slip from his stool and disappear outside.

* * *

I sat in the back room listening to the low murmur of voices from the bar. The sole topic of conversation was me. Bevan stood by the door. Taking his sergeant's words literally, he never lifted his eyes from my face.

I was worried over Shona. However innocent, to an outsider our friendship didn't look good. And in a place like this, no one would understand. I had been there for ten, fifteen minutes when a voice, louder and more agitated than the rest, joined those in the bar.

"Is he here—is he?"

A calmer voice, Dougie's, tried to sooth the other. "Now Joe, you just take it easy. Let the police do their job."

"Has he got my Sarah?"

Other voices joined—agitated, angry—and I saw Bevan shift uneasily by the door. Then I heard Graves. "He's in back. That's where they put him. I saw 'em. They put him in there."

"Right, that's it." Brenda's voice cut a swathe through all the others. "Bar's closed." Through a roar of disapproval, I heard her move through the room. "Doug. See to them over there. Come on—out."

Through universal moans of discontent, I could hear the sounds of glasses thrust down on wooden tables, the heavy tread of feet and the door swing to and fro as people went into the street.

"What about drinking up time?"

"You've had it. And you, Joel Graves, are barred."

"Me!" I could just hear his voice. "What have I done?"

Once more the door banged shut and I heard the bolt thrown across.

A moment later Brenda and Dougie came through. She was wiping her hands on a cloth. "Never seen the like." She looked at me. "That Joel Graves…" She shook her head."

I said nothing.

She tapped Bevan's wrist. "Best get on to your sergeant and tell him we've got a crowd gathering." She opened the door and looked through the room to one of the windows overlooking the street. She lowered her head and squinted trying to get a better view. "Not a very happy crowd."

Before her words were complete, the first brick hit the window. Doug pushed past to see. "They're throwing rocks." He turned to us in the room. His red face had paled.

Another hit the glass. One, thrown harder and with more venom, caught the window at an angle and it burst inwards.

As the breaking glass crashed to the floor, Brenda grabbed Bevan's arm. "Quickly," she said, "before it happens again."

I looked at Brenda, saw the fear in her face and I knew. "Is this what happened to John Black?" But she wasn't listening. Her dull eyes stared into a different time and at another man standing in my place. Brenda's focus returned but before she could reply, I heard a noise from the bar: heavy boots were grinding splintered glass beneath their heels. The mob was in.

I gripped the sides of the chair and looked for somewhere to run. My heart pounded, saliva filled my mouth. There was nowhere to go. Then I heard a voice, a girl's voice, and she said just one word—'Down.' I looked left. The door to the cellar was open.

Bevan's hands were shaking. He was mumbling into the mouthpiece of his walkie-talkie, swivelling left and right trying to get a signal. I jumped up and pointed to the cellar. "C'mon," I shouted, "it's the safest place."

"Not there." Dougie shook his head. Then he looked and for the first time saw that it was open. His mouth dropped and he pulled at the key on his belt. "But the door," he said, "it should be locked. I always keep it locked."

I didn't wait but dashed to the door. After a moment's hesitation, the others followed.

A series of stone steps led down to a long, narrow room. Stale air wafted upwards. Ducking my head under the low plinth, I could see metal barrels and their attendant gas cylinders. A fluorescent light flickered. I paused half way down the steps leaving room for the others to follow and waited while Dougie shut and locked the door from the inside. He sat on the top step, palming the wood as if he could feel what was going on outside.

Bevan stood next to me. "Did you get through?"

He nodded. "They'll be here soon." He looked up at the door and swallowed. I hoped he was right.

I took a step and then another towards the stone flagged floor of the cellar. Peering into the half-light, a breath of air kissed my cheek. I sniffed. There was something on it, an odour—like bubblegum. I looked again. "Shona?"

"What did you say?"

I turned round. Brenda had slipped passed Bevan and was staring into my face. I shrugged. "I thought someone was here—a girl."

"But you called her…?"

"Shona," I said. It was too late for secrets. "She's the girl Graves saw me with." Brenda brought a hand to her lip. Her face was ashen. I gazed into her eyes, my brow furrowing in puzzlement. Then something in my stomach began to swell. I took Brenda's arm and squeezed. "Who is Shona?" She couldn't speak, couldn't move. But an instant later a great sob left her. Her chest heaved and she forced it out.

"My daughter," she said. "The girl John Black took fifteen years ago."

My world lurched. For a moment it seemed the boundaries of reality had changed. Then, just as quickly, a flood of emotions filled me. I looked once more over the dry, musty surroundings of the cellar. "She *was* here. I swear it." Brenda clasped my hand.

Dougie's scream broke our bond. He had been listening and now clamped both hands over his ears and stamped his foot. "No, no, no." The thuds echoed deep into the stone.

Brenda looked to see her husband rocking back and forth. Her eyes narrowed. She climbed the steps until she stood over him and pulled his hands from his ears. "You've never told me. All these years, you've never told me what happened the day she disappeared."

"Nothing."

She tightened her grip on his wrists. "I know when you're lying." She bent close to his face. "Tell me."

"I didn't mean to do it."

Brenda closed her eyes. But there was a new strength inside her. Slowly and deliberately she repeated, "Tell me."

Doug looked up at the closed door of the cellar, pressed his head to the wood—and remembered. "We were on the stairs. She wanted to see them friends of hers and I told her she couldn't go." He moved his head back and forth, his forehead scraping the wooden panel, "but you know what she was like."

"Headstrong," Brenda said. "Like me once."

"She wouldn't listen. She grabbed me and I grabbed her, and then..." He looked back at Brenda and his voice was little more than a whisper. "I hit her."

"You hit my daughter?"

"Just a slap. But she took it bad and ran. She ran so fast I couldn't stop her." Dougie shrugged. "And that was the last time I ever saw her." He shook his head. "Don't you see? I blame me-self. All these years I kept thinking if I hadn't lost my temper, if I hadn't..." He covered his eyes and began to sob.

No one spoke. Like eavesdroppers at confession, Bevan and I looked away. Then something inside me stirred. "Is that everything?"

Doug's eyes dried quickly. And when he looked at me, I saw something dark and bad, something of the man he had once been. "What d'you mean," he said?

"I mean you were fighting on top of the stairs." I shrugged. "Was it just about her going out?"

"I don't know what you're talking about."

"The bruises. Did you always hit her when she wouldn't do what you wanted?"

"Bruises," A sneer crept from his features. "What the hell would you know about bruises?"

We stared at each other. My mind began to reel. I turned quickly and my eyes latched onto the stone flagged floor of the cellar. "She's here isn't she Doug. She's always been here."

The sneer disappeared from Dougie's face, and in its place I saw fear. "You killed her, whether by accident or design I don't know. But you killed her and buried her here—the one place that's your kingdom." I looked away. "And then John Black took the blame because he was different—an off-comer like me."

"But it wasn't my fault. She fell—just fell all the way down."

Silence, as old and grey as death surrounded us. Then an ear-piercing screech. It surrounded us, went through us, reverberated off the walls and reached up to heaven. It was a sound only a mother could make. Then there were other noises too—shouts, a ran, tan, tan on the door and a loud voice demanding it be opened.

Bevan turned the key and pushed it open. Sergeant Jones stood in the frame. One at a time he looked us over. "What's going on here then?" he said.

★ ★ ★

They found Shona McAvoy beneath the stone flags of the cellar. There wasn't much: a few bones, a blue dress and a silver cross she had once worn around her neck.

Handcuffed and taken from the cellar, Doug said nothing. It made little difference—statements from Bevan and myself were enough. Brenda confirmed our story then left to join her sister in Newcastle. No one mentioned my visions.

It transpired that Sarah Cowap was at a friend's house. She hadn't wanted to go home to her father. It was rumoured Social Services were involved.

Shona's bones were buried in the small cemetery adjacent the chapel. I didn't go. I stayed long enough to give my story to the police, packed my bag and was gone on the first train south. It was six months before I found the strength to return.

I bought some lilies and laid them next to the headstone that bore her name. High above a seagull cried on the wind. I watched it circle in the empty sky then wheel away towards the sea. I hoped Shona knew a little of its freedom.

Liz squeezed my arm. "A penny for them?"

"Sorry?"

"Your thoughts," she said.

"Remembering a friend."

"A good friend?"

"Yes," I said, "very good."

Liz nodded. We had met a few months earlier at one of my counselling sessions. She had been temping at the therapy unit and was fool enough to say yes when I asked her to dinner. I was finding it difficult to be without her.

We walked back to the car in silence. On the streets the few people we saw didn't recognise me. If they did, they weren't saying.

As we drove away I paused outside the Barley Mow. I peered through the window into the bar. The new landlord was standing behind the counter. Sitting on a stool beside the games machine, Joel Graves stared at the flashing lights.

"You still haven't told me why we've come?" Liz touched my arm.

"I'll tell you over a beer." I glanced once more at the Barley Mow. At that moment Joel Graves lifted his head and looked out. He saw the car and his brows knitted trying to make out who the driver was. I held his gaze until he turned away and put another coin in the slot. "But not here," I said to Liz. "Somewhere else." I put the car into gear and drove away.

And Greyscar, I left to its ghosts.

Three Steps

by Melissa L. Webb

JOSH RICHARDS TURNED ONTO THE COUNTRY ROAD and slowed down. The trees around him were barely illuminated by the car's headlights.

He looked over at the piece of paper lying on the passenger's seat. Maybe his cousin had given him the wrong directions? There was no way somebody actually lived out here.

"No, this is the right road," he muttered to himself, double-checking the directions. Josh had indeed turned off the highway onto the right road.

He winced at his surroundings. This is why he had spent his twenty-three years in the city. No one should have to venture into a place this dark; but he guessed that's what was done in the middle of Iowa.

Josh sighed as he watched the dark road in front of him. He had enjoyed visiting his aunt and cousin, but he was looking forward to flying back to New York in the morning. A week of being in the tiny town was beginning to take its toll. Moreover, this place had no decent coffee. He was about to go mad from just that.

Suddenly, eyes shone in the headlights. Josh slammed on his brakes and watched as a deer took its time crossing the road. Its eyes never left Josh's as it walked.

Josh shivered as the deer made its way onto the side of the road and stopped, eyes still glued to him.

"Creepy deer," he muttered as he drove past it. Creepy deer. Creepy road. Stupid town. Thank god he had only one more night.

Josh frowned slightly when he saw some light ahead. Why had he let his cousin talk him into going to this party? He could be in bed right now, oblivious to all until it was time to take his flight back to reality.

Josh let out a breath of relief as the road turned into a long driveway. He looked up at the large two-story house in front of him. It was like a beacon of light.

Parking the rental car, Josh smiled slightly at the faint pulse of music coming from inside. He made his way up to the front door and knocked hard, hoping they could hear him above the music. The front door opened and a guy Josh's age stepped out.

"Hey, cuz. I see you found the place," he said through a grin.

Josh reluctantly returned his cousin's grin. "Just barely, Tony. Why on earth would anyone throw a party out here?"

Tony looked slightly offended. "Hey, Paul can't help where he lives."

Josh glanced back over his shoulder with a frown. "I think he can."

Tony laughed. "Come on, I'll introduce you to the rest of the gang."

After the party had ended, Josh sat on the couch with a drink in his hand listening to the story being told.

"And that's how he ended up that way," Karen, Paul's wife, told them. "He had spent too much time in that old building and it had changed him."

"Oh, come on. That never happened," Tony scoffed. "I never heard that."

Paul shrugged. "I did. Only I heard his bed had been made from all of the missing pets in his neighborhood."

April giggled. "Eww, that is so gross." She looked at her sister. "Is that true, Karen?"

Karen nodded solemnly. "That's what they say."

Tony snorted. "It's not true, April. They're just pulling your leg."

"You know as well as I do, Tony, that there are some things you can't explain," Paul said looking away.

Tony looked down at his hands. "The road." He spoke softly.

A hush fell over the group, thick and stagnant.

Josh leaned forward. He knew he was missing something. "What road?"

Tony glanced at him. "It's nothing, cuz."

Josh looked around the room at all the eyes staring at him. There was a look in them he couldn't quite place. "No, it is something. Tell me."

They all squirmed slightly as a sudden weight seemed to fill the room.

Frowning slightly, Paul turned to Josh. "What do you think of our little neck of the woods?"

Josh shook his head, remembering the car ride out. "It's a long way from town," he said and smirked slightly. "It's also really dark."

Paul nodded. "That it is." He glanced over at his wife and then back at Josh. "I take it you don't like our road very much?"

Josh leaned back against the couch. "I can't say I do."

"Yeah," Paul said with a nod. "There's a reason for that." He looked Josh dead in the eye. "There's something wrong with that road."

Josh grinned. "Okay, very funny," he said glancing over at his cousin, waiting for the punch line.

Tony shrugged. "What can I say? It's true. There's something very wrong with the road out here."

Josh looked around at the others. "You guys are messing with me."

Karen shook her head. "Sorry, Josh, but it's absolutely the truth. That road is tainted." She sighed. "I don't know if it just started that way or if something happened there to change it. All I know is that it's bad."

"Bad?" Josh echoed.

"Yeah," April said. "Very bad."

"Okay. You have to be making this up. You live out here," Josh said glancing at Paul and Karen. "You look like you're doing okay to me."

Paul shrugged. "I inherited this house from my great-aunt. I probably wouldn't have bought this place, but as long as we follow the rules, we'll be okay."

"Besides," Karen said, "the land we're sitting on right now is fine. Nothing has ever happened on our property, only on the road."

"Okay," Josh began, still not buying any of it. "So, what are the rules on staying alive on this road?"

Tony looked at him. "During the day, there are no rules. You can walk the road and hike the woods all you want, but come sundown..."

"You better not be anywhere near that road on foot," April finished.

"Why does that make a difference?" Josh asked.

"No one knows," Paul said with a shrug. "But it does. Anyone who walks that road at night is never seen again."

"That's not entirely true, sweetie," Karen said. "Those who are never seen again are the lucky ones. The others, they come back different."

Tony's face looked grim as he glanced at Josh. "I'd call them monstrosities. There is no humanity left in those who come back."

"Like Tom Higgins," April chimed in. "Who's he?" Josh asked.

Paul turned to Josh. "He went hunting on that land. It was just supposed to be a day trip, but he ended up missing for three days."

"When they found him, he was back at his house," Karen told him, "eating his wife and dog."

Josh cringed. "Oh, that's disgusting."

"Yeah, but that's what the road does to you," Tony said with a shrug.

Josh leaned forward, drawn in despite himself. "So, what's out there?"

Paul shook his head. "No one knows. The people who do come back aren't talking."

Karen continued, "But...what is said around town is 'Beware He who walks three steps behind'."

"He who walks three steps behind?" Josh repeated. The words seemed to stick to his tongue. He was quiet for a moment. "Are any of us really safe driving that road at night?"

"Oh, yeah," Paul said. "As long as you stay in the car with the windows rolled up until you're either in our driveway or back on the highway, you'll be fine. That road has never bothered anyone in a car. Never. Only the ones who set foot on the road itself are affected." He looked at Josh and shivered. "I wouldn't walk that road at night for anything in this world, not even to save my own life."

His voice contained such pure honesty that Josh couldn't help but shiver also.

The room grew quiet once again and Josh squirmed in the silence. He cleared his throat. "Well, then. This has been fun but it's getting late. I have an early flight, so...," he said standing up. "I should be going."

The rest of the group got up and followed Josh out to his car.

"It's been good to see you, cuz," Tony said, briefly hugging him. "Don't wait so long for the next visit, okay?"

Josh nodded in sincerity. "I'll try not to. It's always good to see you and Aunt Mary." He turned to the others. "It was nice to meet you all. I had a great time, even if you did try to scare the new guy."

"It's no joke, Josh," Paul told him. "Just keep the windows up and don't stop for anything until you're on the highway."

Josh grinned as he got in behind the wheel. "Okay, I'll keep an eye out for He who walks three steps behind. If I should see him, I'll tell him you say hi." He chuckled slightly as he shut the car door.

The others frowned, but Josh just waved as he pulled down the long driveway.

He knew what they were doing. He had even done it a few times himself. They wanted to get a rise out of the new guy. Well, it wasn't going to work. There was no way he was going to fall for something like that.

As he pulled back onto the road, Josh thought, "Goodbye Iowa. Hello New York City, where the only things to fear are muggers and thieves."

He drove slowly down the road, eyes straight ahead. There might not be any supernatural threat out there, but he stilled needed to keep an eye out for the damned wildlife. Josh remembered that deer with its glowing eyes. He shivered.

"Get a grip, Josh," he muttered. He would not let himself get creeped out over a little ghost story, even if it was extremely dark.

He continued to stare straight ahead, the rental car bouncing along the dirt road. Movement caught his eye, and he turned his head quickly. Darkness. Josh took a deep breath. Now his mind was playing tricks on him.

Gripping the steering wheel even tighter, Josh ignored his fear. A few more minutes and he would be back on the highway headed home.

He didn't know why that story had affected him so much. It was just a silly legend. All small towns had them. It was nothing to be worked up over.

However, when Josh stared straight at the darkness before him, he could almost believe it was a living entity. It seemed to watch him back, as if waiting for him to make one wrong move.

He thought he must be losing his mind. The only thing he needed to worry about was getting back to the city. Fast.

The headlights reflected the stop sign ahead. Josh let out the breath he had been holding. He felt silly as he turned onto the main road. There was nothing out here to be afraid of. It was just a dumb story. He rolled his window down and breathed in the fresh night air. Everything was just fine.

A thud sounded outside and the car shook.

"What?" The car pulled hard to the right. "Just great," he muttered as he guided the car to the side of the road, flicking his hazard lights to life. Just the thing to make this night even worse.

Josh opened the door and walked around to the front of the car. The right tire was completely flat. "Damn," he muttered. "Just what I needed." Well, it could be worse. A simple tire change would fix everything.

He leaned into the car and popped the trunk. He walked to the back and lifted the lid. A road flare, jumper cables, and a flashlight greeted him. Nodding his approval, Josh pulled up the trunk lining. He blinked in shock.

The slot for the spare tire was empty.

"What the hell? Who rents out a car with no spare?" He slammed his fist against the back of the car. He just couldn't catch a break.

The rental company was so getting an earful in the morning. Just see if he was going to pay them now.

Josh flipped open his cell phone. Maybe Tony or Paul would have a spare he could borrow. He looked down at the screen. No service.

"Great." He shoved the phone back into his pocket. "This would never happen in the city."

He grabbed the flashlight from the trunk and slammed the lid closed. What was he going to do now? Ten miles outside of town and his only companions were the shadows the night offered.

He could climb back in the car and wait for help to pass by, but Josh knew his cousin had planned to crash at Paul's house. He wouldn't see any of them until morning and that was too late. He'd miss his flight if he waited that long, and that was just not an option.

It was too far to walk back to town. He turned and looked back the way he had come. The only choice he had was to walk back to Paul's house. A ten-minute walk, and then he could have the guys give him a spare and a ride. It was the only logical choice.

"Beware He who walks three steps behind," echoed darkly through his mind. Did he really want to risk it?

Josh glanced back at the rental car and shook his head. Yeah, like he was really going to spend the whole night on the side of the road just because he was being a big coward. How could he ever live with himself after that? No, walking back to the house was the only choice. He took the keys from the car and locked the doors.

Josh stepped onto the dirt road shining the flashlight around him. The trees surrounded him thickly on both sides, cutting off his view. Just as well; he would rather not get a glimpse into the heart of these woods.

He started forward, sweat building up around his collar. He tried to calm his pounding heart. It was just a road. Roads didn't hurt people. He kept his eyes straight ahead, watching the illuminated spot from his light dance across the ground. That's all there was to it. He just needed to keep walking.

A twig snapped somewhere beyond the road. Josh swung the light beam towards the sound. The trees were empty where the light fell.

Josh shook his head as he brought the light back to the middle of the road. This was ridiculous. Why was he getting all worked up over wildlife? That's all that was out there. No ghosts. No monsters. Just animals.

He continued on, determined not to let the darkness get the best of him. All he needed to deal with was a few more minutes of fear, and then he'd be at the driveway.

Josh froze in his tracks when he heard footsteps along the side of the road. He listened intently for the sound to continue, but only silence met his ears. There was nothing out there.

When he started walking again, the footsteps started once more. Josh swung his flashlight around him. It sounded as if someone was following him from inside the woods. But once again he saw nothing. He shook his head. No one was following him. It was a trick of the woods. They were echoing his footsteps back to him. It was a perfectly normal occurrence.

Josh laughed softly. No wonder everyone was so afraid of this road. They didn't understand the science behind what was happening.

He started walking again, pleased with having solved that little mystery. The footsteps resumed right on cue. He took a deep breath. There was nothing out here to fear.

Josh figured he was halfway there when he heard the footsteps walk out onto the road behind him. He froze. An echo couldn't do that.

"Oh my God." He was too afraid to turn around. Something was on the road behind him. He was sure of it.

Not wanting to die without at least seeing his attacker, Josh screwed up his courage, whirled around, and shined the light on the road.

It was completely empty. He was still alone. The beam of light shook as he turned back around. Fear was being to take over. Every fiber of his body wanted to run. He could be at the house in no time if he just bolted.

"They get you faster if you run," his mind whispered dangerously at him. His heart was hammering and he could feel tears forming in his eyes, yet Josh made his feet start moving. He just needed to keep moving.

The footsteps started up behind him again, closer this time. He ignored the sound the best he could, and just kept walking. The footsteps drew closer still. Josh kept his eyes forward trying to make his mind a blank except for one thought: "I will make it through this."

The footsteps moved even closer until they seemed a hair's breadth away. Josh's body tensed up a second before he felt a hot breath on the back of his neck.

He spun around. Nothing. Once again, he was totally alone. Nothing followed in the darkness behind.

A nervous giggle escaped his mouth. He was losing his mind. The fear of the road had done him in. He needed to get to that house before he went completely insane.

Josh picked up the pace. Everything remained silent around him. No ghostly footsteps this time. He would be okay.

Hot breath seared the back of his neck again. Sweat poured down from him, instantly soaking his clothes.

Josh's sanity threatened to fold. He couldn't go out like this. Not like this. He started to turn around when a weight clamped down on his shoulder.

A screamed died on his lips. He couldn't think. He couldn't move. He was frozen in place as terror engulfed him.

Josh's breathing faltered just enough to snap him out of it. His mind grabbed onto one thought. He had to know what was behind him. He turned his head slowly and looked down at his shoulder.

Long white fingers splayed against his shoulder digging in painfully. The fingers glowed like phosphorus in the darkness.

Josh's vision started to darken. He was afraid he was going to pass out. No, he couldn't yet. He had to know.

But before he could turn around, he felt the thing lean into him. A hot breath whispered in his ear, "You should have listened."

* * *

April looked up as Tony walked into the living room. "I think there's something outside," she told him.

"Like what?" he asked.

She shook her head. "I don't know. I just hear something moving outside."

"Hey, Paul," Tony called out to the kitchen. "April hears something outside."

Paul came into the living room with Karen right behind him. "It's probably a deer. They're all over here at night."

Karen frowned. "I hope they're not eating my roses."

Paul looked over at his wife. "I'll go shoo them away." He opened the front door and flicked on the porch light.

The light illuminated the darkness enough to see a figure lurking past the front porch.

"Hello?" Paul called. "Who's there?"

"Paul," a hoarse voice called back to him.

"Hey, isn't that you're cousin, Tony?" Karen asked.

Tony stepped into the doorway. "Josh, is that you?"

The figure moved into the light of the porch. "Yeah, it's me," he spoke, the words coming out of his ruined lips. He stared at them through bloodshot eyes.

Tony gasped. "What happened, cuz? You look like hell."

Josh looked down at his torn clothes and the dried blood that caked them. He shook his head. "No, Tony," he spoke as he made his way towards them.

They all took a step back to give Josh room to come in.

Josh grinned at them, blood coating his teeth. "I can't look like Hell, Tony, because I'm still three steps away." He stepped across the threshold and into the house.

The Hermits of Hahajima

by Mark Lee Pearson

IT WAS THE NAPALM AGAIN.

Yuuji, teeth bared, fists clenched around the bed sheets, eyes flaming, barked like a fox in a hole, "They're coming! They're coming!"

Naoko rolled off the bed. She grabbed the chair from under the dresser and swung it in front of them for protection.

The napalm cloud bellowed across the room, twisting in circles and casting serpentine shadows across the futon.

Yuuji thrashed his limbs in vain attempts to fight it off. Naoko threw herself onto her husband's convulsing torso. He thrashed again and flung her onto the tatami. Wisps of napalm wrapped around his limbs and mottled his body.

"They're coming!"

"No!" shrieked Naoko. She rolled over and thrust her heel through the paper shoji, shattering the glass behind and bringing Yuuji back to consciousness. The serpentine cloud fled through the broken window, into the night, back out to sea.

The last wisps of the napalm ghost unwrapped itself from their bodies and twisted out of the room. The dust settled in the alcove. Naoko held Yuuji's dripping body close to hers, while outside the tide turned to retreat.

Cool breezes carried the aroma of salt inland. Rasping cicada, bickering gulls and the mild clunk of earthenware pots on lacquered trays echoed in narrow hallways. Naoko's eyelids flickered in the morning light for a moment before she opened them to see her husband lying beside her in a lattice of shadows and sunlight. It took a moment for her to realize the shadows were not shadows at all, but the soil of war: grime, gunpowder, and dried blood.

Naoko picked at her egg roll. Her miso soup and fish remained untouched.

"I am not going back to Chiba," said Yuuji, grabbing his bowl and stuffing rice into his mouth.

Naoko pressed her fingertips on the mahogany table. "It doesn't have to be Chiba. Just back to some kind of civilization."

Yuuji took his time chewing. His dark vulpine eyes unsettled her.

Finally he said, "You have to give it time, Naoko. You'll get used to it." He looked out across the ocean. "You'll learn to love it here."

Naoko turned her face to the window. The wind blew fine strands of long black hair across her pale face. A gull hung in the air over the pine trees. The wind blew it back out to sea. She pushed the wisp of hair from her face, took her plate, stood up and headed for the sink.

Later, in the tatami room, Naoko lay beside Yuuji, aware of the advancing tide, apprehensive of sleep.

"Yuuji?"

"Hmm?"

"Do you think about your father?"

"Not especially."

"Yuuji, I am worried about you."

"I'm not my father, Naoko. It was the war that made him crazy. The War. War isn't an issue now. There is no connection." He reached up to pull off the light, and turned to face the wall, dragging the bed sheet with him. A chill scuttled across Naoko's body. She swallowed hard, pulled a pillow over her breasts and curled up in the dark.

Naoko woke with a start. The digital clock glowed Spartan red: 2:15. Heavy shrouds of dark condensation hung draped across the room.

"Yuuji?"

She sat up and scanned the shadows, heart pounding, throat parched, perspiration forming on her forehead.

"Yuuji? Where are you?"

Barely able to breathe in the room's humidity, she crawled across the tatami to open the window. It was jammed. Chipped and flaking paint came away in her hands. Wrenching it, she slipped and scraped her palm on the frame. She yelped as a splinter of pain shot through her hand.

A dull, seemingly distant explosion shook the room. And there it was again: the smell of napalm. Her heart thrummed to a halt. She turned her head and saw a dark figure standing in the darkness between her and the door, tall, muscular, naked. The flesh of his body was sizzling beneath its napalm veil.

"Yuuji?"

"Yuuji had to go."

The dark, wispy figure stalked toward her, forcing her to back against the window.

"Stop fooling around, Yuuji."

"Yuuji had to go." The voice was sinister. Not like Yuuji at all. He reached out to her. She parried him with her forearm, but he caught her wrists and gripped them until his fingers burned into her flesh.

"Take me back," he said.

"Take you back, where?" The words barely croaked from her parched throat. She struggled but he tightened his blazing grip, wrenching her up to his rigid chest. The napalm stifled her.

"Home," he said.

"Yuuji—"

"Yuuji. Had. To. Go."

Naoko felt her bones about to crack under the pressure of his fingers. His breath was raw on her face.

"Yuuji, wake up!" She wrenched herself away from him and stumbled across the room towards the door. He started after her. She spun around and hollered at him. "Yuuji! It's me, Naoko! Wake up!" Her hands groped for the light switch.

The dark figure advanced through the fog towards her. "Yuuji had to go."

The light flashed on. As the napalm cloud dispersed, tears cut a crevice through the gunpowder and blood that smeared Yuuji's face.

Naoko took him into her arms and held him like a child.

"They were here," he said. "I saw them. They were here."

At the hospital, Tanaka Sensei greeted them with a warm smile and a strong handshake.

"I lived in Europe," he said noticing Naoko's discomfort. "Once you get used to European customs, it's hard to let go."

"It must be wonderful," said Naoko. "I'd love to go to Italy, France…"

"Ah! Yes, we Japanese travel the world, but we long for the homeland. It's in our DNA, you know. Magnetic homogeneity, I call it. Birds of a feather—"

Naoko leaned forward.

"Sensei, my husband is having nightmares."

"Is that so?"

"Yes, but they are not ordinary nightmares. These are so real; terrifying. There is blood. Gunpowder. Napalm. Doctor, I don't know what is happening to us. I am frightened."

The Doctor pondered the idea. "Night Terrors? Manifestations? Here on Hahajima? In the arms of the Mother Isle?" He turned to the window and looked out across the Pacific Ocean. "It's still out there," he said.

"Can you help him?" said Naoko.

"I'm afraid I can't," said Tanaka.

Yuuji, who had been quiet until now, wiped the sweat from his face with a towel and turned to Naoko. "Come on, let's get out of here."

Naoko's eyes were still on the Doctor.

"What is?" she said. "What's still out there?"

"The past, Mrs. Hamaguchi. It's still out there and I believe your husband is in danger."

Naoko shivered.

"Come on, Naoko," said Yuuji, standing.

"The past never leaves us," said the doctor. "We can will it away for a while. Like an unwanted gift, we can stuff it in a cupboard and close the door on it. But sooner or later the cupboard is full and then everything comes tumbling out."

"I'm not sure I follow you," said Naoko.

"I am talking about the war, Mrs. Hamaguchi. The Imperial War in East Asia."

Tanaka Sensei turned to Yuuji. "Tell me about your father."

"What has my father got to do with anything?" He shot a look at Naoko and barked, "You told him."

She shook her head and opened her mouth to speak, but Yuuji turned to Tanaka.

"This is ridiculous! That war was over years ago. Before I was even born. What on earth does it have to do with me?"

"It has everything to do with you, Mr. Hamaguchi. It is the fault of the man as much as it is the fault of the nation. We try to push the past away, but the onslaught of war is unrelenting. It is always trying to find a way to return to the present. The war has found its way out of that closet and into your blood. It is your responsibility now."

"This is absurd," shot Yuuji. "Come on, Naoko. Let's get out of here."

"Wait," she said.

Tanaka pushed a small white name card across his desk. "Go to this man. His name is Edogawa. He can help you."

The NHK news reported Typhoon Number Four heading in from South East Asia. Yuuji pulled the shutters down. Naoko lay on the tatami smoking Hopes. J-Pop blasted from the speakers. The Giants played the Tigers on the large screen. Yuuji stood in the kitchenette eating noodles from a paper cup. At ten Naoko laid out the futon. She curled up in the darkness listening to the wind tear across the ocean, howl along the beach, reel through the village, rattle the shutters. Edogawa's number lay crumpled in the bottom of the trash can.

At 2:45 AM Naoko still hadn't slept when the thumping came from the room above her. Outside, the typhoon battered the house. The shutters shook in the wind and branches cracked against the roof.

Naoko lay tense, holding her breath, listening. The thumping stopped, but there was something else. Straining her ears through the storm she could just make out what appeared to be a fox barking, a baby crying, a scream, a gunshot.

She rolled off the futon onto hands and knees, ears pricked, suppressing her breath. The floor above her shook as if an entire troop had stormed into the house and was turning over the furniture, looking for men to fry, women to rape, babies to skin alive.

Another gunshot. Naoko's hands scrabbled for the lamp. Her fingers grappled with the switch. The electricity was out. The phone was out, too. Her cell phone showed no signal.

An explosion shook the entire house. Plaster rained from the ceiling and the thunder of footsteps hurtled down the stairway. She dove behind the sofa and pushed it in front of the paper screen.

A fist pounded the screen and ripped through the paper, filling the room with a heavy cloud of napalm.

"Where are you, bitch?"

Naoko scrambled into the closet and pulled the door shut just before Yuuji kicked his boot through the screen. He was decked out in a khaki army uniform and had a white band around his head. Even in the dim light she recognized the wartime logo: The Rising Sun.

Yuuji leapt onto the sofa, mud from his boots splattered on the hemp covers, and vermillion blood festooned the tatami. Peering through a crack in the cupboard door, Naoko traced the blood to the open gunshot wound in his right shoulder and drew a sharp breath.

"I know you are in here, bitch. I smell your—"

Another explosion rocked the house. Yuuji's eyes darted around the room and fixed on the closet. Through the crack, she watched him take a step toward her. She drew back, holding her breath, and bit her lip.

He charged the door, wrenched it open. She rose to meet him, smothered him with a blanket, brought him down struggling, whipping his body across the floor like a furious snake. He threw her off and she landed on her back, rolled away from him and finding the strength, got back to her feet. He charged her, yelling. She slugged him square on the chin.

Yuuji went down, but came up fast and was at her before she had a chance to run. He hurled himself at her, slammed her into the wall and pinned her there. His hands tore at her skirt.

"Yuuji!"

"Bitch!" He tore at the silk and his right hand forced its way into her crotch. His left forearm pushed hard against her throat.

"Yuuji," she could barely spit the words out, "wake up!"

Fury spun in Yuuji's eyes. He spoke through clenched teeth. "Listen. To. Me."

The slow realization of what he pressed against her pubic bone petrified her to the spot.

Napalm breath on the back of her neck. Hand grenade in her vulva. "I'm listening, Yuuji. I'm listening."

His hand was shaking; the grenade was hot against her. "You have to take me," he said. "You have to take me. If you don't take me, I'll kill you, bitch. I'll blast you out of existence." He released the pressure of his forearm and Naoko caught a glimpse of his shoulder. The wound was three inches across; a combination of blackening blood and torn flesh peppered with black soot. His temples were manic, pulsing. Yuuji had gone.

He worked the sharp pin of the grenade into her. All her senses trained on that little ball of deadly explosives.

Then, through a sudden flush of tears she found herself yelling, "Quit torturing me you asshole and tell me where it is you want to go."

"To Her. To Her. To Her."

"Who?"

The room was spinning in a universe of stars. Their eyes were barely millimeters apart. She searched his for any traces of her husband that might remain.

"To Her. The homeland."

The light flashed on as electricity was restored to the island. Startled, Yuuji loosened his grip on the hand grenade. It fell. It hit the floor. The pin popped out. Naoko stood paralyzed, horror pressed like a dry chrysanthemum onto her face. Three, two, one—

The grenade imploded into nothingness. The Rising Sun logo bled off Yuuji's forehead. The white band faded into his skin. The uniform dissolved from his body, leaving him naked and prostrate on the tatami.

Naoko's legs collapsed beneath her. The two of them sat among the clutter of the room breathing heavily as the typhoon crept back out to sea.

Yuuji's mother, Fujiyo Hamaguchi, wore a murasaki kimono, emblazoned with birds of blue and white, wrapped with an orange obi. She sat upright beside her daughter-in-law in the Chiba City Memorial Hospital and spoke in soothing tones.

"It's not your fault. We cannot help the way things turn out."

"But if I'd persuaded Yuuji to deal with it instead of just standing by and—"

"Yuuji is just like Father, and Grandfather. Stubborn. The Hamaguchi women just have to endure that. It will make us stronger, and in the end it will make our men stronger."

Naoko looked up at the old woman's wizened face. It still had the ornamental beauty of a porcelain doll tinged with sadness.

"No. I'm done with suffering," she said. "It's time to change. I can't sit there and watch it happen like you did."

Mrs. Hamaguchi looked down at her hands. Naoko immediately regretted the force with which she had spoken.

"You are young, Naoko-chan. I had no choice."

Naoko spoke in a more placating tone. "Everyone has a choice."

"Now, maybe. But not in my day. Not when there was the war on."

"Was your husband in the war, Mrs. Hamaguchi?"

"Yuuji never told you?"

"He doesn't talk about it."

"Poor Yuuji." Mrs. Hamaguchi sat for a moment contemplating the Edo period painting of Mount Fuji which hung on the wall.

"Will you tell me?"

Mrs. Hamaguchi smiled and Naoko relaxed.

"It is long and very complicated, and I don't know if I can remember all the details, but I will try."

Naoko nodded, urging her to continue.

"The day I married Yuuji's Father was both the happiest and saddest day of my life."

"How can it be both?"

"Father had been called to war and was to be dispatched to Shikoku the following day where he would wait for orders to be shipped out to Guam.

"He was in the navy?"

"South Seas Forces. We were devastated. We had no idea if we'd ever see him again.

The ceremony went without hitch. Father so handsome, so strong. He never let it be known there was a tempest in his heart. But, I knew it. I knew him.

"After the ceremony, Grandfather and Grandmother were locked in bitter argument over something. It continued through the meal and then after we had all eaten, Grandfather stood to make an announcement in front of the guests.

It was astonishing, pronounced with dignity and love. Every member of the wedding party was moved to tears."

"What did he say?" said Naoko.

"Grandfather announced that he would take Father's place in the draft."

"Was it authorized by the military?"

"It barely mattered. It was 1941. They needed men in South East Asia. And it is difficult to turn a willing soldier back."

"Father let him go?"

"He contested, of course. We all contested. But Grandfather was adamant. He had made his decision. To the dismay of his wife, his children, and his friends, he took up the burden of duty and on the sixth of November 1941 headed for South East Asia in place of his son.

"Grandfather was stationed in Guam. He wrote to us from Shikoku before he left telling us how proud he was not only to go off to serve the emperor, but also to save his son's life. After that we received one more letter, in 1942. He wrote mainly facts about how well the operations in Guam were going. He promised to write again, but we never heard another word."

Mrs. Hamaguchi stopped speaking to collect her thoughts. Naoko passed her a handkerchief. She wiped her eyes and continued.

"He was missing in action. It grieved us all. Not the least Father. He said that it should have been him and not Grandfather. Said it was not fair that a man as noble as Grandfather should take the place of a coward. He believed himself to be a traitor to his family and his country.

"After Yuuji was born, we all thought Father was getting over his grief. He acquired a large tract of land, where we now live, and he put all his time into building the farm and a future. But I could see that the burden Grandfather had taken for him weighed him down more than ever. He rarely left the farm, and at night he would shut himself in his room and brood.

"As Yuuji grew up, I saw that darkness manifesting in him too. Father put pressure on Yuuji to take over the family heritage. Yuuji thought the pressure to fulfill his father's demands too strong. Eventually it drove him out of the family home.

"Little by little, Father was driven to despair. He locked himself away and wouldn't speak to anyone. There was nothing I or anyone else could do to stop him. Slowly he drove himself crazy with grief. He attempted suicide and eventually he was institutionalized.

"As for Grandfather, I believed for a long time that he would return and put everything right. Twenty years after the war ended they were still finding soldiers wandering around the jungles across South East Asia, from Myanmar to Saipan. Men who believed the war had never finished. I had hopes that one day he would find his way back to us.

"I believed that Grandfather returning would bring Father back from the edge of despair and, in time, bring Yuuji back home to continue the Hamaguchi line. I still wait."

Naoko stood in the doorway of the ward smelling disinfectant, cleaning fluids, pain. Yuuji sat upright in bed staring at the wall. He looked fragile with one arm resting on his abdomen, the other somewhere in a past memory, still holding her hand, still running fingers through her hair.

"I love you, Yuuji."

Yuuji turned to face her.

"But it is time to face the world. If you want to hide away on Hahajima, that's fine. But I'll not be a part to your running anymore. Your family needs you. Your mother. Your father. It's time to heal the past."

Yuuji bowed his head.

She touched her hand on his cheek and raised his face to her. She ran her fingers through his hair, kissed him, lay down beside him and wrapped him in her arms. Soon they both slept.

Dramatic peaks overlook vast plateaus and dense jungle. A small village on the edge of a jungle surrounded by coconut trees. An ancient Banyan. Thatched huts line the lakeside and wooden pontoons stretch out onto a small lake. It is morning; the sky is tinged with mandarin shades. From the village walks a shadowy figure.

The figure approaches. It is a soldier with what appears to be a machete in his right hand and a bayonet slung over his shoulder. There is something eerie about the soldier; guilty satisfaction in his swaggering gait.

Yuuji shook Naoko awake. There was urgency in his voice.

"He's back, Naoko. He's coming for me."

"I saw him," said Naoko. "He is coming for us."

Edogawa was a small man with an ancient simian face and oversized ears. He lived in a tidy minshuku situated beside a temple by the coast road on Hahajima.

Naoko handed him a small gift and he invited them inside. He led them along a narrow passage lined with woodblock prints and ushered them into a tiny four mat room.

They knelt around a low maple table overlooking the sea and he served wheat tea from an earthenware pot.

Outside the sea birds bickered, and down the hall the sound of canned laughter came from a television set. For a long while Edogawa sucked on his unfiltered cigarette and sipped his wheat tea. Finally, he placed his teacup on a saucer.

"Let us not waste any more time on formalities," he said, looking at Yuuji. "You said there was a soldier after you. I can help. But first a history lesson. OK?"

Yuuji nodded for Edogawa to continue.

"During the war our brave soldiers went into Asia to fight for the freedom of our empire. Many men died, but there were survivors too. Among them were men who had apparently committed atrocities in the name of our emperor. These men returned from the war only to discover that they were being sought by the Allied Forces. General MacArthur wanted to put them on trial, after which they would be executed for their crimes. Of course, these men were afraid and many of them sought sanctuary here on Hahajima.

They built themselves shelters in the foothills, on the beaches, in the forests, in caves, as far from the American bases, as far from civilization as they could. They lived as hermits. And cut off from civilization, they died as hermits. Many of them are still out here, their bodies hidden on the beach and in the foothills and mountains. They were safe here."

"What has that got to do with what's happening to me?" said Yuuji. He was getting uncomfortable in his formal kneeling position, so he stretched his legs out under the table. Naoko poured the old man some more wheat tea. She offered Yuuji more, but he declined.

Edogawa continued:

"It has everything to do with you. Some of the soldiers who died left girlfriends, wives, children and families. Their will to reunite with their families was so strong that it passed over with them into their death.

"Now it is said they haunt the island looking for a gateway back into the world and back to their families."

Naoko shivered.

"Are you cold, Mrs. Hamaguchi? There is a strong wind today. Shall I close a window?"

"No, go on."

"You, Mr. Hamaguchi, are a gateway. Somewhere on this island is the body of a man who returned from the war and lived his dying days as a hermit. We have to find his body and lay him to rest. You are going to take us to him."

"But I don't know where it is."

"Of course you do Mr. Hamaguchi." Edogawa's broad smile stopped the world in its tracks and there was nothing anyone could do but trust him.

Edogawa provided them with a room. It was small and drafty; four mats in size with a large window overlooking a shrine.

"At least we have the gods to watch over us," said Naoko.

"We're going to need all the help we can get."

At 3:45 AM Naoko woke to see a shadow of a man standing at the window, looking out.

"Yuuji?"

"Yuuji had to go."

Naoko leapt out of bed, bolted to the door.

"Mr. Edogawa. He's back. The soldier has come back."

Edogawa emerged from a room down the corridor. "Where is he?"

"In our room. Standing at the window."

"Did you wake him?"

"No, I did as you said."

"Good, come." He looked at her, smiling. "You need a coat."

He handed her a long black trench coat. She slipped it on over her nightgown and followed him outside to the shrine.

"Now, we pray to the gods," Edogawa said, clapping his hands together.

Naoko bowed her head, closed her eyes, clapped twice and prayed.

There was movement in the shadows around the minshuku.

"There," said Edogawa.

Naoko opened her eyes. She followed his finger to a dark figure darting through the shadows.

"Come on," he said, taking her hand and whisking her along the pathway with uncanny agility.

Yuuji was about fifty yards ahead of them, running towards the beach road. Edogawa wasn't far behind, but Naoko had dropped back. Yuuji veered off the road and disappeared into the trees. Naoko stopped and bent with her hands on her knees to catch her breath.

"Come on," Edogawa called back to her. He raced down the bank in pursuit, bounding through the undergrowth, dodging the trees.

Naoko recovered and followed them, tripping and stumbling through the undergrowth. She slid down the bank, lost her balance and landed with a thud on the sandy beach. She picked herself up and scanned the beach. Edogawa was about forty yards in front of her. He had stopped and was looking at an opening in the rocks.

"They are in there," he said as she caught up with him. "You must get yourself in shape if you are going to have that baby."

"I'm not pregnant."

"Oh no?" said Edogawa, smiling.

They stood peering into the narrow cave. It was barely large enough to crawl into.

"We follow him in there?" said Naoko.

Edogawa dropped to his hands and knees and crawled head first into the cave.

Naoko squeezed through the fissure and scrambled along through the dark passage after him. The sharp shingle scraped her knees and tore the skin from the palms of her hands.

But she kept her momentum, afraid to stop in case she lost Edogawa. The pressure of the entire island threatened to bear down on her, crush her, squeeze her out of existence.

When she finally came to a juncture where the roof of the cave opened upward and she was able to stand, she called out in a whisper.

"Mr. Edogawa?"

A light shone back towards her through the darkness. Edogawa had a flashlight and he seemed to be searching for something.

"Look." Edogawa's voice echoed in the hollow cave. "There." He was motioning his flashlight ahead and as Naoko's eyes grew accustomed to the light she saw her husband.

Yuuji knelt in the darkness of the cave, dressed in full Imperial uniform, tears streaming down his cheeks onto the Rising Sun flag laid out in front of him. His mouth moved in prayer.

Before him was a skeleton, still dressed in a tattered Imperial uniform, the right arm of the jacket pinned up to cover the missing limb. His belongings were scattered about the cave; cigarette cartons, a canteen, a bayonet. In his single hand he held two pictures. One a portrait of Emperor Hirohito: the sovereign for whom millions had honorably died; the nation's divine master, who had pumped war into the hearts of the Japanese people; the man who had ordered his soldiers to drain the blood from the veins of Asia. The other picture was a black and white photograph of a beautiful young girl.

The following spring Naoko and Yuuji Hamaguchi returned to Hahajima Island. Yuuji was working with a new prosthetic arm and was preparing to start a new job in Chiba. Naoko was full of burgeoning hope for the new life she carried in her womb.

They made their way up to the old minshuku to greet Mr. Edogawa, but when they arrived in the vicinity, there was no trace of the old building. All that remained was the small shrine where they had scattered the ashes of the soldier the previous fall.

At the shrine they burned incense and offered solemn obeisance for the exiled soldier. They clapped their hands together in prayer for the beautiful girl that a nation's fate had torn from the lone soldier's hands. They lowered their heads in respect for Yuuji's grandfather, the man who was willing to sacrifice his freedom and his life for the sake of his son. They quietly remembered the soldiers who sacrificed themselves in the war for their country, their emperor, their god. But it was only when Yuuji prayed for his father, the man locked deep in a prison cell of despair in a sanatorium somewhere in the suburbs of Tokyo, that tears began to roll down his cheeks. The tears he wept were heavy. They were tears of forgiveness.

Naoko took Yuuji's hand in hers. Her other hand rested on her swollen abdomen

"A new start."

Yuuji turned to her and smiled.

"A new start."

Nobody in the village could shed light on the whereabouts of the old man who had led them to the lost soldier. The people of Hahajima claimed to have no recollection of anyone called Edogawa, so they decided to pay a visit to Tanaka Sensei. He welcomed them with his usual convivial smile and served green tea and sweets around a low table looking out across the Pacific Ocean. They knelt and watched the gulls gliding across the bay and spoke in quiet reverence of the ghosts that inhabit the past and the future, and when they told him of their puzzlement concerning the extraordinary disappearance of Edogawa, Tanaka Sensei smiled grimly and said, "Edogawa had to go."

House of Dreams

by Michael Sebastian

L OS ANGELES WAS PLAYING ITS PART beautifully on the day
Jennifer Vale arrived at her new apartment. She parked
the Cherokee at the top of the hill and got out, pausing to take
in all of Hollywood spread below her. Blue skies, seventy degrees, palm trees rising up into the sky like balloons at a kid's
birthday party—it was just as she'd always pictured it.

The building stood on a dead end overlooking Hollywood
Boulevard. Old and brick, it rose up from the surrounding stuc-
co, a relic from a bygone era in a city with amnesia. Who knew
what stars had lived under its roof on their way to immortality.

Jennifer lifted a box from the back seat and headed up the
steps to the front door. She was about to put the key in the lock
when the door swung open two inches. An eye appeared.

"Dominick," a voice hissed. "Is that you?"

"Uh, no, my name's Jennifer Vale. I'm—"

"You're late," said the frail voice. There was a note of fear
in it. "They're expecting me at the studio."

"I'm not Dominick, ma'am," she said louder. "I'm moving
in today. Can I come in?" She gently pushed the door open, but
it slammed back.

"Don't look. They've given me someone else's hands." A withered, bony hand shot out of the darkness and grabbed Jennifer's wrist hard. "These aren't my hands, Dominick!"

"I'm not Dominick!" Jennifer thrust the old lady off her and opened the door. A change came over the woman's face, like she'd been tricked.

"You're not Dominick."

The old woman hurried back to her apartment, glancing over her shoulder, and slammed the door. Jennifer heard the deadbolt click.

Poor woman, thought Jennifer. Having to live all alone and crazy. Maybe she even had been a star once.

Jennifer saw a door marked MANAGER. She had yet to meet him. She'd viewed the apartment during an open house, picked up an application from a stack inside the door, and finalized the lease at the management company's office. It was then, signing her new name with practiced illegibility, that this whole move to LA had finally hit home. Everyone had always told her she would be a star. And now, here she was. She was really doing this.

Jennifer knocked on the manager's door. The entryway reverberated with the sounds of other tenants rehearsing monologues and performing vocal exercises. There was no answer, so she went down the hall to the elevator, her footfalls resounding deeply on the old wooden floor. Taped to the elevator was a note—OUT OF ORDER.

Perfect. She didn't want to leave her things in the car overnight, and there was no telling when the elevator would be fixed. She walked back to the entryway and looked straight up the immense staircase. The right angle turns stacked on top of each other like an accordion. With determination she started up the stairs with the first box.

Jennifer elbowed open the door to her studio apartment. It was smaller than she remembered. She set the box down and walked over to the window.

"Hi there."

She jumped. A young guy about her age was standing inside the doorway.

"Sorry," he said. "I thought I heard someone. I'm next door." He held out his hand. "Collin."

She laughed off her shock and embarrassment and took his hand. "Jenny. Jennifer," she corrected.

"You need a hand?"

"I couldn't ask. The elevator's broken."

"All the more reason," he said. "It's always broken. I'm used to it."

She smiled, relieved to have the day's seemingly insurmountable task lifted from her.

* * *

Collin was overjoyed to learn that Jennifer was an actress. He himself was an aspiring writer-director.

"When I'm the next Tarantino, you can be in my movies. You'll be my Uma."

She smiled. "It's a deal."

Finally the boxes were all moved in and stacked around the cramped studio apartment. Jennifer thanked Collin as he left. She took out her cell phone to call her parents and tell them she'd arrived safely, but the phone wasn't getting a signal. She'd heard that about old buildings. The walls were built too thick or something. She would have to get a landline.

She started a bath, pouring aromatic salts into the old fashioned freestanding tub while she massaged her sore shoulders. She lay for a long time with her eyes closed until a shiver ran through her body. The water suddenly felt cold. She hadn't been in there that long, had she? It wasn't just that it had gone luke-warm—it was freezing. Shivering, she got out and dried off.

That first night Jennifer couldn't sleep. She was too excited as she envisioned her meteoric rise to stardom, playing her talk show appearances in her head, the red carpet premieres, her Oscar acceptance speech.

She must have finally drifted off to sleep because she woke around four to the clack of a typewriter coming through the walls. She wasn't sure if she was still dreaming, and sleep soon tugged her back under.

★ ★ ★

The next day Jennifer picked up her headshots at the pho-tographer's studio and drove around looking for a job.

The first place she tried was a hipster coffee house down the hill from her apartment. Inside, guys in baseball caps pecked away at their laptops. Jennifer was hired on the spot. Mostly actors worked there, the manager told her, so getting a shift covered when she had an audition would not be a prob-lem. Jennifer could not believe her luck. She took it as a sign of things to come.

Already the city seemed less daunting. She returned trium-phant to her apartment building and tried the manager again. No answer. She bent near the door and thought she could hear the low howl of air flowing through a cavernous space.

The elevator was still out of order. She took the stairs two at a time and knocked on Collin's door. He was slow in an-swering. When he finally appeared it was with sunken eyes and a wan face. Jennifer's smile faded.

"Jeez, you look terrible. Are you feeling okay?"

"Long night," he said. "Is that them?"

Collin took the manila envelope and slid out a glossy black-and-white.

"Now that's a movie star if I ever saw one."

Collin had to get to his night job at a video store off Sunset, but he spared a few minutes to help Jennifer stuff envelopes. They sat on the rug in her apartment surrounded by half-unpacked boxes. She asked about their curiously absent manager.

"He's never there," Collin said. "My AC broke last summer. It took three weeks to get it fixed."

Jennifer stapled a résumé to the back of a headshot and paused. Set down in black and white, her credentials suddenly seemed embarrassingly thin. A few high school plays. A short film she had acted in for the local college.

"Do you think it matters that I don't have much experience?"

Collin shrugged. "Gotta start somewhere. Might as well start at the top."

Jennifer smiled and resumed her work.

* * *

She woke in the middle of the night to a thrumming sound. Light from the bathroom spilled into the room from around the half-closed door. She got up in a daze and went over, the noise growing louder. She pushed open the door. Water poured from the faucet into the almost-full tub. Had she left it running? No, that didn't make sense. She shut the water off and flipped the light switch. Great, something was wrong with the old pipes. How long would it take to get the absentee manager on that?

* * *

Jennifer's first morning at work was overwhelming, but by late afternoon a lull had settled over the coffeehouse. She went outside to check her voicemail and was elated when she heard a man introducing himself as Mort Riskin, an agent. She called back immediately. Mort had an audition lined up for her that afternoon if she could be in Burbank by four.

Jennifer tingled with excitement as she pulled up to the Warner Brothers gate and told the guard her name. He checked a clipboard, then gave her a pass for her windshield and directed her to the appropriate building.

In the waiting room sat a row of girls who looked vaguely like Jennifer. Some had their moms with them, hovering, fussing over their hair and makeup. Most were alone. No one talked as they sat trying to memorize their lines. Jennifer's heart pounded, her hands sweating. Finally, they called her in.

* * *

"Great news!" Mort's voice came over the phone as she drove back to the apartment. "They loved you. They want you back tomorrow to read with the cast."

Jennifer squealed and nearly crashed into the back of another car. This was it; she could feel it.

She went straight to Collin's apartment. He flung open the door and said, "You are looking at a professional screenwriter. Go ahead, you can touch me if you want."

She leapt on him excitedly and told him about the callback. "Let's celebrate," she said.

"All right, but just for a minute. The studio gave me notes. They want a polish ASAP."

They sat on Jennifer's bed and drank champagne, discussing what they were going to buy with their first paychecks.

* * *

Jennifer awoke to the clack of Collin's typewriter. She looked at the clock—4 a.m. "Col-lin." She pounded on the wall. "Audition," she called. "Sleep."

The typewriter stopped. She let her head fall back onto the pillow.

The clock radio snapped on with loud static. Jennifer started awake.

Snippets of voices came through faintly as the radio tuned—which shouldn't even be possible with its digital tuner. Abruptly it caught on a station and a muted horn sang over a languid Middle Eastern rhythm from the big band. Somehow she knew the song was called "Caravan" performed by Bunny Berigan and His Boys on the Saturday Night Swing Club.

Jennifer quickly shut off the radio. The apartment was silent again. She stared at the green glow of the clock, waiting for the radio to snap on again. The wiring must be screwy in this place too. She suddenly couldn't wait for that paycheck so she could move to a one-bedroom in a newer building. Sense of history be damned.

Then she noticed the light in the bathroom.

Collin must have left it on during their celebration. She was beginning to detect a pattern of thoughtlessness on his part. She got up and padded barefoot to the bathroom. At the threshold she stepped in something wet. Water was coming from under the door. The pipes! She threw open the door. Her heart jolted.

A girl lay in the tub, her slip dancing underwater. The faucet roared, water spilling over the full tub and onto the tile. She had short hair and pale skin. Her forearms were slashed from wrist to elbow. Her head lolled to the side, mascara-dripping eyes staring right at Jennifer.

Jennifer woke screaming. She caught her breath and looked around the apartment. A dream. Just a dream. But something was wrong. It was too light. She checked the alarm clock—flashing 12:00. She cursed and threw off the covers. She checked her cell phone—11:32. Two hours late. She dressed hurriedly and ran down the three flights of stairs to her car, checking the signal on her phone the whole way.

When service returned, she had four new messages. She listened as she sped toward the freeway. First the producer's assistant had called wondering if she was stuck in traffic. Next Mort wanted to know where the hell she was and demanded she call the producers. Then the producers had called again, saying sorry they'd missed her but that they would have to go with someone else. Finally Mort informed her that she was no longer his client. By the time she had merged onto the freeway, her career was over, dead before it could begin.

* * *

Jennifer arrived late to work and immediately regretted having come at all. She went through the motions, barely aware of what she was doing. A voice roused her from her trance.

"This isn't soy."

She turned from pouring a coffee. A man stood at the counter, holding up his to-go cup.

"What?" she said.

"I said soy milk in this latte."

There were two types of customers at the coffee shop. The laptop junkies took up all the tables and didn't tip, but they at least kept to themselves. Then there was the Industry trash. They were something different altogether.

"Sorry. Just let me finish with this customer."

"No. I was first. If you'd done it as I asked the first time, I wouldn't be here. Now make it right."

She wanted to flip the cup of hot coffee right in his face. She did the next best thing, tossing her apron at him and saying, "Make it yourself." Then she left.

Jennifer didn't know what had gotten into her. She'd never acted that way. How could she snap at a customer and walk out on her job like that, even with such an asshole, even after the day she'd had? She was in a lousy mood and felt like making it worse.

She marched right to Collin's apartment and pounded on the door. He answered, his smile immediately dropping when he saw her face.

"Thanks a lot. I missed my audition because of you."

"What? What're you talking about?"

"You. Clacking away all night on your typewriter so I couldn't sleep. You cost me the part."

"Jen, I write on a laptop."

But she wasn't listening. She stormed back to her apartment and slammed the door. She fell into bed as if pulled there and did not wake until morning. But instead of feeling refreshed, she was groggy from too much sleep and the thought of the previous day. How close she had seemed, how quickly it had vanished.

She knocked on Collin's door. He answered, cell phone to his ear. He looked tired, overworked, yet full of manic energy, talking in an Industry voice she'd never heard him use. When he hung up he said, "We got the green light. Marty had some last minute notes."

"Wow, it's really happening for you, huh?"

He shrugged. "My time I guess. How you holding up?"

She shook her head. "I'm thinking I made a big mistake. Maybe I should just go home."

"You can't give up now." He came over and held her by the shoulders. "After just one set back? You think anybody became a star on their first shot?"

She looked up at him and her doubt melted away. "Want to stuff some envelopes?"

"I'd love to, Jen. But that polish…"

Jennifer said she understood and went back to her apartment to start in on the new round of headshots. Despite Collin's pep talk, she felt tired, drained. She put on a pot of coffee with some beans she'd taken from the shop.

She felt lonely and wanted to call her parents, but they would just tell her to come home. And Jennifer knew she would go if they asked. She'd have a normal, boring life and would always know she could have had something more.

She stared at the open cell phone in her hands. No bars. That solved that, but she couldn't stuff any more envelopes either. She drove over to the New Beverly to catch a Marilyn Monroe double feature, but fell asleep during the first film.

* * *

She woke in the dark. The alarm clock read 10:05. That couldn't be right. It would be light out by now. She sat up and reached for her cell phone. 10:05 p.m. She'd slept twenty-three hours.

Jennifer climbed out of bed as if buried under a heavy weight. Must be coming down with something, she thought as she made a big pot of coffee. But she didn't feel sick and had none of the usual cold symptoms, just a drained, lethargic feeling like being underwater. Each movement required great energy and will. Wasn't mono supposed to be like that?

She had a bite of cold pizza, but it was tasteless. She took a hot shower, then tried to get through some headshots. But she soon gave up and answered the call of her bed.

She slept, she woke, she slept, all out of sync with the rising and setting of the sun. She was unable to resist the tug of sleep.

Night. Jennifer woke needing to use the bathroom and dragged herself from bed, stumbling through the dark with slit eyes. Washing her hands, she glanced in the medicine cabinet mirror. She started. It was her, but it wasn't. Her features seemed to meld with someone else's—her nose a bit too wide, the eyes too dark. She flipped on the light and her own reflection looked back at her.

Jennifer splashed cold water on her face and finally felt somewhat awake. The scare had accomplished what the gallons of coffee had not. She had no idea what day it was or how long she had been in her torpor, but whatever she'd come down with seemed to be passing. She would see a doctor about it tomorrow, just to be sure. But first she would call Mort Riskin and beg him to give her a second chance. She could do this. She knew she could. The clock read 10:30. She was about to go next door and ask Collin if he could recommend a doctor, but he would still be at work.

Jennifer drove down Sunset looking for the video store. On a weeknight the Strip was not the same hotspot where lines stretched around velvet-roped clubs. It was transformed into a forgotten, entropic place where junkies and muttering homeless wandered the streets.

Jennifer alternated between scanning the street and scrolling through her cell phone's contacts. She found Mort Riskin and hit SEND. A chime sounded followed by a recorded voice: "The number you dialed is not in service. Check the number and dial again."

She scanned the phone's record of missed calls. Finding Mort's, she again pressed SEND. Again the same voice told her the number did not exist. She called Information and asked for the Mort Riskin Talent Agency, Los Angeles.

"I'm sorry, there's no listing."

Jennifer shut the phone, too tired to make sense of this right now. She spotted the store on the corner of a small side street, a glowing beacon in the nighttime wasteland.

She went inside but didn't see Collin anywhere through the stacks of DVDs. She asked the guy working the counter.

"Collin? He stopped showing up for work six months ago. Didn't even call or anything. Everyone assumed he OD'ed or went back home or something."

Nothing was making sense. Her head ached. Back at the apartment she knocked on Collin's door. He answered, cell phone to his ear, and let her in without looking up. He was talking excitedly about some crisis with the script.

When he hung up he said, "Don't have much time. Leo is threatening to walk unless he gets the changes he wants. Marty's trying to pacify him, but I'm really under the gun here."

Collin did not stop moving as he spoke. He popped some pills from a vial on his computer desk, then brought a stained mug over to the kitchenette. Collin's eyes looked sunken. He snapped his jaw back and forth unconsciously as he poured water into the coffeemaker.

"You getting any sleep?" Jennifer said. "You seem a bit overworked."

"Living the dream," Collin said as he flipped the ON switch without changing out the coffee grounds.

Jennifer drifted over to the desk. It occurred to her that Collin never seemed to have problems getting a signal on his cell. She picked up the phone to see what kind he had. She flipped it open. The screen was blank. She pressed the power button. It didn't respond. She pressed it again.

The phone was dead.

Collin came back into the room. He was looking at her. She set the phone down and started backing toward the door.

"You can't leave," he said.

"What?"

"It's gonna happen. Just look at me."

She nodded as she felt her back touch the door. "You're right," she managed. "Well, I'll let you get back to work."

She turned the knob behind her and was out the door and back inside her own apartment throwing the deadbolt. She leaned against the door, catching her breath, trying to make sense of her thoughts. There was an insane person living next door. He'd been in her apartment. On her bed. He could have...

She had to move. She would pack her things tonight and be gone in the morning. Her parents would cover the rest of the lease if she explained the situation.

A burst of static. The clock radio snapped to life. That same strange swaying jazz song blared. Jennifer turned. The dead girl lurched out of the bathroom, puddles forming with each step, open gashes trailing blood down her forearms.

Jennifer backed into the wall, knocking over a poster frame. The dead girl reached out a hand. Her mouth opened as if to speak but only coughed up water.

Jennifer whirled and grabbed her car keys off the desk just as she felt the dead hand on her shoulder.

All at once images, thoughts, feelings, an entire life flashed through her. Her name was Beatrice McClusky and she wanted more than anything to be a movie star but was stuck working as an extra at MGM, but one day a producer told her to meet him after her scene ended and she slept with him because he was charming and powerful and yes, she thought that maybe he would give her a line to say, because that was all she needed and then they would see that she was a star, but she didn't get a line, and then one night the producer invited her to a party, only once she got there he handed her off to another producer and told her to "be a good girl," and there was always another producer or director or star and always the promise of a line until one day they stopped calling altogether and she realized she never would be a star, so she turned on the radio and took a warm bath.

And then Beatrice McClusky was gone. Jennifer was left with the weight of all the dreams that had died within these walls, feeding this place, this evil.

Jennifer ran. She leapt down the stairs two at a time. But when she reached what should have been the ground floor, she stopped. She leaned over the railing and peered down into a bottomless staircase.

She hurried back up to the nearest floor. The number on the apartment door read 505. A higher floor than when she'd started. She ran back down the steps, one floor, two floors, five, seven, ten. She checked the apartment number: 909. She'd descended up to a floor that did not exist.

Fine, she thought, and started climbing the stairs. She walked until her legs burned. She didn't know how many floors she had put beneath her, but when she checked the apartment number she was still on nine.

Exhausted, hopeless, she collapsed. She was trapped. She was going to die here. Or go insane like Collin.

Ding. The elevator doors slid open at the end of the hall. No one got out. The doors stayed open, waiting.

Jennifer got to her feet and walked down the hall. It was the smallest elevator she'd ever been in, like a coffin. Deep red carpet covered the walls. The control panel had just one button, marked M. She pushed it. The doors shut.

She had lost all sense of time and direction. Perhaps ten seconds went by, perhaps an hour. Finally, the doors dinged and opened. An empty hallway stretched out in front of her. At the end was a door marked MANAGER.

As she walked toward it, she could hear the slow, uneven clack of a typewriter. She tried the knob. The door creaked open and she entered. The dim apartment glowed red, but no light source was visible. Dust layered the furniture an inch thick. Cobwebs crisscrossed the room. Stacks of newspapers the texture of dead leaves crowded the floor making it difficult for Jennifer to move. As she navigated the towers she scanned their headlines:

FAMED PICTURE DIRECTOR ARRESTED FOR MURDER
Wild weekend ends in girl's death

BENEDICT MURDER TRIAL BEGINS
Witness describes "illicit love nest"

BENEDICT PICTURES BANNED NATIONWIDE

KEY WITNESS ADMITS BLACKMAIL PLOT

BENEDICT NOT GUILTY!
Jury: we owe this man an apology

BAN UPHELD DESPITE VERDICT
Hays office: director does not represent values of this industry

BLACKLISTED DIRECTOR MISSING

As Jennifer entered a second room, she saw a man bent over a desk, his back to her.

"Hello?" she called.

The man did not stir, just continued pecking away at the typewriter.

Clack clack clack.

She drew nearer. Stringy gray hair clung to his skull, spilling over his hunched back.

She called again, louder.

Clack clack clack.

She was close enough now to see over his shoulder and read what he was typing.

> INT. MANAGER'S APARTMENT. *The door opens and Jennifer enters. A withered old man sits hunched over a typewriter. She approaches.*
>
> JENNIFER: Hello? *She nears and looks over his shoulder at what he is typing.*

Jennifer recoiled. The old man turned slowly from the typewriter. His face was like nothing she'd ever seen, as if every drop of water, every drop of life, had been drained from his body. Deep lines cracked his loose skin. His eyes were milky white, his diseased gums toothless. His dead tongue lay useless.

He let out a dry croak.

Then Jennifer saw his legs—or the legs of the chair—for the two had become indistinguishable, melding together, fusing seamlessly into the grain of the floor.

Jennifer opened her mouth to scream and everything went black.

* * *

Everyone had always told Kelly Newfield she was going to be a star, and now here she was, in Hollywood. Carrying a box of her things, she approached the building that would be her new home. A faded beauty heavily made up exited and smiled at her.

"Moving in?" said the woman. "Let me guess—actress."

"How'd you know?"

"Oh, I can tell. You have that star quality." The woman smiled, then started down the sidewalk. She turned and added, "Stop by three-o-three later. I'll get you in touch with my agent."

"Really?" Kelly couldn't believe her luck. Her first day in LA and already she had a line on an agent.

"Sure," said the woman. "Mort Riskin's the best in the business."

Night of the Wild Hunt

by Eliza Granville

T HE STORM BEGAN GENTLY ENOUGH.

At first it was little more than a whisper, so docile it could hardly be called a breeze. Out of the heart of Wales it came, whistling under its breath, minding its own business, snaking lazily eastwards to meet the muted warning of a red-sky-in-the-morning dawn. Narrowing his eyes against the watery sunlight, Owain Cadwallader watched it preen the feathered poplars marking the slow incline of the Rhayader road.

He wasn't taken in. Already his bones were grumbling and aching; over the years Owain's battered frame had become better tuned to the moods of the weather than any barometer. Besides, the eruption of his suppressed grief always echoed the rousing of The Wild Hunt. *Yesi Mawr.* His spirits plummeted. Not again. Dear God, not again.

A sick churning began deep in the pit of his stomach. Sweat gathered to lodged in his eyebrows. His vision slewed until the farmyard tipped and distorted, all perspective lost, familiar becoming unfamiliar, as in the tangled backwaters of a dream. Owain's heart pounded as he fought his fear, striving to replace it with rage by repeatedly slamming alternate fists into the byre door. The knuckles wept blood and razor-edged pain flared, whiplashed, sped nerve-end to ganglion. And still fear won.

Owain's shoulders slumped as he trudged back across the yard sucking his wounds. Years ago a day such as this had stripped him of everything but an agony of festering memories, impossible to forget. Decades slipped by, but every rising storm scraped raw the half-healed scars, forever shackling him to the past.

From bitter experience Owain knew that his best chance lay in numb oblivion.

Levering off his mud-caked boots, he padded over the chilly, back-kitchen flagstones, anxious to avoid Ma Bullock's lackadaisical cleaning and tittle-tattle tongue. Holding his breath, he fumbled at the back of the cow-drench and rat-trap cupboard, the only place the prying old biddy kept her nose out of. Just as his fingers tightened round the bottle's neck, the low drone of muted voices drifted in from the hall. Owain froze. He swallowed hard.

No. It was too early.

Nightfall would bring the familiar clamour of dead voices. This was a stranger's baritone rumble, pitched so low he couldn't distinguish words. What kind of man called on folks at this crow-fart hour? And who came to a farm so far off the beaten track that even the postman left mail at the end of the lane?

Owain crept across the kitchen and peered cautiously round the door. Nothing to see but a panoramic view of Ma Bullock's slow-moving floral backside, but her mouth was running on like the mill leat with the sluices up.

"Ain't nothing been changed round here for years. Bit like cleaning some museum. Time stood still, know what I mean? Bit touched, he is. Will have everything left just as it were when..." Her voice dropped to a theatrical whisper. She completed her shuffle forward and now Owain could see the massive figure silhouetted against the window. "*Ever* so sad it were. First his poor Mam, who from all accounts never hurt nobody in her life, Gawd bless her, then his Dad...less said about him the better...and to top it all the young brother gone and done away with himself."

"Terrible. A tragedy."

The stranger's voice was as insincere as it was deep. He moved restlessly, letting in a sliver of daylight, so that his hand, resting on the hall table, was thrown into sharp relief. It was a huge hand: square, knotted, crawling with coarse black hairs. Owain's heart lurched and became a wild bird, battering blindly against his rib cage. It was his father's hand. Terror engulfed him as the hand rose. He threw himself away from the door, hardly able to breathe.

Dwu! Dwu! It was starting already. And he remembered every word.

"See that bloody stable's mucked out before I come back. Properly, too, or you'll feel the back of my hand."

Owain scuttled halfway across the back kitchen before common sense prevailed. Of course it wasn't Rhys. Rhys Cadwallader was dead and buried. Long dead. Nearly half a century dead. Pulling himself together, Owain strode back and flung open the door.

"What's all this then?" he demanded, scowling.

"Oooooh, Mr. Cadwallader!" Ma Bullock clutched at her cardigan buttons, defensively flicked at an imaginary cobweb, and turned her discomposure into a simper. "Oh, you give me such a fright. You really did."

The intruder emerged from the shadows. Owain forced himself to stand his ground. With the light full on him, the stranger could have been his father's double—same build, same pugnacious jaw and midnight swarthiness, same air of hardly suppressed violence. He was a by-blow perhaps, certainly a blood-relative. But the eyes were different. This man had a shifty look about him, whereas Rhys had cultivated an arrogant, regal glare.

"Ain't I descended from Cadwallon, ancient King of Wales?"

And when the man spoke, it was clear that he was only some fool Englishman.

"Jaz Treadgold," he growled, extending the hairy paw. Owain ignored it, stuffing his own raw-knuckled hands deep into his pockets. Treadgold gave an almost imperceptible shrug. "Having a spot of trouble with the car. Couldn't get help on my mobile—no signal. Your good lady very kindly let me use the phone."

Ma Bullock flushed an ugly deep ruby port.

Owain's scowl grew steadily blacker. "Missus Bullock ain't *my good lady*. Her comes up from the village to do the cleaning."

"Ah, right, my apologies. So you're on your own up here?" Treadgold's eyes narrowed speculatively. "We were just having a little chat about your old bits and pieces. Any knick-knacks you want to part with, by the bye?"

"No."

"Or larger pieces gathering dust—kitchen dressers, say, davenports, or marble-topped washstands? Got a few contacts in the trade as it happens—I'd be glad to help you out. People pay good prices for this sort of stuff nowadays, enough for a damned good holiday in the sun, or a cruise, perhaps. Settle the bills. Let your hair down a bit."

"No."

"Take this old screen, for instance. Pretty piece but a bit knocked about, needs restoring. I could offer you, let's see..."

Treadgold rapidly scanned Cadwallader's worn cords, the ravels of wool dangling from his elbows, the self-inflicted haircut. He coughed and pursed his lips. "How does fifty pounds sound?"

"You deaf or what?" demanded Cadwallader. "That screen was my Mam's. I don't want your money and you ain't touching her things. Everything here stays exactly as it is."

"Fine. Absolutely—this is your home, your decision." Treadgold's tone remained pleasant as he ratcheted open his bunched fist. "But how about outside? Any old farm equipment poked away in corners? Any staddle stones or stone water troughs? Cheese moulds? I couldn't help noticing that splendid old cheese press. And, er, this lady says you've got sheds full of..."

Owain glared. "I don't want to sell nothing."

"Seems a pity to let them rot," Treadgold persisted. He craned his neck and his eyes flicked slowly round the parlour as if taking an inventory.

"I ain't got time to stand here and fiddle-faddle the morning away," snapped Owain, jerking his head towards the door. "Some of us got work to do. Heard tell that the only way to get rid of a *knocker* who won't take no for an answer is to set the dog on him."

Treadgold's nostrils dilated. "No need for threats."

And again Owain saw his father in the other's quick rage, in the instant acid-yellowing of the dark skin, in the scarlet fury veining the whites of his eyes, the way the man's lips compressed to a mean reptilian gash. His own mouth was suddenly dry. A drink, God how he needed that drink.

"Show him the door, missus."

While Ma Bullock waddled off to force back the bolts, Owain dived into the back-kitchen and pounced on the bottle with shaking hands. By the time she came back, looking much put-out, the spirit had cauterised the worst of the fear.

"Oh, Mr. Cadwallader, I'm ever so sorry." She delicately averted her eyes as he drained the second glass. "He *said* as his car had broken down. I didn't know he was a dealer."

"Ah. Well, what's done can't be undone. Don't matter now."

They both waited to see if he would pour a third measure.

Owain sat and let the day collapse round him. The gauzy actors assembled just as the light began to die.

"Slummock!" roared his father. "Lazy bitch! Don't you never get no further than giving the place a cat-lick and a promise? You could eat your dinner off my mother's floors. And look at the state of that sink."

"I'll do it for you, Mam," slurred Owain, fumbling for the scouring powder.

"Better than a girl, ain't he?" sneered Rhys. "Can't think who sired the bloody little runt."

"Shut your evil mouth," Owain snarled into the empty shadows. But he fancied he heard his father unbuckling his belt. Knocking back his drink, he scurried through the door. Outside, the breeze had become a chilly, knife-edged wind growing in strength as he stumbled from one chore to the next. Tail-ends of trapped screams wove in and out of its thin whine. Billowing cumulus clouds boiled in from the west, silvered broccoli heads rapidly deepening to menacing shades of slate.

As twilight thickened, an oppressive heaviness began to weight the air. Draggled ewes stampeded through the thickets of blackthorn, summoning their lambs with urgent bass calls as they made for the deeper shelter of the valley bottom.

"You going to stand there gawping all day?" bawled Rhys, his voice thundering over their cries. "Get extra bedding in for them stock, you daft sawney. Jump to it or I'll give you what for."

From long habit, Owain ducked away from the blow. "Leave me be," he muttered, under his breath, "bloody slave-driver. Don't I always manage it all single-handed?"

"Just do it," begged Mam's wraithe, twisting her pinny into tight little knots. "Don't say nothing, son. You know what he's like if you give him any back-chat."

"Ah, I'll do it to keep the peace. But one of these days, by God, one of these days the worm will bloody turn."

Owain slashed viciously at the tight blue baler twine. The compressed wheat straw exploded among the fidgeting legs and wetly enquiring noses of the young beasts.

His father rapped on the stalls. "*Barley* straw, I said, you wasteful sod."

"Bugger off, you." Owain threw in a second bale for good measure. "One of these days, God help me, one of these days..."

The storm whipped itself into a frenzy, gathering strength from the darkness, echoing ancient battles as it roared over the Black Mountains to wreak havoc the length and breadth of the Welsh Marches. The dead rode on its back, gathering souls as they went. On the upper hill-slopes massive oaks whirled and danced, bending their aching backs to claw at the black air. Rain fell in torrents. Lanes turned into streams, sodden with blood-red clay. Further afield, lorries were overturned, thousand-year-old trees sucked from their moorings, whole roofs swept up and scattered across the countryside. It was the Wild Hunt. It was the Devil's work. It was Man's comeuppance for meddling with the forces of nature. And it was the cue for Rhys Cadwallader's reappearance.

"Ah, one of these days," mumbled Owain, staring blindly out into the night. "One of these days I'll learn him. I'll give him one hell of a basting and larruping..." Dispensing with the glass, he tipped the bottle up with such force that whisky dribbled from the corners of his mouth and ran along the gouged folds of his neck.

When the wind finally slackened, he strained his ears for the first sound of cartwheels grinding their way up the farm track. Instead, he heard the dog's urgent barking. Stumbling through the back-kitchen and into the pitch black dairy, he tried to focus on the yard. A single light dipped and swayed in the tractor shed. Taff's frantic wolf howls punctuated the circling wind.

"Bloody English cattle rustlers," snarled Owain.

It was a well known fact, had been since Norman times, that no animals or women were safe from the savages living on the wrong side of Offa's Dyke. Owain blundered back through the clawing darkness and fumbled for the phone. Damned thing was dead. He'd have to see to the *Saesneg* vermin himself. Cursing softly, he scrabbled for the twelve-bore and a pocketful of cartridges.

As he slid outside, the wind tore the door from his grasp, jamming it wide open against the flags. The cold was so shocking after the steamy warmth of the kitchen that he almost turned back, but anger and pig-headedness spurred him on. Icy needles of rain penetrated his clothes; within minutes he was soaked to the skin. The warm whisky glow faded abruptly. Soon his whole body felt numb. Bent double, Owain fought his way against the rushing torrent of deep orange flood water pouring down from the upper meadows. The drains gurgled and overflowed. A thick mat of filthy, cow-mucked straw swirled round his feet. One bloody boot sprang a leak.

Beneath the Dutch barn, Taff yanked desperately at the end of his chain, strained forward, up and war-dancing on his hind legs. Already the sheepdog was wet and skinny as a giant rat. His eyes bulged with hate, and foam speckled his muzzle as tobacco brown fangs snapped blood lust. Released, he shot forward, a pied bullet piercing the darkness. A single high-pitched scream rose above the snarling and barking.

The wind shovelled Owain past his fear.

He saw a small pick-up had been backed alongside the old Fergie tractor. Two skinny young fellows strained under the weight of the pump-trough being eased up the tail-board. The back was already crammed with stuff from round the yard: the other stone trough, some hop-dogs, a couple of mildewed saddles, the old curd-mill, several hundred-weight of cast-iron cheese press...even the worm-eaten hand winnower.

"What you playing at, you thieving bastards?"

The reaction of the first was almost comic. His jaw dropped. "Shit—he said there weren't nobody here."

The other ran forwards, squaring up. "Get out of it, Grand-dad, unless you want to get hurt."

"I'll have your hide for this," promised Owain, catching sight of Taff's plumed tail lying in the shadows. He raised the twelve-bore.

"Bloody hell, the old bastard's tooled up!"

The trough slid back down and shattered against the concrete as Owain struggled to keep the barrel level. Both youths ran, darting behind the cattle feed, and were instantly swallowed up by the thick shadows.

Then he noticed the tarpaulin had been yanked off the ancient cart. And there was Treadgold, looking it over, standing by the front wheel as if he'd just driven in and jumped down.

"Calm down." He waved a wad of banknotes under Owain's nose. "Put that thing away. I've got your money."

"Told you plain as daylight that I weren't selling, you bloody hook-fingered git."

Treadgold laughed. "It'll be my word against yours, old boy. People your age get forgetful. We had an agreement, remember?"

For answer, Owain raised the shotgun and took aim.

And immediately Treadgold lunged forward, bellowing abuse and flailing his arms. Caught off guard, Owain staggered and dropped to his knees, knocking his head on the side of the pick-up. Brilliant white light spiralled behind his eyes. He sped backwards through time and space, watching the scene from a great distance.

With a violent slam, he came back into himself. He crawled to the cartwheel, hauling himself unsteadily to his feet.

It had never been so real.

As always, the lantern was only strong enough to light a small circle round the cart. Beyond that there was nothing except the battering rage of a February storm. The usual stench of whisky hung between them, but this time Owain couldn't make out whether it was him or the other figure swaying.

"That you, Dad?"

Rhys had already jumped down. Now he straightened to his full height. "Where's Evan? Seeing to the horse is his bloody job."

"I packed him off to bed, Dad. It's late. He was exhausted."

"You did what? Who the hell are *you* to give orders? Get the lazy little sod out here right now."

"Think harder," advised Treadgold, grinning. "You'll remember selling it all to me in a minute."

"No," said Owain. "I won't."

"You bloody well *will*!" bawled Rhys, and smacked him hard across his mouth.

"You bloody well *will*!" echoed Treadgold.

"And when you've done that, get these feed sacks unloaded."

"Unload it yourself," said Owain.

"You having a brainstorm?" demanded Rhys. "Do as you're bloody well told. And jump to it."

"I'm not unloading anything," Treadgold sneered. "You'll remember selling all this to me shortly, just see if you don't."

"I never will."

"Don't rile him, Owain, love," whispered Mam, and he could still feel her trembling in the darkness. "Leave Evan sleeping and I'll see to the horse. You get your Dad inside. He'll never know. Go on. Then we'll get the sacks unloaded between us when he's settled."

Owain struggled with a jumble of thoughts. Remembering? Foreseeing? It was no longer clear. But he was certain of the result. No two ways about it. If Mam tried to take in the mare, she'd be trampled. Then Rhys would be kicked to death trying to calm the terrified beast. And poor daft Evan would take on the guilt and string himself up over the stable. He looked up at Rhys and felt the blood and the savage hatred swell in his mouth.

"But do you remember what I said to you?" he spat, jabbing the barrel into the huge man's chest. "Didn't I swear that one of these days you'd pay for the hell you've put us through?"

"You? You ain't man enough, you poor little crink." Rhys bellowed with amusement. He slapped the great square hand against his thigh.

"What the fuck's the matter with you, you mental old bugger?" screamed the dealer. He ripped the weapon from Owain's hands and kicked it under the pick-up. "You need locking up." He sidled backwards, half-crouching behind the pick-up as he raised his clenched fist. "You come near me and I'll give you a bloody good hiding."

"I said you'd get what's coming to you," shouted Owain, his fingers sliding towards the broken mattock handle. "Now I'll learn you. By God, ain't I going to give you chiack. I'll warm your bloody hide. Cripple you, I will. You'll think twice about lifting your bloody hand to Mam or Evan or me again."

"Daft sawney," said Rhys, turning his back. "Can't think who sired you. Some passing tinker, shouldn't wonder."

"What are you on about?" shrieked Treadgold, "You never said anything of the sort. All right, forget the junk, keep it. It isn't worth that much anyway. I'll get the lads to put it back. Just lay off, will you?" He turned to run.

Owain leapt after him, bringing the handle hard down on his skull. A savage joy exploded inside him as Rhys landed face down in the swirling soup of straw and muck and flood water. The club rose and fell. Thin threads of scarlet curled lazily round the few bubbles frothing the puddle's surface.

Slowly he became aware of the two frightened white faces staring at him. He stepped impassively over Treadgold's prone body. "I gave him fair warning. Now put everything back and clear off my farm. You hear me? If I see you here again, you'll both end up six foot under."

Somehow Owain stumbled back to the kitchen. For a long time he dozed, close to the range, soaking up its warmth while his clothes steamed. Gradually the storm died, passing on into the heart of the Black Country, leaving only a light rain which pattered against the glass like gentle tears of relief. As the first pale hint of day lightened the sky, he saw that the turmoil had left the land energised, potent, and strangely peaceful. He felt at peace, too. It was over. One of these days had come at last— and finally gone. The past was finished with. The ghosts laid.

Ghost in the Rear-View
by Jeff Kozzi

THE EARLY SPRING AIR CARRIED A CHILL. Not cold, like a bitter winter night, but the kind of chill that runs up your arms and spine without penetrating to the bone. Or maybe that was an after effect of her cold soullessness. Truth told, I can't say for sure it was her that first time because she wasn't quite put together enough for positive identification.

I was driving home from work, a three-to-eleven shift on the front desk. It's possible I imagined her, because I had a drink after work. The thick cloud cover absorbed most of the light thrown from the city. A drenching rain had left glistening puddles on the roads as only those sudden New England spring storms can do. I was tired. I tried to rationalize that night away, any way I could: the beer, the complaining guests, being tired and aggravated.

I always saw her on that short, relatively undeveloped stretch between exits 24 and 25, right after the graveyard that runs from Branch Avenue all the way to the bus terminal. I checked the rear-view mirror that night like I would any other to make sure no one came speeding past on my right.

Instead of seeing headlights on the road behind me, there sat a skeleton in the back seat staring at me through the mirror.

Think more rather than less of me because I admit I screamed. I jumped hard and fast enough to bump my head on the Jeep's roof.

I swerved over two lanes. I was lucky no other car was there. I checked the mirror again, wanting to dispel whatever hallucination had gotten into my head. The skeleton reached for me with one hand. A gold and emerald ring rolled loosely on the third joint of her middle finger. Almost swerving off the road, I jerked my head around.

The skeleton was gone.

I never believed in those things. I still don't want to believe in them, and I still scoff at those idiots who go on television and tell how their house was haunted by dead little children. I wasn't about to go on television and tell some melodramatic announcer that my seven-year-old Jeep Laredo was haunted, not even by a respectable ghost, but by a bare skeleton.

My mistake was telling people at work the next afternoon. Everyone except Rachel laughed, even harder when I told them I slept with all the lights on. That was mostly a lie anyway, because I didn't get much sleep. I stayed up listening to the house. It settled occasionally, and the sound reminded me of my grandmother's old creaking bones. That terrified me even more, although I don't think the skeleton in my Jeep could have been Grams because it was taller and sat up straight in the seat, not hunched over.

The next night I drove home more carefully, and not just because I had mustered courage with a few after-work brews. For every twenty feet the car rolled down the highway, I must have looked in that rear-view mirror three times. No skeleton visited me, thankfully, but I still didn't sleep quite right that night.

The third night was brighter than either of the two before it, and between glances at the road and glances in the rear-view, I looked for the graveyard off Branch and North Main to see if I could spot the tombstones. I figured maybe a subliminal peek at the graveyard had mixed with whatever song might have been on the radio had made me imagine a skeleton in the mirror. I spied no ghost-white headstones through the bare trees, and no skeletons in the mirror. Within a few days, I forced it from my mind. I had other things to do with my life than scare myself.

She was back about three weeks later, even more ghastly than the first time. She was no longer just a skeleton. Wads of rotting flesh hung off her. Black stuff oozed from her eye sockets. Rotted organs dripped between her ribs. I still saw bone, gray in contrast to her teeth. I stared into the mirror, horrified but transfixed.

A car's high-pitched horn blared furiously. I had almost collided with a Volkswagen as I stared into the mirror at the rotting corpse. I swerved back into my own lane. I held the wheel steady and stared into the mirror again. The cadaver's head was moving, and it raised a rotting hand over the edge of the bucket seat. That's when I spun to face her directly. I swerved far enough to hit the rumble strip. The traffic risk was for nothing, because nothing sat in the seat that the mirror had said was occupied. I checked the mirror again, but she was gone.

Another sleepless night plagued me, followed by several more. Between check-ins at work, I told Rachel because she believes in all that cockamamie. She listened with wide-eyed fear and chills that I shared even though the lobby air conditioner wasn't yet on for the season. Rachel made a faithful sounding board, but offered little in the way of advice. The following night she asked if I had seen it again, but thankfully I hadn't. She asked the night after that too, with some genuine concern for the haggard, dark-eyed look that had settled on my face with the disruption to my sleep. After that, she let it rest, and I caught up on my sleep as the general business of life took my mind away from my horrific imaginings.

Some weeks later, the ghoul returned. It was like she was staying away just long enough for me to forget about her, then coming back to haunt me as if I was the butt of some prank her little graveyard friends had dared her to make. I almost pissed myself that night because I didn't see her in the rear view first. I heard her. She made a hissing nose, not like a snake, but more like an angry, rabid alley cat. I guess her prior visitations hadn't left my mind as thoroughly as I had led myself to believe. When I heard that unhuman sound, I didn't suspect a burst tire or turn around to the back seat to see what made that noise. I looked right into the rear-view, knowing the cadaver would be there.

A cheekbone jutted through a rip in her rotting flesh, but she was, that third sighting, something much more than the skeleton I first had seen. Skin on the hand that reached for me held the emerald ring. I swerved in the road again, this time because I whirled to catch her before she could spirit away. I needed to see this recurring horror directly, but in the second it took me to turn, she disappeared. The hand that I had swung over my right shoulder to slap away her rotted, air-grasping fingers connected with nothing. She must have been with me longer that third time, or I had stepped on the gas when I heard her hiss, because I missed the exit and had to backtrack from Pawtucket. The drive home seemed longer, not just for the unwanted detour, but because the Jeep reeked of rotting death.

I was up until dawn that morning, shivering despite the late spring warmth.

Rachel suggested I call a car-history bureau to see if the Jeep had been in an accident before, but that wasn't necessary. I had bought it from my neighbor after admiring it nearly every day for the six years since he first drove it off the showroom floor. I knew that it had never been in an accident, much less that anyone had died in it.

The fourth time I saw her, there was no doubt she was a she. I flicked the directional for the right lane turn and checked the rear-view. She scared me most that time because I had come to expect a cadaver in decomposition, not a twenty-something girl sitting quietly in the back seat. I jumped and screamed, although not necessarily in that order. I bumped my head and swore, then looked in the mirror again.

Her eyes glowed brighter than the back-lit illumination of headlights behind me. A massive scrape marred her face from temple to chin. A hunk of her nose was missing. Whatever had scraped her had also taken off her ear and left a blistered wet pulsating membrane in its place. A section over her cheekbone was just plain gone.

I gasped.

"Why?" she asked.

I turned towards her, almost side-swiping the truck that had gained on me since I had slowed to study her mutilated face. The driver blasted me with automotive obscenity. My heart raced as I swerved back to the left, looking in the mirror.

"Why?" she repeated.

I turned to face her directly but she was gone.

I pulled over right before the exit, shaking. It took a long time for my heart to stop hammering against my ribs. I drove the rest of the way slowly, with constant looks in the mirror, but she didn't reappear.

Rachel saw how shaken I was the next afternoon. We talked about it over our dinner break, away from the prying eyes and ears of the people who had taken up calling me "Ghostbuster." To my surprise, she whipped out a day planner. "You saw her last night? Hmmm, well that's odd."

"What?"

"There's no pattern to it. Two Tuesdays, a Wednesday and a Thursday. All different dates, three or four weeks apart."

"But always coming home from work."

"About the same time every night?"

"Yeah, about. You know me, sometimes I'm here later."

"Maybe you should just go right home from work. You can't wait until you get home for a beer?"

I resented that. "It's not like I'm drinking myself stupid. I'm just socializing with the wonderful people I work with."

"And that's putting you by that graveyard right around midnight."

"I've been driving by that graveyard right around midnight five or six nights a week for more than two years now, Ray. Why should I start seeing this ghoul now?"

"Let's go to the library tomorrow. We'll look through the obituaries about the time you started seeing her."

That search came up with nothing. No twenty-something girls had died around the time I started seeing her.

I no longer stayed after work, but went right home, completely sober. The skyline around the commute became obscured with the trees' thickening leaves. I thought just two shift drinks had been enough to activate some morbid imagination. When the fifth week passed without another unearthly visitation, I began to relax. I was no alcoholic. If I had to forgo a drink to have unhaunted rides home, I was more than willing to make the sacrifice. Anyway, I didn't like my coworkers as much since they'd taken to calling me "Casper."

I was sober the next time I saw her. Actually, I heard her first, but this time she asked that plaintive question, "Why?"

I jumped, screamed, swore. She had been the furthest thing from my mind that night. The traffic was heavy, with more cars on the road in summer when teenagers with later curfews cruised the city for sex and other trouble. Instead of the rotting smell, a mist of a sweet, strange odor filled the car, something like my little sister's lip gloss or hair spray. I shivered. I shook my head, checking lanes on either side of me, but I didn't look in the back seat. My hands trembled, but I locked my elbows to keep the wheel steady. Then I looked in the mirror.

The ghost was a pretty girl with pleasant features, a shade of blond that may have been natural, not too much make-up, just small jeweled studs in her ears. I looked for spots of rotting or missing flesh, but I saw none. Her face was whole. Her hand appeared in the mirror, reaching for my shoulder. The ring sparkled with an ethereal green hue.

"Why?" she repeated.

"That's what I want to know!"

"Why did you do this to me?"

I screamed at her. "Why are you doing this to me?"

Her mouth opened to issue response.

Another horn blared. When I looked over my shoulder to discern the threat, she vanished, leaving only the smell of lip gloss and an unnatural chill. Another driver threw something against my car and whizzed around me. My directional was still on, flicking towards the right, and I followed it, although I'd missed my exit again. I pulled into the breakdown lane to steady my nerves. It took a long time.

Rachel's next suggestion was pragmatic. "You always see her on the same spot on the road?"

"Yeah. By that graveyard off the highway, right by my exit."

"Don't take the highway."

I followed that advice, successfully. Occasionally, when coming home from other business at other times of the day, I'd travel by the highway just to see if she would appear by day, but she never did. I was carrying the experience of her visits with me, though. My vow not to indulge in a quick drink with the guys had started a more anti-social tendency. I was furtive and paranoid, haunted by that girl and her repeated question. My fears only subsided with time as the summer days waned. I didn't want to think about Halloween coming, and I had already reserved the night off, to stay at home and toss candy to the begging little ghouls rather than risk seeing a real one pleading "Why?" in the rear view mirror.

I started taking the highway again on days when I actually managed to forget being haunted. Whenever I found myself inexplicably on the freeway, I would start checking the backseat directly. I had never laid eyes on her without the mirror, so I thought that was safer than checking the rear-view. She didn't appear.

That is, she didn't appear until late November. I'd gotten over my stupid fears by then. I told myself it was some disturbance in my mind that I never recognized, one that must have solved itself.

The preternatural cold and the smell of lip gloss and hair spray hit me first. I checked the mirror. She sat with her arms crossed over her pink satiny pull-over top and light cardigan sweater The emerald ring glistened. She was staring out the window, as if annoyed that I hadn't acknowledged her sooner. She looked even younger than she had before, like maybe she wasn't twenty, or even eighteen.

"Why are you here?" I demanded.

"I hate you," she said.

That took me aback. My hands, shivering with the sudden cold, fell off the wheel for an instant before I regained my grip.

"Why?" she asked.

My fear had turned to fury. "Why what?!"

"Why?" she repeated.

I whirled to face her.

She was gone.

I avoided the highway more diligently than before, all winter long. The car's heater didn't work well, so I was cold driving home even without the ghoul in the back seat. I wondered if she had done something to the heater, or if my changed route somehow brought on her cold but prevented her from forming in the car.

Spring started thawing the winter. I had never seen the sullen spirit when someone was in the car with me, or in the day, so I had started taking the highway from time to time. The frequency gradually increased. It's slow getting around Providence without the highway. Downtown is center to the city limits. Only the highways cut a direct path, so alternate routes sometimes spin you into almost the opposite direction before turning you back where you really need to go.

I had resumed taking the highway long enough to have gotten over most of my fear when I saw her that final time. The road was quiet; it was a Sunday night, and I was filling in a shift for a little overtime. Since it wasn't my night to work, I shouldn't have even been on the road then.

I slowed, then changed to the right lane. Looking ahead, I saw a car in the breakdown right before my exit, hazard lights blinking a bloody hue on the highway. My blinker added an eerie yellow tinge.

The cold came upon me more thoroughly than it ever had before, accompanied by that sickeningly sweet candy-girl cosmetic smell. I was going to look in the rear-view and maybe intone the name of Christ to drive her away, but her cold, cold hand dropped on my upper shoulder before I looked. I jumped, screamed, bumped my head, actually did piss myself that time, and intoned the name of Christ unlike how I'd intended. Her hand moved up my shoulder, reaching for my neck.

"Why?!" she screamed.

I lost control over my shivering body. The car swerved. My urine already felt frozen in my shorts.

She kept screaming. "Why?! Why?! Why?! Damn you, why?!"

I struggled, too cold to move fast. As I drifted partially out of the travel lane, the driver's door of the broken down Buick opened. The crunch sounded oddly distant, as if muted by the cold. I spun, traveled sideways, vainly tugged on the wheel against the impact that sent the Jeep rolling over the Buick. I landed right side up on the grass that ran between the road and the graveyard.

My seat belt saved my life.

I should have gotten out to help, try to help, see if I could help. Instead, I sat shivering in the Jeep, checking the rear-view mirror, constantly relieved no one was there.

I didn't respond to the emergency lights. The paramedics and police found me shivering in the seat. I stepped out on my own when they pried the door open and threw blankets around me. I couldn't quite hear their voices through the constant cold.

"Shock...Buick...Dead...Girl..."

I stumbled around the mashed Buick. I had pushed it clear off the road. The paramedics nudged me back, but I pushed past them. The Buick was empty.

The cold clung to me as I turned away from the demolished car.

Traffic was diverted from the right lane. People drove slowly, savoring their glimpses of carnage. The paramedics had parked the ambulances to block the sight from the road as they lifted the stretcher with a jerky, careless motion. A hand fell out from under the sheet. The emerald ring glistened bloody brown in the flashing red lights.

On Shadowed Grounds

by Kevin McClintock

Auschwitz-Birkenau Investigation

2:25 a.m., 13 March
Arrive at John Paul II International Airport Kraków-Balice

3:45 a.m., 13 March
Bed down at inexpensive hostel for quick bite to eat; sleep

Noon, 13 March
Brunch, equipment check, roll-call

2:25 p.m., 13 March
Stop at outside vegetable / fruit market for supplies; bottles of water

3:30 p.m., 13 March
Rent three Chevy vans, leave Kraków for Birkenau

5:59 p.m., 13 March
Arrive outside Birkenau, former German Nazi concentration camp

6:19 p.m., 13 March
Team leader Michael Smith calls all PIT members for customary "group huddle"

THEY MADE THEIR WAY—the famous five, as their fans liked to call them—atop an automated flatbed train car, staring at the camp around them as they bumped across the rusted railroad tracks.

Slipping from his head his famously soiled PIT ball cap to scratch at his sweaty scalp, Michael Smith gestured for the group members to collect around him. The production crew fired up their cameras and shuffled into place to tape Michael's words for the upcoming episode.

Anderson Jorris, as usual, was standing at Michael's elbow, gazing off at the fading sunlight. Also—as usual—Carson Reavis was the last of the team to walk up to them, still worrying over the equipment while coiling an orange extension cord around the crook of his elbow. It was his job to make sure every tiny piece of equipment was unpacked correctly from the storage bags in the back of the three vans.

It was cold. Most of the Americans were bundled up in heavy coats, slipping on gloves or zipping folds up to their chins. They'd been warned about the harsh Polish wind, and only now, here on the frigid plains, were they getting their first, true taste of it. None welcomed it.

Michael gazed at the desolate camp around them. By far the most striking feature was the brick-lined structure straddling several railway lines that veined the camp's outer perimeter. At the top of the entranceway loomed a tower with a now defunct spotlight. The others were quietly squinting against the wind at the distant building, which lay roughly a mile to the east but was closing rapidly. It was a foreboding structure, despite the green grass and fading blue skies.

"I don't like it," Sarina Powell whispered, slowly turning away from the building. She had her arms wrapped around her mid-section, visibly shivering. Television viewers had recently listed her as one of the "hottest babes" on television. Normally, she wore low-cut shirts, but not out here, not in the grip of the Polish winds. Of the five investigative members, Sarina was most sensitive to the paranormal. While some viewers thought she hammed it up for the cameras, fellow PIT members trusted the woman's instincts. Too many times and in too many cases, Sarina had announced the presence of a spirit's moment just seconds before an orb flashed by, a shadow moved or an EVP recorded. Anderson jokingly called her a human ghost detector.

"It may be because of its history," Michael said, putting an answer to her spoken uneasiness. While none of the group's words were scripted, they knew in the back of their minds that everything they said and did would be recorded. Later, their words and actions and—yeah, even their screw-ups—would be cut and pasted into an hour-long episode.

"Agreed," Wesley said, gesturing toward the distant camp. Normally the comedian, he was eerily stoic.

"We're all aware of the camp's history," Michael said. "Try not to let it influence your work, guys."

Michael and Anderson had founded PIT when it was just a two-man operation staged from a trailer in the corner of a vacant lot. Now, PIT merchandise annually raked in $5 million. Anderson was the "good guy" to Michael's "bad guy"—a relationship that had translated well enough to the television screen and cable audiences.

The two had high hopes for this particular investigation. According to the sponsors statewide, anticipated ratings for their Poland adventure were expected to be the highest in five years.

They continued to ride in silence. Entering the camp atop the train car had been Michael's idea. He wanted them to experience the same feeling of uneasiness the Jewish refugees had felt as they approached the camp's looming stone entrance. It was working all too well. The squeak of the wheels below them and the quiet of the Polish camp in front of them had unsettled even him. Standing three inches over six foot, bald and muscular to boot, Michael wasn't easily spooked.

"Creepy-ass building," Anderson said.

And it was an evil-looking structure. Its red, brick-lined windows resembled eyes, and the opening at the bottom that allowed the train cars through was almost an opened maw—the twin wings of the structure reaching out on either side like grasping arms.

"I'm going to read," Sarina suddenly announced. In her hands was a book written by Tadeuszx Borowski, a camp survivor.

The bolts crack, the doors fall open. A wave of fresh air rushes inside the train. People... inhumanly crammed, buried under incredible heaps of luggage, suitcases, trunks, packages, crates, bundles of every description. Monstrously squeezed together, they have fainted from heat, suffocated, and crushed one another. Now they push towards the open doors, breathing like fish cast out on the open sand... A huge, multicolored wave of people loaded down with luggage pours from the train like a blind, mad river trying to find a new bed...

The silence was broken only by the metallic squeak of the car's wheels atop the rails.

"Jesus," Wesley whispered, suppressing a shudder.

The train car slowly made its way beneath the tower.

"More than a million Jews," Sarina said, a small tremble in her voice. "They were all brought here to die."

AUSCHWITZ-BIRKENAU INVESTIGATION (CONT.)

6:23 p.m., 13 March
Teams gather up equipment, stacking extra tapes and batteries inside their "utility" belts

6:25 p.m., 13 March
A scream is heard by team member Wesley. He says it's faint, but appears to be coming from the crematorium

6:26 p.m., 13 March
Michael orders all PIT members to activate night vision goggles and to keep walkie-talkies in-hand at all times

6:37 p.m., 13 March
Teams move out to begin respective investigations

The camp was huge, even if abandoned. It covered twenty-two square miles. It had been a rather somber tourist attraction for quite some time. Until paranormal activity was first detected ten years ago—mostly moving shadowy shapes, voices and even screams.

"Where to first?" Carson asked Michael, who was zipping up Sarina's pack and giving her a pat on the shoulder.

"The pond's the closest. We'll go there, where the remains of the dead were scattered. If we have time, we'll make our way over to either the barracks or the latrine."

"Gotcha."

All five members had their night-vision cameras in place. The two PIT co-founders shared a thermographic camera— Michael holding the camera, Anderson the monitor. Behind them stood Wesley, in charge of the mini-DVR recorder. To either side walked Carson and Sarina, each holding EVP recorders. Carson also had the map. He'd pause from time to time, peering at it, before gesturing in the right direction. Twice they found themselves veering left toward the distant crematoriums.

"Sense of direction sucks tonight," Michael said. It was understandable. Ninety-nine percent of their investigations involved rural homes or derelict buildings. About the only experience that even compared to this was a haunted Boy Scout's camp in eastern Kansas.

It was hard going. Prickly weeds snagged their clothes and slowed their progress. Sarina stumbled into a pothole the size of a children's swimming pool, damn near damaging her EMF detector. All of them were tired by the time they reached the edge of the so-called "ash pond."

"PIT team at the ash pond, south side, 8:03 p.m. CST," Michael whispered into his recorder, which he kept inside an old pocketknife sheath on his belt. Next, he broke out his video recorder, turning it on. Artificial lights were pretty much banned during investigations since they tended to royally screw up a person's natural night vision. Periodically, Michael would tear away to focus on various distant objects, from a leafless tree to one of the hulking shadows belonging to a distant camp cabin.

"This place is definitely creepy," Anderson muttered, glancing down to check his EMF reader.

Sarina spied the movement. "You getting anything?"

"Nuthin'. Smooth as a babe's butt."

No doubt the producers would at this point put in a premade clip of either Michael or Anderson speaking about Electromagnetic Field Recorders, and how the handheld machines recorded electromagnetic fluctuations. Allegedly, spirits or entities trying to manifest would pull energy from wherever it could be obtained, causing a sudden spike in EMF readings.

From time to time, Carson would call out a "flash," warning the others to shield their eyes before he snapped off pictures. On rare occasions, the random camera clicks would catch a floating orb or splash of ectoplasm, proving the machines could pick up objects the human eye would never see.

"So what's the deal with this pond?" Anderson asked.

"They say there are manifest— Wait..." Michael held up his arm.

The others stopped in their tracks, straining, staring about in the darkness.

"What is it?" Anderson whispered.

Michael didn't know. It had sounded like branches snapping underfoot from the nearby ridge of trees off to the east. "Something," he said, gesturing in that direction. "Over there. Movement."

"Want us to head on over and give it a look?"

Michael shook his head no. "Keep an eye on it for now. I'd rather you stick to the pond."

Nodding, Anderson made his way to the east, walking slowly so the camera hugging his hat wouldn't bounce too much and make the viewers back home motion sick.

It didn't take him long to report back.

"Hey guys," his voice crackled over the radio. Michael paused to grab it up from his belt.

"What is it?"

"Lot of movement and sounds out here on the edge. I may need some back-up."

"Movement?"

"Lights."

Michael nodded. He turned to Wes and Carson. "Stick with Sarina. Check out the pond, then head on over to the White House when you can. We'll get back to you when we can."

The others nodded. The White House was one of the smaller crematoriums, the last built by the Nazi's before the end of the war.

Michael jogged over to Anderson who periodically flipped on his flashlight to guide him.

"Spooky out here when you're all alone in the dark," he called out to Michael.

"We've seen worse," the PIT leader said. "So what's this about a light?"

"It was out there," Anderson said, gesturing off toward a lumpy tree line marking the eastern borders of the abandoned camp. "Gone now."

"Might come back again."

The other nodded. It'd happened before.

As usual, the two men were trying to talk casually, a majority of their words intended for the cameras and legions of fans who tuned in each week to their show. The last episode of *Ghostly Excursions* had garnered nearly 15 million viewers, the most in the program's history.

As they moved, a light winked on. It appeared far away, floating flush with the distant horizon.

"That your light?"

"That's my light."

"Let's walk toward it."

The two trudged across the rough ground, using their flashlights to avoid ravines or holes capable of snapping ankles.

Michael's radio suddenly chirped at his side.

"Yo," Michael said.

"Hey," It was Sarina. Her voice sounded stressed.

He exchanged looks with Anderson. "Got something good for us?" he asked her.

"Something's happened…"

"What?" Michael felt a sinking in his gut. Whatever it was, it couldn't be good.

Silence.

Maybe someone had twisted an ankle or busted up a kneecap in the dark. It happened from time to time.

"Where the hell are you guys?"

"Just north of the ash pond—and well, for a while we couldn't find Wesley."

"Okay…" Michael said. "So where the hell did he go?"

"We didn't know. One minute he was here with us, the next he was gone. So we backtracked and found him on the other side of the pond, near a clearing in the tree line."

"And?"

"Somebody knocked him out, Michael."

The PIT leader rubbed his face with his free hand. "Okay—Jesus, is he okay?"

"He's up, but…"

"Spit it out, Sarina."

"Something… some*one* cut him, Michael. Cut into him."

The two PIT leaders stood, stunned.

"Yeah," she continued, "it cut into his stomach. Pretty deep, too."

"Like—slashes? An animal, maybe?"

"No—symbols."

"Symbols?" Anderson barked, listening at Michael's elbow. He sounded skeptical.

Carson's voice came over the radio. "It's a swastika, guys. Cut it into Wes's stomach. Used a knife or razor or something. Didn't see anyone, me or Sarina, and Wesley claims he didn't see anyone either."

"So he's awake now?"

Sarina was back on the radio. "Yeah, but he's in a lot of pain, and there's a lot of blood. And… we keep hearing things out here. Words and footsteps and… even conversations, but whispered."

Michael caught Anderson's attention and mouthed, "We're not alone." He turned back to the radio. "Okay Sarina, we're on our way back."

"We're just east of the ash pond, 'bout a half-mile from it."

"Can you or Carson shine a light to guide us in?"

"Yeah, Carson will."

A few moments later, the two men spied a stabbing light in the distance.

"We see you guys., We're on our way. Hang tight."

They began retracing their steps.

"She said a swastika, right?" Anderson asked him, working to keep up.

Michael nodded.

"Would Wes do that to himself?"

"What do you mean?"

"Maybe as a joke. You know, to scare the others?"

Wesley was a wacky guy, their newest member, but none of this was in their script, and neither thought Wesley would do anything to jeopardize his growing success on the show.

"No. Someone did this to him."

"So you think it's a person."

"Sure as hell ain't a ghost, Andy. Ghosts don't cut people."

"Some do."

"Not like this. Someone's out there, playing games with us."

They jogged in silence for a good minute or so before Michael grunted and stopped. "What the hell are they doing way over there?"

Carson's light was shining brightly, but it wasn't growing brighter as they labored to close the gap. In fact, over the last minute, it had slowly steered away from them, and now seemed to be winking from among the tree line to their right.

"Why are they moving?"

They continued their jog, punctuated only by harsh breathing and an occasional curse. Again, the two men stopped. Michael sounded irritated.

"The light's moving," he said, bending over to catch his breath.

With Anderson gasping beside him, he clawed out his radio and smashed down the button. "You there, Sarina?"

"I'm here."

"Why the hell you guy's moving your light?"

Silence.

"Sarina?"

"Michael, we haven't moved since we last talked to you."

"But you have," Anderson said into the mouthpiece. "You guys are leading us almost due west now, toward the tree line and the burial ground."

"No—we're by the pond, Michael. Where are you guys? We keep hearing noises. Chuckles and... and sounds like babies crying or something."

"Okay, hang tight." He cut the link.

"What the hell are we following?" Anderson whispered.

"I don't know."

"It's drawing us away."

Michael clicked the radio. "Sarina, tell Carson to shake his flashlight really fast."

"Okay."

The two peered at the distant light. It hovered motionless in front of them, pulsating. Almost like it was breathing.

Michael was growing impatient, snarling into the radio. "You guys doing it?"

"Yeah. Can you see us?"

It was Anderson who finally spied it, and tapped Michael's shoulder. "Over your shoulder, to your left."

There, almost behind them, they spied Carson's dim light, which was making a sloppy figure-8 in the night air.

Michael's blood iced over.

"So who the hell," Anderson whispered, swiveling back to the pulsating light, "is *that?*"

They didn't stick around to find out; they turned and ran toward Carson's light.

"It's gone," Anderson said at one point, panting as he glanced back over his shoulder. "The light."

Michael just nodded. The two of them nearly made Sarina scream when they finally stumbled into Carson's beam of light.

"What took you so long?" Wesley asked.

"There was another light," Anderson said, gasping. "Tried to draw us away from you guys."

Carson processed what he'd just said. "There's been some strange shit out here."

"You said something about babies?"

"Yeah, and voices, too—male and female. Moving shadows. Screams, even."

The four PIT members surrounded Wesley who was on the ground and wrapped up in a blanket with an extra coat snug around his shivering shoulders.

"How you doing?" Michael said, leaning down over Wesley, placing a friendly hand on his forehead.

"Hurts," he said. His eyes were closed, the single word spat through gritted teeth.

"What happened?"

Wesley's eyes were blank holes in his head. "Can't 'member."

Carson moved up and peeled back Wesley's bloodstained shirt. Michael audibly gasped at the ruined stomach.

"Yeah," is all Carson could mutter. The hated Nazi symbol, still weeping blood, was larger than Michael had anticipated. The slashes themselves were rather neat. It wasn't sloppy like a pocketknife would make.

"Okay," Michael said, rising slowly to his feet with a tired and drawn-out sigh. "Let's call it a night."

AUSCHWITZ-BIRKENAU INVESTIGATION (CONT.)

9:23 p.m., 13 March
Wesley has recovered enough of his wits to—unsurprisingly—crack jokes about his wound, saying he'd always wanted a tattoo

9:27 p.m., 13 March
Members erect a "base camp" of tents and a canvas shelter on the road which leads to the crematoriums at the back of the camp

10:02 p.m., 13 March

Other members begin rudimentary data analysis, mostly reviewing digital camera shots and audiotapes

11:32 p.m., 13 March

Members bed down, though one will stay awake to "keep watch" over both the team and equipment locked inside the vehicles. Michael is convinced that someone—a human, and not an entity—is trying to pull a few pranks on them

1:15 a.m., 14 March

Anderson hears a series of screams that are so loud, so distinct, that they can't be ignored. After some discussion, the two co-founders trudge nearly four hundred yards to the latrine located inside the camp

"Okay, this appears to be it," Michael said, as he and Anderson ducked through a wired gate and entered a large, windswept courtyard where the former camp prisoners had been held behind barriers of machine gun bullets and barbed wire.

"Yeah," Anderson said. "Spooky place."

"Says something in German above the door over there."

"Do you speak German?"

"Are you kidding me?" he said, giving him an eye-roll. "C'mon, we'll take a quick peek."

The two moved up to the door, pausing to unlimber equipment—Michael with the DVR, and Anderson with EMF and EVP gauges in either hand.

"Ready?"

Nodding, Anderson pushed open the door, rusty hinges protesting. When the wind caught the wooden door, it banged inward, causing the two investigators to duck and wince.

"That was subtle," Michael quipped.

"Smells funny," Anderson said.

"Like a sewer."

Years ago, the two had trudged through a haunted sewer system beneath Lee's Summit, Mo., chasing phantom lights that turned out to be workers holding flashlights. But that was below a modern city. This was a 70-year-old abandoned camp?

"Doesn't make any sense," Anderson whispered.

Lit by the green of their goggles, the two could see the building had been haphazardly pieced together. It was typical of the type of thrown-together buildings the Germans constructed for people they believed inferior. The building's interior was mostly comprised of rotting timber held together by nails and termite spit.

Michael began a few EMF sweeps.

"Anything?" Anderson asked him.

"Nothing above point five," he said, frowning. He slowly made his way over to the far left latrine trench. There, he stopped short.

"What is it?" Anderson asked, moving up to his friend.

"Got a spike, Andy—six point eight now. And climbing." Anything between 2.0 to 7.0 milligauss signaled potential paranormal activity.

"And there's no electricity here." EMF detectors had a nasty habit of reading man-made power sources. But nothing man-made was working within 60 miles.

"Creeping up to seven," Michael hissed at Anderson, without ever taking his eyes from the tiny screen. "EVPs, good buddy."

"Already on it." Anderson moved over to a latrine trench. "Hello? Anyone here? My name is Anderson. I'm an American. We helped defeat the Germans. Can anyone communicate with us? We're here to help you."

He paused.

"Can you do something or maybe say something to show us that you're here?"

Anderson stiffened, turning to Michael with a shocked expression. Michael was down on his haunches, shining his pen light along the cracks of the floor.

He spied his friend's expression. "What?"

"Did you *hear* that?"

"No."

"It was a voice."

"Really?"

"From *behind* you."

Michael instinctively turned. Turned again. Swallowed hard. Adjusted a suddenly sweaty grip on the video recorder.

"Could you please repeat what you just said so I can hear it, too?"

Seconds later, a faint, human moan sounded.

He spun back to a beaming Anderson, excited. "Heard it that time."

"A moan," Anderson said, nodding. "Sounded like a moan. Think you got it on tape?"

They huddled together as Anderson rewound the machine and thumbed the 'play' button.

"Out," he whispered seconds later, his eyes large and white as he stared up at Michael. "It said 'out.'"

He pushed past and made his way over to the middle concrete latrine trench. "Sounded like it came from in here, Mike." He was moving holding the EMF detector just a few inches above the spill holes. "It's holding steady at seven—Jesus. I haven't seen a reading hold like this for so long. Makes me—"

In front of them, a human baby wailed from within the latrine trench.

Anderson gasped and dropped the EMF detector. Next to him, Michael skittered back a few feet. The sound was so foreign, so inexplicably out of place, so incredibly creepy, that both stood dumb for long seconds, their mouths wet and gaping.

"It can't be—no way in *hell*," Michael hissed. "That's coming from the far end."

He dashed forward, pulling up near the copper gate at the far end of the latrine. All three trenches were hollow, and black as night inside, periodically pimpled with openings just large enough for a person to urinate or void. Grabbing his flashlight from his belt, he peered down inside. Grunting, he then popped off the copper grate and climbed atop the latrine.

"Whoa buddy," Anderson said, moving forward.

"Going down in there. Keep your light on me."

"Maybe we should—"

The baby wailed again. This time, it sounded like the infant was in pain.

"It can't be," Michael was saying, leaning and peering down into the hole. "It's gotta be a joke of some type. You know, maybe a recording, like those bastards did to us at that bar & grill in San Francisco last year. I—"

Down at the other end of the trench, Anderson inhaled sharply. He brought up the light, shining it wildly. "Dude—something moved down in there."

Michael pushed his legs down through the hole. The latrine trench's top came up to his chest. It was roomier, in fact, than he'd first thought.

"What'd you see?" he finally asked.

"Don't know."

"A shadow?"

He nodded. "Maybe."

"Where?"

"Halfway down—saw it through one of the holes."

"Which hole?"

"Third one down, toward you."

"Okay. Shit—okay." Michael ducked down into the latrine, his flashlight splashing up through the holes. "Don't see anything." His voice sounded muffled. He shuffled forward a step, clicking off his flashlight and pulling back down his night-vision goggles.

"Damn dark down here." He shuffled some more.

"You're slowly coming toward me," Anderson said.

"Still nothing," he said. He was breathing hard now, bent over as he was inside the trench. "Too cramped for an EMF reading in here. What do you have?"

"Let me check. Hold on."

Michael paused, waiting.

"Okay, I've got a four point eight," Anderson said. Down inside the trench, Michael remained quiet.

"Got a four point eight," Anderson repeated. "Michael?"

"Something's in here with us." Michael's voice sounded strained.

"What is it?"

"I..."

Anderson could hear Michael shuffling around in there.

"Michael?"

"Something's down in here. Movement..."

Anderson checked his temperature gauge. "It was seventeen outside and..." What the hell? He looked at the display window. The screen said it was six degrees. But that couldn't be right.

Michael shuffled a few more steps toward him. "About where did you see your shadow?"

"Maybe a tad bit ahead of you, buddy. It was just a black mass, looked like. Pulsating."

"*Pulsating?*"

"Yeah—"

"You mean... like breathing?"

"Almost. Yeah. I guess you—"

"Like the light from the trees earlier."

"Yeah, but—"

A baby's piercing wail sounded immediately behind Anderson. Down at the far end, Michael screamed. Panicked by the sounds behind him, he instinctively tried to climb up through one of the spill holes; only his head could fit through.

"Don't get *stuck*," Anderson gasped, making a complete, wild circle before reaching out to his friend.

"It's down here—or something." Michael's eyes were wide and panicked.

"Mike?"

But Michael had fallen back down inside the trench. His goggles were skewed sideways on his forehead.

"It's here," Michael said, his voice sounding like a dead thing. There were suddenly frantic noises from inside the latrine. As Anderson moved up to one of the holes, he saw Michael scrambling past, down on all fours and spooked.

Anderson took an EMF reading. "Jesus—it's spiking. Get outta there, Mikey!"

It was too narrow for Michael to turn around, so he was backing up, retreating, still on all fours, his face fogged by his own icy breath.

"Get out, Mike," Anderson yelled, his voice cracking. He was running alongside Michael beside the trench, urging him on. "Get out now."

"Oh Jesus oh Jesus oh Jesus oh Jesus..." Michael was leaving behind plenty of skin and blood, but he didn't feel or care. He was frantically eyeing the black cloud in front of him.

And it was moving now. Moving toward him. There was a smell down here, too—of sulfur. Like fresh shit.

Breathing hard, Michael continued his bloody slide backwards toward the opening. At one point, his camera slipped off his neck, and he watched it bounce away from him.

Moments later, Michael let out an ear-bleeding scream and hurled himself from the hole, wrenching his left leg as he went up and out, flopping down on the floor. There, he curled into a fetal position.

"Michael?"

The PIT co-founder rolled over onto his side.

"*Michael?*"

"The camera," he gasped.

Turning, he went over to the latrine and looked down into the hole. For a second, he thought he saw something there, something black, something coiled and waiting for his hand to reach down in there.

He hesitated.

"Get the camera," Michael said, groaning as he began to rise to his feet.

With shaking hands, Anderson clicked on his penlight and evaporated the darkness. Nothing was down in there but the battered DVR camera. He snaked a hand through one of the holes and pulled it out.

"Anything in there?" Michael asked, up in a sitting position now, gasping for breath.

"Nothing," Anderson whispered. "Nothing was there." He reached out to his friend. "How you doing, buddy? What'd you see?"

"It... a figure, crawling—hands and knees and—it had like a head... head that swiveled, you know... and it just stopped and crouched down and threw like... like its *arms* over its head and... Jesus, it was sucked back out... like, it was just gone. Like that." He tried to snap his fingers.

Anderson just stared. He'd never seen Michael like this before. Never.

"Just *gone*," Michael said, spitting out the words through blue lips. "Just like that..."

Auschwitz-Birkenau Investigation (cont.)

4 a.m., 14 March
   PIT members are stirred from sleep by distant wailing and screaming sounds. It's an army's worth of screams; at least twenty to twenty-five distinct voices, and untold "fuzzy" ones

9:13 a.m., 14 March
   Team members eat breakfast. Most are still spooked, whispering about the noises they heard or recorded five hours earlier

10:32 a.m., 14 March
   Michael and Carson recon ground previously covered the night before. Nothing unusual is found inside the latrine or around the ash pond

1:18 p.m., 14 March
   Because the sun won't set for another five or so hours, Michael and Anderson decide to begin reviewing material recorded from the night before

5:02 p.m., 14 March
   Michael and Anderson meet with Carson and Sarina for evidence review

Michael and Anderson made their way over to a tent. Inside, Carson and Sarina were hunkered over a folding metal table, lounging on two cheap wooden chairs in front of a lone laptop.

"You guys about wrapped up?"

Carson laughed. "You bet. Some of it is... well, it's pretty unbelievable," Carson said, shaking his head. He elbowed Sarina. "You want the honors?"

"First, there was that scream from last night—pretty much woke us all up. We caught that on the wireless." She gestured toward one of the computer monitors, which was split in half by an electronic, jagged line. When she clicked the play button, the line jumped with each recorded sound, usually a snore from the one of the sleeping PIT members or a natural noise somewhere in the background, mostly caused by the wind.

"You'll want to listen to this," Sarina said, pointing to a lone spike in the middle of the flat line. "Here it comes."

For several seconds, a woman's scream of sheer terror sounded from the tinny speakers.

Sarina clicked the off button. "We all heard it. And we were all accounted for—nobody was away from the camp when this happened. And as far as we know, there was no woman here aside from myself. So..."

"So it's unexplained," Anderson said.

"'Less it's a prank," Michael added. "Can't dismiss that. Maybe a couple Polish kids out punking us. Maybe the same nut job who cut up Wesley."

Sarina shrugged her shoulders. She had no answer for that.

"What else have you got for us?"

"Three really good EVPs," Sarina said, tapping the mouse of the laptop on the table. "This first one was caught by you, Michael, when you and Andy first stepped onto the path."

"No kidding?"

"Yeah, you had your recorder on as you guys were walking along. Now, you'll hear Anderson ask you something about your flashlight, and then you'll hear it..."

The speakers crackled and hissed with white noise. Moments later, a little girl's voice temporarily drowned out the static.

"Is that English?" Anderson asked.

Michael shook his head. "No way."

"It's Polish, actually. I sent the text off to the University of Krakow through my iPhone and they confirmed it. It's a little girl's voice asking about her mommy."

The two men just shook their heads.

"Okay, here's the second one."

After a few moments, a man's voice babbled out a long line of Polish words.

"Those last few words sounded the same," Anderson said.

"Good ears," Sarina said. "Again, I've gotten this translated. It says, 'Spare my child, please, please...' and then repeats the word 'please' four more times."

"And where was this caught?" Michael asked.

"Right after you left the ramp. Okay, moving on," Sarina said, cueing up the third EVP. "You guys again on this one, late last night, when you were inside the latrines."

"This is the voice that told us to get out?"

Carson and Sarina nodded. They listened to it. Michael and Anderson nodded in unison.

"But we ain't done," Wesley said. "We've got something on video. This was from your camera, Michael—from the latrines last night."

"Yeah, that's the camera I dropped when I panicked," Michael said.

"You'll see the camera fall and... there, that's Michael's hand, and then you see things rocking for a couple of seconds, and then..."

A black mass flowed toward the camera. It was solid enough to ink out a light from one of the spill holes above. Then, just as quickly, it seemed to suck in on itself and reverse direction, fading quickly from view.

"Wow..." Anderson said. His face was slack. "Rewind that."

Carson nodded, manipulating the buttons.

"It's a solid mass—see that?" Michael said. "*See?* See how it blocks out the light right... there?"

"Yeah, hell yeah," Anderson said.

They watched the black mass move again.

"I got the distinct impression it wanted to hurt me," Michael said, his voice barely above a whisper. "Never felt anything like that before."

"None of us have," Anderson said with a slight shrug.

Auschwitz-Birkenau Investigation (cont.)

5:17 p.m., 14 March
Team members gather up equipment, stacking extra tapes and batteries inside the "utility" belts

5:29 p.m., 14 March
Team leader Michael Smith orders members to activate night vision goggles and to keep radios on at all times

5:31 p.m., 14 March
Due to his injuries, Wesley is left behind at the vans to monitor equipment

6:29 p.m., 14 March
The four investigators reach the outskirts of the Crematorium #2 ruins

"What the hell is *that*?" asked Carson, pointing off into the gloom ahead of him. They all followed his gesture. Michael, bringing up the rear, felt the hair along his neck prickle.

"Jesus," Anderson said, fumbling for his camera, "It's the goddamned light we saw last night."

"Yeah," Michael said softly, clicking at it with his own camera. "The one that tried to lead us off into the forest."

The light seemed to shimmer, almost in answer.

The four took a dozen steps forward.

"It's moving," Sarina said.

Michael nodded. "You guys taping this?"

"Thermal and mini-DVR."

"Good show."

"It's leading us toward the Crematorium," Carson said.

"Stay back—don't get too far ahead," Michael said, his voice a whispered hiss. "I think this is how the bastards got Wes last night."

"Don't want it disappearing."

Michael grunted. "Don't want *you* disappearing."

They followed the light.

"Wait up," Carson whispered, holding up a visibly shaking hand. "Do you hear that?"

They did.

Cries.

Infants crying.

"Not again," Sarina said with a groan.

"From the crematorium."

As the ruins of the Nazi-constructed gas chamber slowly crystallized into view, the light they'd been chasing brushed up against the rubble heap and winked from sight.

"Went inside," Carson said, pointing.

As the PIT members searched the rubble, Sarina began reciting a passage from the memoirs of Alexander Ehrmann, an 18-year-old Jewish prisoner during the summer and winter of '44:

> *It started to get daylight, and we moved on to an area where there was barbed wire on both sides. We walked down an alley, a sentry so often spaced out. We kept on moving, prodded to move faster. We were told, 'You will be coming to an area where you will be given a bath and change clothes and you'll be told what to do.' We were walking, and beyond the barbed wire fences there were piles of rubble and branches, pine tree branches and rubble burning, slowly burning. We're walking by, and the sentries kept on screaming, 'Lauf! Lauf!' and I heard a baby crying. The baby was crying somewhere in the distance, and I couldn't stop and look. We moved, and it smelled, a horrible stench. I knew that things in the fire were moving, there were babies in the fire.*

"Why the hell would you say something like that now?" Carson sounded disgusted.

"So everybody knows what was done here," she answered. "And why these grounds are haunted."

"Stay focused, guys," Michael snapped, stepping forward and gesturing at the rubble. "Let's head in through there."

"What about the signs?" Carson asked.

Standing sentinel around the rubble's perimeter were black, modern signs showing a human with a red bar slashed through it—no trespassing.

Michael shrugged. "We have full authorization from the Polish government to go wherever we want... we're going inside."

He sought out Sarina. "Hey—you're our expert on this type of thing. You want to lead us?"

She nodded, softly stepping over a rope boundary and walking over to the top of a half-dozen steps leading down into a stone-lined trench, well below the ground's surface.

"This is where the Jews were brought in," Sarina said. "Men, women and children were marched here from the ramp in '42 and in late '43 from railroad box cars directly to this spot. Guess it saved the German guards from having to walk the extra thousand yards with rifles in their hands."

"Me and Andy've got the thermal running," Michael said. "Sarina and Carson, use EMFs and EVPs."

One by one, the PIT members walked down the spongy carpet of mildewed stone and grass that at one time had been a concrete floor. Their eyes were level with the ground.

Carson slowly walked away from the group, whispering questions into the air, collecting EVPs. Sarina moved ahead, searching for strange electromagnetic spikes.

"What did they do in here, Sarina? Was this the actual gas chamber?"

Sarina shook her head. "This was the last of the world they would ever see."

The others shivered.

"What's your temperature reading?" Andy asked Michael.

"Steady at 38 degrees."

"Gotcha."

"Anything on the screen?"

"Zilch."

To either side stretched brick-lined walls. They gingerly stepped over bits and pieces of scattered rubble.

Toward the end of the chamber the three men and single woman stopped short. Facing them, a mound towered above their heads—a looming, massive shadow of rubble in the dark.

"Sarina?"

"After the prisoners were stripped naked in the room behind us, they were herded into the gas chamber in front of us."

"Not much of it left," Carson said in a suddenly tired voice.

"There's an opening," Andy said, gesturing at the thermal screen. "I see heat bleeding through a small hole. Right there? See it?"

"Okay, get behind me," Michael said, "and I'll lead us in. We should be able to wiggle down in there."

This was the only portion of this once sprawling complex that was still roofed, or at least had the remains of a roof over it, Michael observed. Nothing more than a crumbled mess now, deteriorated in places from the falling rain and muck of the harsh Polish season.

"There were once pillars in this room, supporting the roof," Sarina was saying. "But they were hollowed out."

"Why?" Carson asked.

"Because the Nazi's would drop the poison into the pillars from the roof."

One by one, the PIT members wormed their way through the narrow opening. Covered with grime, they crept down onto the floor that was slippery with mold and damp algae.

"Smells strange in here," Anderson said, before turning to help Sarina through the opening.

"Like..." Michael sniffed. "What?"

"Meat?" Carson ventured.

"Blood," Sarina muttered seconds later.

"EMF readings?" Michael asked, his breath fogging the air in front of his face.

"Three point eight."

"Temperature?"

"Just under 30 degrees," Andy said. "Wait—29. No... 28 now. What the *hell?*"

"Did you hear that?" Michael asked, stopping, peering up above him, way up into the darkness.

The others froze.

"What? What'd you hear?" Carson asked.

"Sounded like a bang," Michael said. "Like a lid shutting."

"Thought I heard a chuckle," Anderson added. "Just now."

The others strained to listen, silently turning their heads in several directions.

"Where from?" Anderson finally asked his partner.

"Outside the building, sounded like."

"Nobody's out there, Mike. We're all in here."

"I *realize* that. But it came from *outside.*"

There was another sound now—like sand being poured into a pipe.

"Now I'm hearing that," Anderson said.

"Me, too," Carson said. "Above us."

Everybody looked up. Except for one member, that is. Sarina quietly made her way over to one of the brick walls, running her right hand across its smooth surface as she began to speak again in her dead voice. She was weeping, and reciting the Jewish memoirs from memory.

"As soon as the people inside realized what was happening, they struggled to get away from the gas seeping over them. There were

peepholes—tiny little filtered pinpricks in the walls—for the SS to observe what was happening inside—"

"Stop it, Sarina," Carson whispered.

"—And when all were dead," Sarina continued, *"the Sonder-kommando's would open up the chamber doors to let the gas and stink out. Then, with faces covered, they would pull out the bodies, one by one by one. They would shave hair for use in German industry and pull out gold fillings from teeth—"*

"Sarina?" Michael said, turning to her.

"What the hell's wrong with you?" Carson said with a hiss, moving toward Sarina.

"Listen," Michael barked from the corner of the chamber.

It was a dense, spurting sound, the type of sound a military smoke grenade makes.

"Oh shit," Michael said, the thermal camera clattering to the ground at his feet as he lurched toward the small opening. He stumbled one way; another way, but he couldn't find the exit.

"Where the hell's the opening?" Michael screamed, as the air around him grew thick with smoke. "I can't *find* it."

Sarina continued to speak in that dead voice of hers, eyes closed now, and her back pressed against the wall.

"After a while I heard the sound of piercing screams, banging against the door and also moaning and wailing. People began to cough—"

Michael called out her name, covering his mouth with his shirt, his eyes shut and tearing from the smoke and smell. He bumped into a panicked Anderson, and then knocked a hyperventilating Carson to the ground.

"Their coughing grew worse," Sarina continued, *"from minute to minute, a sign that the gas had started to act. Then the clamor began to subside and to change to a many-voiced, dull rattle, drowned now and then by coughing. In ten minutes, all was quiet. Zyklon B*

was adopted as a killing agent because it offered an easy death, yet the victims showed the marks of a terrible struggle."

All of the PIT members were prone on the floor or struggling on their hands and knees by the time Sarina's words finally morphed into belch-like coughing.

★ ★ ★

"Hello?" Wesley called out, squinting through the harsh glare of the sun.

Only the crickets greeted his words.

"Are they in there?" He was breathing hard from the excursion. Wesley hadn't slept a wink since the group had headed out the day before to Crematory #2. He'd waited with growing dread as the moon slid across the sky, cradling his radio and periodically urging one of them to speak.

None did.

When dawn chased away the darkness, he'd trekked alone across the abandoned camp, his heart in his throat.

At least there hadn't been a struggle. There were no scattered equipment and no...

Bodies?

When he spied the opening at the bottom of the collapsed crematorium, he didn't hesitate to peek inside. Grumbling, he ducked out, unclipped his flashlight, and ducked back in.

There, he just stared.

The four PIT members were down there, lying prone on the ground. They appeared to be sleeping, not a trace of bruising or blood on the floor around them.

Deep down, however, Wesley knew his friends were dead, and not sleeping, for their bodies had been neatly stacked.

That's when Wesley raised up his head to scream.

The High Priest's Cat

by Christine Lucas

Thebes, Egypt, circa 1620 BC

A SHADOW LOOMED over the sleeping human—*his* human. Nedjem tensed at the foot of the narrow bed. Being the High Priest's cat had its downside. Sure, good food was at paw's reach, the cushions were soft and the gardens cool, and willing females dwelled in the kitchens and storage rooms. Still, the Lord Embalmer and High Priest of Anubis attracted all sorts of spirits. Some were just lost, others confused and a few of them pure evil. This one smelled bad, like a bloated corpse floating among the reeds at the banks of the Nile.

Muscle after muscle, Nedjem rolled onto his belly, his eyes focused on the ghost. He put all his strength in his hind legs, ready to leap on the intruder. Ankhu, his human, stirred in his sleep, his hand brushing off an insect that wasn't there—just a grotesque face of smoke and mist. Nedjem's fur stood, his spine tingling in the presence of the *akh*—the spirit that should be in the afterlife and not among the living. He growled a warning, raising his forepaw, claws exposed.

The spirit turned and looked right at him. The ethereal head grew bigger, its jaws stretched wider than a crocodile's.

No sound came out—only a stench worse than anything the cat had ever smelled.

Nedjem hissed, his back arched, his fur fluffed up, the incessant tingling only adding to his distress. He clawed at the monstrous face but met nothing but smoke. He rose on his hind legs and clawed at it with both forepaws. The ghost recoiled, his mouth now twisted as if laughing. With a long sigh, it dissolved into the night.

The sleeping human stirred and rolled onto his side, mumbling something. Nedjem sniffed the air. The ghost's stench lingered in the room. Some elements in it smelled familiar—tar, pine wood, oil—but its origins evaded him. He scratched his head, then his back. The persistent tingling at the root of every hair on his body warned him that they hadn't seen the last of it.

He leapt off the bed and onto the windowsill. Occasionally licking his forepaws, he scanned the gardens below and stood guard until sunrise.

★ ★ ★

"Murderers! May Ammit feast on your hearts!" Ankhu stopped reading, crumbled the papyrus, and threw it across the room.

Nedjem looked up, still drowsy from his afternoon nap. The High Priest's words meant little to him, but the sound of crumbled papyrus made his paws tingle. Where had it gone? He stretched his neck, his yellow eyes scanning the floor. There it was, under the window. His tail twitched. The heat made any sort of movement a burden. But still, crumbled papyrus was a rare treat. Humans kept it out of his reach, for reasons incomprehensible to his feline mind.

He yawned and glanced at his human sitting at the desk by the window. The High Priest perspired anger and distress. Perhaps he should go and purr against his legs? *Too hot to move.* Or perhaps he should just lie on the bed. He rolled onto his back and stretched. A new scent, a mix of rotting fish and flatulence, announced the High Priest's faithful servant.

"Your cup of wine, your grace." Short, without one hair on his wrinkled body, the old man limped into the room.

"Leave it on the table, Khemes."

Khemes approached the desk and the stench waxed stronger. Nedjem rolled over, all senses alert. It smelled of a predator nearby—a big, scaly beast with huge teeth.

Even the High Priest wrinkled his nose. "In the name of all the Gods, what's that foul smell?"

The servant hung his head. "The new salve for my leg, your grace. The physician gave it to me just this morning. He swears that nothing heals crocodile bites as fast as their waste."

Crocodile—Nedjem knew that word, and what it stood for. He hissed his objections. He tolerated the jackal masks and statues in the High Priest's residence, given his human's status in the service of Anubis. But the accursed serpents belonged to the Temple of Sobek—he'd have none of them around, not even their waste.

Ankhu smiled and patted his lap. "Come here, little one. Don't worry, there's no crocodile around."

Give it time. This stench will attract a few, sooner or later. Nedjem measured the distance from bed to windowsill. *Too far.* So instead he jumped off the bed and indulged his human by curling up on his lap. It was less comfortable than usually— the High Priest was tensed, his muscles stiff, and his hands rough against Nedjem's fur. He sniffed the cup, but wrinkled his whiskers. He turned at Khemes and mewed. *Where's my milk and fish?*

The servant stood oblivious, scratching his chin.

Nedjem turned to Ankhu and mewed again.

"Relax. You're safe here." Ankhu sipped his wine, his face drawn. "You're so lucky, little one," he said, his voice weary. "You were saved. The others weren't."

But where's my milk?

Khemes waited patiently by his master. "The others, your grace?"

"Phoenician smugglers were caught transporting sacred animals up the Nile to carry them to distant lands. Mostly young crocodiles, ibises and cats." His knuckles turned white around the alabaster cup. "When the pharaoh's men closed in on them, they threw the caged animals into the Nile to dispose of the evidence."

Nedjem's heart fluttered, and the thought of supper vanished from his mind. *Caged.* He knew this word. It meant nothing good—only hunger, thirst, and terror. He lowered his head on his forepaws. The human's lap was not as soft as the cushions, but it was safe.

"But they caught them, didn't they?" Khemes took the empty cup.

"That they did. One killed on the spot, the other two imprisoned. And the pharaoh's men managed to save some of the animals. But not all." He stroked Nedjem's back. "Those rescued have found shelter in the shrines and temples, like you did, little one, nine months ago."

"The same gang of smugglers, my lord?"

"I do not yet know. They will be interrogated in prison. But the thug who trapped Nedjem was Cretan, not Phoenician, and died in prison shortly after his capture. His inmates beat him to death. His face was so disfigured when the guards found the corpse that even his own *ka* would never recognize it. We never found his accomplices, if he had any."

Khemes took a step backwards. "Will you need anything else, your grace?"

Ankhu dismissed him and the servant left, dragging his injured leg. The High Priest gazed out of the window at the languid flow of the Nile. He held Nedjem against his chest, stroking his head.

Nedjem managed a timid purr. But a strange chill crept under his fur, despite the afternoon heat.

* * *

The ghost returned that night. Nedjem stood guard atop the windowsill and had almost dozed off when the same stench filled the room. He stretched, the tip of his tail twitching wildly. Shreds of darkness detached from the corners of the room; black tendrils swirled in a blasphemous dance, weaving into the evil form. It hovered over the bed, its crooked hands reaching out to the sleeping human.

Was the ghost thicker tonight?

Unlike last night's mist and smoke, tonight it seemed to consist of loose mud—black, poisonous sludge, unlike the fertile mud at the banks of the Nile. Several small objects swam in it: rotting carcasses of minnows and frogs, decaying leaves, bone fragments and animal waste. When the ghost turned and faced Nedjem, its empty eye sockets harbored an eerie, wicked glow. The cat shivered and glanced downwards, measuring the distance to the ground.

Too high.

The ghost reached out to him, its hands twisted like a hawk's talons.

Nedjem dared another glance downwards. *Still too high.*

And I can't leave the High Priest now. He saved me from that thug's cage.

The ghost hovered closer to the window. Foul mud dripped on the linens of the bed and on the floor, leaving dark stains.

It tilted its head, its abnormal angles crowned by tendrils of sludge, mimicking long strands of hair.

"I know you..." Its voice echoed distant, like a whisper from the depths of a well. *"He broke the cage and took you..."*

Nedjem arched his back and hissed a warning. He now knew the evil spirit or, rather, the human it had once been. Its current form meant little to him, but now he recalled the stench: a mixture of cow dung, tar, cheap ale and oil. He had seen others of its kind—trappers and poachers—rubbing their skin with animal droppings to cover their human smell. How had he missed this before? The painful memories he had denied for nine months flooded in.

Careless play among the reeds, chasing flies and frogs, running, pouncing on his sisters. A sudden, tight grip. Callused hands, dirty, black nails, hairy man. His mother's desperate calling, his sisters clawing through the bars of the cage.

Why?

Days in burning heat, thirst and hunger. Birds screeching, the smell of reptiles too close, the stench of death even closer. Don't just lie there. Please, mew. Please, get up!

Humans shout, metal clanks on metal, the lock breaks, the cage opens. Pale, soft hands pick him up, the comfort of a smooth, hairless caress almost as soothing as milk. Almost.

The Cretan thug had returned.

The ghost's mouth twisted. "Soft bed... good food... while I'm denied peace! Burning, yearning, cursed!"

Nedjem raised his forepaw, claws fully exposed, and hissed another warning. *You got what you deserved!*

He met the ghost's hungry snarl, his growling more confident now. Of all the rescued animals, the High Priest had chosen *him*. He would *not* cower before any foul spirit.

The ghost chuckled. "I feasted on the dead smuggler's heart. They left me to rot, the cowards! His mates will soon follow, and I'll devour their black hearts too. When we meet again, stinking runt, I'll feast on your master's heart and rip you apart."

The first sunlight colored the horizon pink and the ghost dissolved into the breeze, its cackle stretching on to a whisper, its stench lingering on.

Runt? Nedjem blinked.

He sat down, raised his hind leg and sniffed his privates. He blinked again. *Stinking?*

He glanced over the rooftops of Thebes, his spine tingling. When that foul spirit returned, he wouldn't meet it alone.

★ ★ ★

The guard bearing the bad news arrived a couple of hours later, while Nedjem appropriated pieces of dried fish from Ankhu's neglected breakfast. The two Phoenician smugglers had been killed in prison, their throats ripped open, their skulls crushed. And while the High Priest seemed relieved, Nedjem was now racing against the sun. Come nightfall, the thug's ghost would return as promised. He licked his human's plate clean and set off.

Nedjem spent the better part of the morning on the city streets. He sprayed corners and doorways, leaving his scent all over Thebes, alerting his kin of the danger, requesting assistance, preaching revenge. After a hurried lunch of raw carp under a fishmonger's bench, he grabbed a second fish under the merchant's glare and set off to a harder task. Leaping from boat to boat, careful to keep his paws off the water, he crossed the Nile and headed to the necropolis.

A jackal sat at the entrance of the tomb, its head resting on its forepaws. It looked up when the cat approached, sniffing the air. The canine scent agitated him, but Nedjem saw what human vision couldn't. Beyond the matted grey fur and the scratches on the ugly muzzle, the jackal glowed with an eerie light, the color of green jasper, Anubis' sacred stone. It stood up, its body stretching too tall, its eyes more perceptive than a mere canine's.

"Visiting relatives, little one? Have you brought food for the dead?" The jackal spoke with a deep voice, masculine and ancient.

Nedjem put the fish down, the fur along his spine fluffed up. The stench of old death, dried bones and embalming fluids urged him to flee. When his own human returned home, smelling like that, Nedjem spent the night in the gardens. But he couldn't this time. He had to face the guardian of the tomb where the denizens of Thebes brought their beloved pets to spend eternity, sailing aboard the Solar Barge to the blessed afterlife. His deceased kin rested there, cats and kittens, forefathers, brothers and sisters, wrapped in scented cloth, amidst offerings of fish and meat and milk.

He eyed the canine creature. Although the guardian had used human words, Nedjem had fully understood. But he had no voice to speak, no words to answer the guardian. Instead, he pawed the fresh fish.

"An offering, young one?

Nedjem licked his whiskers. He pushed the fish with his muzzle closer to the guardian.

The jackal's yellow gaze darted from the cat to the fish and back. "An offering, then." For a moment that stretched on, the green glow burned brighter. Then it withered away, and the jackal sat back down, its form now ordinary and mundane. "It is done. Return to your home and human, little one."

Nedjem ran off without one glance back.

★ ★ ★

"...Khemes, clean the floor. Khemes, go find the cat. Khemes, did you find the cat? Poor Khemes has a bad leg, and his old bones can't search every corner and hole in Thebes. Hathor bless your soul, my lord, but why would you ever name that cat 'Sweet One'? He never listens to his name, anyway... Poor Khemes broke his back searching for the cat, while he's probably sleeping under a bench or tree in the garden..." The servant bent over to look under a table, groaned and supported his back with his hand to stand upright, never ceasing his mumbling.

Nedjem stood hesitant just outside the kitchen's door, his ears drawn back. Had he made a mistake coming in this way? He had hoped to sneak in unnoticed, steal himself some supper and then clean his fur of the town's mud. He looked and smelled like a common alley cat now. What was Ankhu's rambling servant doing here? Nedjem wrinkled his nose. And what had he rubbed on his skin this time? Pigeon droppings? At least he no longer smelled of reptiles.

"Ah, there you are, boy. Your master was worried sick. Where have you been all day?" He reached out to pick him up.

Master? They keep saying this word. I wonder what it means. Nedjem sniffed the servant's hands. *Definitely bird droppings. You're not touching this fur.* He stepped back and whimpered. *Feed me.*

Khemes served him generous portions of milk and dried fish and left. Nedjem ate in peace, then groomed each hair to perfection before returning to his human to await the night and the coming battle. Too agitated to rest, he paced the length of the room over and over again, jumped on the desk, off the desk, on the windowsill, off the windowsill, until weariness settled into his body.

He curled on his cushion at the foot of the bed. His lids grew too heavy; the cushion grew too soft. Then the stench of the untimely dead hit him hard. He jumped up with a hiss.

The ghost had become a walking corpse. It towered over the sleeping human, its flesh ashen, its grin too wide. It waved over Ankhu's face. He gasped, as though short of breath, but didn't wake up.

Nedjem hissed a warning, but the corpse ignored him. It waved again and a thin, luminous mist came out of the human's mouth. It swirled for a moment, then formed a little bird, fluttering wildly. That was part of the human soul: the *ka*. Ankhu would not survive without it. Nedjem flexed his muscles, his eyes focused on the corpse's neck, and growled one last warning.

The dead hand squeezed the ethereal bird, and Ankhu started to choke in his sleep.

Nedjem jumped on the corpse. His fangs dug into its neck—dead flesh that made him gag. But he did not unclench his jaws, only scratched with all four sets of claws. The corpse shrieked in anger and released the *ka*. Crooked fingers grabbed the cat's body, pulling him off. Nedjem held on as tightly as possible, but the inhuman strength overpowered him. It squeezed his body until Nedjem's vision blurred from the pain. He released his bite. Before he could attempt a new attack, the corpse flung him across the room. The impact thrust the air out of his lungs. Something cracked, and sharp pain pierced the right side of his chest.

Panting, hurting, Nedjem managed to pull himself up. Across the room, Ankhu sat up on the bed, eyes wide, clutching his neck. His eyes darted from corpse to cat and back. Between coughs, he managed a few words.

"What? How?"

"You sent me to prison! You sent me to death!" The corpse reached out and grabbed Ankhu's throat with its left hand, its right clawing red circles on the exposed chest. "I'll rip out your heart!"

Nedjem blinked, the pain in his chest hindering his movement. That thug had once put him through torture, days of hunger and terror. He was not a kitten any more. He would *not* yield this time. Putting all his strength in his lower back and hind legs, he leapt on the windowsill. The sharp pain made his vision blur. He glanced upon the sleeping town, raised his head and yowled.

The corpse released its deadly grip; its face twisted in rage.

Louder than the mating call, deeper than the food-demanding mew, more desperate than a kitten's cry, Nedjem's yowl echoed through streets and alleys, calling his kin.

And the cats of Thebes answered.

Big cats, small cats, young and old, striped and spotted, males and females, they ran to Nedjem's aid. They climbed up the ivy of the High Priest's residence, up the stairs, through windowsills and cellars. They crossed rooms and hallways, paws soft on the paved floor, bodies agile among statues and furniture, their path noiseless, their eyes reflecting the moonlight a thousandfold.

Across the room, Ankhu had retreated to the other side of the bed, still gasping. Now the dead thug turned its attention to Nedjem and his kin.

"What's this?" It waved over the cats crowding in the room, on the floor, on the furniture, every spot covered by breathing, growling fur. "You've called for help?" It snarled, fetid drool dripping down its chin. "I'll gut you one by one!"

Nedjem charged first, with a deep, throaty growl. He aimed at where the corpse's jugular should be, but his fangs closed around dried skin and sinew. Despite the foul taste, he dug his fangs deeper, cutting, tearing and spitting out bits of flesh. Several of his kin joined in. Then the corpse managed a blow to his already injured chest. Panting, Nedjem retreated under a chair and licked his wounds.

How could they kill what shouldn't be living?

Across the room, his human sat on the floor, his eyes closed, his lips moving to a silent prayer. A jackal howled somewhere outside and the night breeze carried the scent of frankincense and myrrh into the room. The corpse shrieked. Nedjem's eyes narrowed. Amidst the charging and shredding cats, others joined the attack; ethereal, translucent felines, his deceased kin had come to his aid. Not just those resting in the tomb, but also those who had died caged, or had been taken away from the Land of the Nile and died under different stars.

When one living cat limped away to a corner to lick its wounds, two ghost cats charged. Bone by bone, sinew by sinew, they tore the dead thug to pieces, until nothing was left but ashes and dust to the night breeze. The cats departed, some limping, some bloodied, to return to their hearths and lick their wounds. And so did the ghost cats, to board again the Solar Barge.

In the welcomed silence of the room, Nedjem made his way to his human's lap.

"Are you hurt, little one?" Ankhu stroked Nedjem's back, his touch slow and careful.

Nedjem whimpered, and after three rounds he managed to curl up without hurting.

"I'll take you to the physician." He tried to get up, but the motion hurt Nedjem and he whimpered again. "Fine. We'll go in the morning."

Content, Nedjem rested his head on Ankhu's thigh, and managed a tentative purr. It didn't hurt, so he purred louder.

In Thebes, no one messed with the High Priest's Cat.

Reckoning

by C. Dennis Moore

JODY RETURNED HOME for his mother's funeral. He stood outside that day, in the middle of January with the wind chilling
his ears so bad they felt like they were on fire, just wishing the
minister would get on with it, put her in the ground already, so
he could get into the car and out of the cold. Jody'd left home
the week after he graduated high school and had talked to her
only a handful of times since then. Instead of spending time
with a mother he'd grown only more distant from over the
years, Jody had spent his time tracking down the father who'd
abandoned them years earlier.

Now he stood looking at the box she was to be buried in,
feeling little more than the biting winter wind It took way too
long for the dozen or so people in attendance to say their final
goodbyes. By the time the last prayer was spoken, Jody was
shifting from foot to foot, half in trying to keep warm, half in
trying not to piss his pants.

She went into the ground, and he drove quickly out of the
cemetery and back to the house.

It wasn't that he didn't like his mother. The first few years
of his life had been fine, but as he got older things changed.

He couldn't say how, but he knew there was a point where his parents stopped looking at him as their child, as the perfect blank slate on which they could make the image of a responsible adult. They started seeing him as the kid who needed a bath, who needed to eat, who needed new shoes for school. He knew that point arrived for his father, when his new job introduced him to new friends, and those new friends introduced him to new substances, and those new substances introduced him to new ideas. The stay-at-home dad became too stoned or drunk or busy philosophizing with his friends on the ills of the universe to get off the couch and care for his family. Jody's mother had played around with the new friends early on, too, but she soon realized that wasn't the life for her. She became the head of the household, sometimes working multiple double shifts in a week just to make the bills—although sometimes Jody thought maybe she worked so much just so she wouldn't have to be home, but that left him there by himself in the middle of the mess and for that, sometimes, he hated her.

When he got into town, he'd almost stayed in a motel, but the last minute flight across five states had taken what little savings he had. His aunt Marcy had picked him up at the airport and Jody was now driving around town in his mother's '73 Delta 88 and staying in her house.

He didn't think of it as his house—although that's probably what it was now. He hadn't thought of it as his house in a long time. So when he got back to his mother's house, he parked the car and ran inside, stood in the bathroom sighing in relief for a long time. He flushed his mother's toilet, then went to sit in his mother's living room. He slid out of his coat, then realized the house was freezing and put it back on.

The house was built in the very early 1900s, then renovated in the 60s by a neighborhood housing firm that took old

213

houses, made them livable again, and sold them cheap to middle-income families. The problem was the work they did was full of cut corners. Boards were nailed in without being plumb. The pipes were a joke, the wiring a hazard. The basement had a dirt floor and the foundation down there... Jody had few clear memories of his father, but he did remember being in the basement while his father tried to winterize the house. He'd pulled wadded up bundles of *clothes* from the holes between the bricks down there. Jody was five and didn't understand the problem at the time, but he remembered his father's contempt and disbelief when he found they'd tried to insulate the house with *clothes*. That had been before the people started showing up and his father stopped going to work.

If his mother had left the house to him, Jody decided, he was selling it the first chance he got.

He checked the thermostat and saw the house was only fifty degrees. He turned up the heat, but nothing happened. He found a fireplace lighter in a kitchen drawer and went down to the basement to check the pilot light.

He hadn't been down there since he was a kid. It smelled of stale pine and he found a dozen old car fresheners hanging from the ceiling. He wondered if his mother had been trying to mask the rotting lumber the housing company had used or the dead rats in the walls. Probably both. There were empty poison boxes at each corner. He opened the furnace, lit the pilot light, then climbed the stairs again. The heat kicked on and he stood there in the kitchen, his shoes and socks off and his bare feet over the grate.

He looked around and wished again he'd had the money to stay somewhere else. He wondered if aunt Marcy would mind if he stayed with her. He didn't plan on being in town very long, only until the reading of the will, and everything else he could take care of back at home.

As if she knew he'd been thinking of her, Marcy called.

He told her he was doing fine—he didn't have the heart to tell her he really didn't feel much of anything resembling loss—then he decided against asking if he could stay with her.

"So you'll call me, then, if you need anything? You know we missed you around here all these years."

"I know. Missed you, too," he lied.

"Okay, then, I'll call you again tomorrow. The will's going to be read either tomorrow or the day after," she said.

And then, before he knew he was going to ask it, Jody said, "You don't think my father will show up, do you?"

No one, as far as Jody knew, had even mentioned his father since the man vanished twenty-eight years earlier. Jody had been seven. He'd been trying to track him down, not because he missed the man, but because he simply wanted an explanation.

"I don't see why he would," Marcy said. "Far as I know, she never had any contact with him. I don't know where he is, and I doubt he knows what's happened. Even if he did, he didn't care enough to stick around, huh? So why should he come back now?"

"Yeah," Jody said. He didn't know if he was disappointed or not.

He said goodbye and hung up, then turned to go to the living room and froze.

Standing in the bathroom doorway, naked and shivering, was a young boy. He was soaked, as if he'd just climbed out of the tub without a towel to dry off. His arms were wrapped around himself. His lips were blue and his eyes focused on something across the room.

Jody took a step toward the boy. He'd never given ghosts a second thought, and wasn't sure if he should now either because he knew this couldn't be a spirit. It was him. He was six or seven, but it was definitely Jody.

"Ghosts are dead," he said under his breath. "I'm right here."

He took a step closer and the boy was gone.

Jody stood staring at the spot trying to will the vision to return, but it never did. The vision was from stress, he decided, an old memory, returning so suddenly it had seemed to be there before him.

He sat on the couch for an hour, clearing his mind. It was early still, but already getting dark. The house was finally warming up. Jody was thinking about his parents.

He'd grown up a stranger to both of them. The rift with his mother, he could never explain, they'd just never grown close. And his father had simply vanished one morning with his friends. With his mother working all the time, his father's friends were over every day, almost all day. Once in a while one would leave to get more beer or some food, but they spent most days in the living room, passing joints around and listening to Little Feat's *The Last Record Album*. If someone brought something other than pot, they'd put on Jody's dad's *Dark Side of the Moon* record. They'd sit around discussing the cosmic topic of the day, religion or politics and how the state of the world was, in the long run, bad for the universe. "What the world needs is more positive energy floating around." It wasn't strange for little Jody to wake up in the morning and have to tiptoe through the bodies passed out on the living room shag.

Then one day he woke up, went downstairs, and the room was empty. He made his breakfast and sat on the floor, happy and childlike, watching *Jabberjaw* and *The New Fred and Barney Show* for a change. His mother came down and told him, "Your father's left. Him and his buddies. They won't be back."

And that was that. Jody never brought it up, and his father never tried to contact them. Thirty years later, Jody had no idea where he might be, even though he'd been searching off and on since leaving home. But his mother might, he realized.

They'd never talked about it, but that didn't mean she hadn't heard from him. Maybe he'd written all the time and she'd just kept it from Jody? Now would be the time to find out, wouldn't it? If he had written, would she have kept the letters? Maybe. Where? In her room?

He climbed the stairs and went down the hall, but instead of entering his mother's room, he turned the other way at the last second and stepped into his old bedroom.

Whatever he'd encountered downstairs had followed him up here. The room was empty except for the bed. Lying on top of the covers was young Jody again. He lay awake, staring at the ceiling. Then he suddenly sat up and looked toward the door—Jody shrank back, fearing the ghost would see him (It's not a ghost, he reminded himself)—then got up and ran out of the room.

Before it could pass through him, Jody leapt out of the way and fell into the wall behind him, knocking a picture to the floor. The glass cracked.

The boy ran down the hall, but vanished before he reached the stairs.

Jody stood there, numb, watching and waiting. Was he imagining all this because of the day? He'd thought earlier it was the stress of his mother's funeral, and he wanted to keep believing that it was. He wondered if she'd ever seen a spectral Jody running the halls of this house during the years he'd been gone.

And, he wondered, if he was alive and well, as he believed himself to be, how could there be this… ghost, okay he had to use the word because what other word was there, how could there be this ghost of his seven-year-old self?

When he looked into the room again, the bed was gone. There was nothing.

He crossed the hall and went into his mother's room, closing the door behind him.

He started by looking through her dresser drawers. He felt like a burglar looking for the good jewelry, but he knew that with her gone, he'd have to do it eventually anyway. Why not start with looking for letters from his father hidden under her clothes. But the dresser revealed nothing.

Same with under the bed. Some dust, a single slipper.

In the closet he found a few old boxes, and he spent the next couple of hours on the bedroom floor, sifting through them, trying to piece together the bits of his mother's life. There were old pictures of Jody—and yes, the boy he'd seen tonight was definitely him at, according to the dates on the pictures, seven years old. He discovered old paycheck stubs and by comparing some of them, realized that in 1979 his mother had held, for a brief period, three jobs at once. Why had he never known that? And if she'd been struggling so hard, why hadn't she simply sold this house and gotten them someplace smaller? In case his father came back, he'd be able to find them? He didn't know.

He found old Christmas cards from aunt Marcy, some dated as recently as this past year.

He found everything—pictures, grade cards, broken watches, old jewelry. Everything except one scrap of evidence his father had ever contacted Jody's mother.

"Nothing," he said, shoving the boxes aside and getting to his feet. He looked around the room, wondering if he'd missed anything, knowing he hadn't. Still, there had to be something somewhere in this house.

Out in the hall, he heard footsteps running down the stairs. The basement. The footsteps had sparked the thought, but they also scared him. He listened at the door. So far, he'd only seen himself at seven, but who was to say that was all he'd see? If his own ghost could be here, why not someone else's as well?

I just need to get through tonight, he thought. I can leave in the morning, go see the town. If the reading of the will isn't tomorrow, I can cash in my plane ticket, stay in a motel tomorrow night, and drive Mom's car back home.

If she left it to him, that was. Who else was there? Marcy had a car already, and a nicer one than Jody's mother's.

So he just had to get through tonight. He looked at the clock beside his mother's bed. It was only 9:00.

Jody stepped into the hall and met no one. He walked down the stairs undisturbed. He entered the living room and there he was, seven years old, eating cereal and watching cartoons. The child sat eating from an invisible bowl and smiling at a blank television screen. Then he put down his spoon and looked over at Jody.

Jody froze as the boy nodded once, then turned back to the television. That must have been when his mother gave him the news about his father. From the looks, he'd reacted much the same to his father's abandonment as he had to his mother's passing.

Jody went into the kitchen, headed for the basement, and happened to glance down the hallway. There was the naked boy again, standing wet and freezing in the bathroom doorway.

That's when they tried to baptize me, he thought, and stopped.

How did he remember that? He didn't know, but suddenly he saw the events of that day as if they'd happened earlier this evening.

In 1976, he sat at the kitchen table with a Superman coloring book when his father and one of his friends came in to say they had a surprise for Jody. They were going to baptize him into their circle and once they did that, Jody would be able to sit in the living room with them and listen to their discussions. Jody had brightened at the thought of being treated like an adult, and he'd agreed eagerly.

They took him into the bathroom, ran the tub full of cold water and stripped him. His father grabbed his feet, the friend grabbed his hands, and they lifted him horizontally, then plunged him into the water, holding him under, Jody thrashing and wanting to cry. He didn't know why they'd waited so long, but they finally lifted him out of the water and set him back on his feet. They had to hold him, because Jody wanted to pass out. The friend drew a symbol on Jody's forehead with his thumb and said he baptized him in the name of the sun, the moon, and the stars and that Jody was now one with the cosmos. They left him there, shivering, and went back into the living room.

Jody had stood there for a long time, afraid to move, afraid to have to walk past them in the living room, but he had to get dressed. The clothes he'd been wearing lay on the bathroom floor, soaked from all the splashing.

Finally, he'd grabbed a towel, dried off, and walked very quietly, his head down, through the living room and up the stairs. He didn't come back down until his mother came home from work and called him for dinner.

He ate quickly, then tried to go back up to his room again, but his father stopped him and made him sit next to him on the couch. The friends passed a joint back and forth in front of him and talked about things he couldn't begin to understand.

Edwin Starr's "War" was on the stereo that night, and one of them said, "Positive vibes, strong energy, the world, she needs more of that stuff. If she don't get it, she's gonna start to get sick, and when the world gets sick, we all catch it, you know what I'm saying?"

Jody didn't know what they were saying.

"Put me out there, man, I got all the energy you need. I give the universe my energy."

Jody's mother called him to bed. And that's where the second vision came from.

He remembered lying in bed that night, afraid to turn off the lights. He couldn't say why, but something about listening to those people talk had scared him, so he stayed up. Some time after 12:00 he heard the bedroom door open across the hall and his mother's footsteps going down the stairs. Suddenly he heard a scream, quickly stifled, but by then he was already in the hall. He stopped in the middle of the stairs and asked, "What's wrong, momma?"

His father and everyone else were passed out on the living room floor. Open on the coffee table was a box of rat poison standing next to a bottle of what his father called The Good Stuff.

"Did you see a rat?" he'd asked.

His mother sniffled, looked up at the box on the table, and said, without turning toward him, "Yeah, Jo, that's what I saw. I'll take care of it, though. You go back to bed."

"Wake Daddy up," Jody said. "He can get it for you."

"Yeah, I might do that," she said, then waved him away. He slowly climbed the stairs and returned to his room.

He finally dozed off very late that night and slept with the light on. When he got up the next morning—very late morning—he'd had the living room to himself.

Then his mother had shared the news about his father, and that had been Jody's life.

Why had he forgotten that stuff? Because at the time, it was normal day. Other than the baptism, everything was business as usual. No, not everything. His mother didn't often get up in the middle of the night and go downstairs, and he could only imagine that she did because his father never came up. Even partying into the night, his father always came up to bed.

But not that night.

What did she do with the bodies? The answer came immediately. He went into the basement and right away saw the indentation where the bodies had decayed in the dirt. Over the hole, stood his mother.

In her nightgown and robe, she sweated and cried as she shoveled dirt. Her face said she wouldn't stop working until it was done.

"Mom," Jody said to the image. She didn't look up. Was this a real ghost, or just another image like the ones of himself? Or, and he had never considered this before, maybe that's all ghosts were, memories, images, unspent energy. Was that what made it possible for him to see the ghost of himself?

The questions flooded in as he stood there looking down at the spot where his father's body lay under the dirt floor.

Why had his father done it? Why hadn't she called the police? How did she do it? How did she live in this house all those years?

Jody looked up to see his mother leaning the shovel against the concrete wall, then walking slowly up the stairs.

He wondered about the strength it had taken to haul the bodies down here, and then dig a hole big enough for all of them. How many had there been? Three, he thought. Or four. He went to the wall and grabbed the shovel.

He dug with a will, tearing off his shirt when he couldn't stand it sticking to his back, enjoying for a second the cool air in the basement. Three feet down he struck something. He dug first one direction, then the other, widening the hole, then taking it down further, carefully, to uncover the bones. His mother had used lime when she put them in the ground, and all that was left were the bones. He bent over, trying to think of anything other than throwing up.

His search was over, it seemed. He thought of all the time he'd spent trying to find his father—internet searches, databases, any and everyone in the US, Canada, and Mexico he could find with his father's name—and all along he'd been here, done in by his own stupid delusions, trying to make the world a better place by giving it his energy.

Jody stood up and clutched the shovel in both hands. He didn't notice the tears on his face. If he had, he would have wondered why he was crying over a man he'd hardly known. Was this why his mother had done it? Better Jody think his father had skipped town than killed himself?

"You stupid assholes!" he screamed at the bodies in the floor, then swung around and brought the flat of the shovel down on them. Someone's ribs shattered and dust flew up in a puff. "Stupid fucking dopeheads."

He said this last quietly, to the friends who'd invaded his father's life. For a second, he let his anger overtake him and he hated those people. Then he thought of his mother. She'd turned her back on that life when she could just as easily have gone down the same path. This had been his father's choice.

Jody shoveled dirt back over them. Let them wallow in their shallow basement grave. He hoped their souls—worse, he hoped their energy—would be stuck under there forever. He covered the grave again, set the shovel against the wall where his mother had left it, and climbed the stairs. Jody had spent enough time letting his past intrude on his present. When he passed through the kitchen, the bathroom doorway stood empty.

Talk to Me

by Jamie K. Schmidt

THE BEER BOTTLE HIT HER KNEE and clunked to the stage. Tess kicked it back into the audience and kept singing. Pyrotechnics flashed in time with the drum beat as she dodged another flying object. Last night a Viagra bottle broke Mark's nose. The gig paid this month's rent, though. And it wasn't like it was her nose. Mark faced the audience sideways tonight and swung his bass to make a harder target.

Tess closed the set three songs early with a fake, "Good Night, Boca Raton! You've been the greatest."

The lights went to black and the band tripped over each other to get off-stage while the crowd surged forward.

"Your security is the pits," Tess informed the night club manager, who was cringing in the wings.

"I think they like you," he said. "There haven't been any knifings this week. And if you guys showed more skin you wouldn't be getting half the abuse you've been getting."

Tess rolled her eyes as her drummer, Betty, used her drumstick to flash a boob at him. Heading back into the janitor's closet that doubled as the dressing room, Tess let out a long slow breath.

The cracked and grimy mirror over the slop sink showed her a woman who was twice her age. Hard living and an even harder death ravaged her face. Tess pretended not to see her.

"Your eyeliner looks like hell."

Tess ran the water to block out the image's cigarette and whiskey voice. Rummaging into her backpack, she plucked out the cold cream and smeared it over her face.

"You'll never get a recording contract if you keep playing dives like this."

Concentrating on taking the elaborate face paint off, Tess refused to be drawn into the conversation. She wiped it off with brown paper towels that seemed to take off the first layer of skin too.

"You missed a spot by your ears."

Tess closed the door on the image and hefted the backpack. The back door of the club had a few groupies hanging out. Forcing a smile, she shook hands and signed a couple of autographs.

"Tess, you wanna come to a party?"

"Tess, I've got some stuff that will make you fly."

"Thanks, thanks, everyone, but I've got an early start tomorrow. We'll be in the studio," she lied and backed away towards the street. Luckily, Betty and Mark were right behind her and Tess slipped away as more fans started streaming towards them from the club.

She walked five blocks before she felt she was far enough away. Tess slipped into a bus stop's seat and leaned her head back against the plexiglass. Song lyrics teased her brain, enough so she got the gist but not the actual words. When the bus roared up in a cloud of blue pollution, she had the bass line down in her head as well.

Tess sat in an aisle seat and ignored the dead man in the reflective glass of the bus's window.

"You're not bad, you know."

She caught a glimpse of him out of the corner of her eye. For a corpse, he looked good. He was probably a CEO who had a heart attack, if that suit was any indication. The music in her head was lost, though, when he continued to speak.

"I know a guy who could help you. He's a promoter. I could get you in."

Tess looked around the bus. This time of night there were few people. None of them looked like they would bat an eye if she started talking to the window. Still, she took out her cell phone and held it to her ear. Facing the window, she met the ghost's eyes.

"I don't normally do this," she said.

"It's rude to ignore people who are speaking to you."

"It's ruder to bother..." Tess looked around and lowered her voice, "the living."

"Am I bothering you? I'll go."

Tess shrugged and put away her phone. She faced front again. But he didn't leave. Where was he going to go?

She felt him staring at her as she got off the bus at her stop.

Tess was careful to avert her eyes from any puddles in the street or the reflections in the windows that she passed. She could sense them watching her. But the local ghosts had long since given up trying to talk to her.

At the foot of her apartment complex's stairs sat a waif like girl, rocking back and forth. As she went to go inside, Tess's foot brushed the girl's arm. Tess flinched. The girl was corporal.

"Nice night," the girl said and grinned up at Tess with broken teeth. She was wearing a stained pink party dress that matched her eyes. Her satin shoes were muddy. Tess could see track marks on her arms through the worn tulle sleeves.

"This isn't a good neighborhood," Tess said. "You might be safer at one of the local shelters. Or even at one of the twenty four hour stores."

"I'm waiting for Nando," she said. Her breath almost gave Tess a contact high.

"I'll send him down." Tess shook her head and let herself into the foyer. After a quick peek into her empty mailbox, she rode the rickety elevator to her apartment. The hallway smelled like a rodent's wet dream and the mold made her nose itch.

Her apartment door was unlocked and Tess banged it shut behind her.

Nando looked up blearily from a line of cocaine. Tess could see a vague face in the mirror under the white powder, but she looked away before the ghost could engage her.

"Your girlfriend's waiting for you on the stoop." Tess watched in revulsion as he sucked up the drug and then chased it down with a gulp of whiskey from the bottle.

He offered it to her, wagging it by the neck.

Tess took a sip and sunk down on the couch.

"I almost saw him yesterday." Nando smiled. He held out a bag of pills to her. "I bet the reason why you can't see him is you're so used to blocking the ghosts. This will help you expand your mind."

"Or blow it out my ears." Tess pushed the bag away from him, but took another pull on the bottle.

"Rough set?" Nando said, his body shuddering before he jumped off the couch.

"No blood."

"Come to the party with us."

"No thanks," Tess said. "You know that's not my scene."

"Rock and Roll Thunder is going to be there. It's a private party. Invitation only."

"Yeah?" Tess said. "How did you score it then?"

Nando waved the bag of pills again. "I don't always get paid in money."

"No, I think me and Jack Daniels here are going to have our own little party."

"Don't be such a morose little hypocrite."

Tess gave him the finger.

"You can get bombed on free booze. I bet by dawn you'll have played a set with Rock and Roll Thunder and convinced them to hear your demo tape."

"Yeah, right," Tess said.

"It's called networking, darling. You should really switch over. Alcohol is a downer, the drugs are an upper."

"It's called mourning," Tess shot back. "And it usually lasts more than three months."

Nando kicked over the coffee table with a sudden violence. "I mourned," he said. "I wore black. I went to the church—which was more than you did."

"I didn't want to see Kestrel like that."

"No, you wanted to see him through the looking glass." Nando searched the room with his eyes, but there wasn't a reflective surface in his line of sight. "But you haven't seen him yet, have you?"

"Maybe he doesn't want to be seen."

"Or maybe you're not looking hard enough."

"Fine," Tess said. "I'll go to your stupid party."

Nando's rage ebbed out of him. Aside from a few jitters along his shoulder, he seemed to be back to normal. "You're going like that?"

"Let's just go." Tess brushed by him. "Lock the door this time."

They could hear the bass of the music a few blocks away. Nando turned off the car stereo so they could appreciate it. It sounded like a gigantic heart beat. Tess was in the back seat, leaning up against one window and staring out the opposite side. She had rolled down the window to avoid any supernatural contact. The smoke that wafted in smelled like marijuana with sweet motes that she couldn't place.

The girl in the pink dress, Myrna, took deep breaths as they stepped outside. A uniformed guard took Nando's keys and parked the Cadillac amongst the Mercedes. Tess put her arm through Nando's.

"We're off to see the wizard?"

After the security guards scrutinized the invitation, they were allowed in. Tess broke away from Nando and Myrna as they made their way to the buffet table. Walking towards the driving sound of the band, she slid the heavy glass sliders aside. A ghost in the door had been doing his best Edvard Munch's "Scream" impersonation, or maybe it was Macaulay Culkin's "Home Alone."

Rock and Roll Thunder was aptly named, the drums booming out into the Florida night. People were dancing around the pool and the pungent smell of sweat was thick. She snagged a fluted glass from a passing waiter and enjoyed the frenzy of the band's music. No one threw any projectile weapons at them, and if the audience was self medicated, at least they were an amiable lot. Tess saw a few starlets intent on destroying their careers through booze and drugs and indiscriminate nudity. Or maybe they were making sure that the flashes from the paparazzi would put them on the front lines of the tabloids. No such thing as bad publicity. Tess considered taking off her top and rushing over there. Instead, she drained her glass and sank into the nearest folding chair. It gave her a good view of the pool where a dead body floated naked in the center. Every now and then it would lift its head up and wave to her.

When the band took a break, Tess' ears felt numb and her heart still beat in time with their latest hit single. But she could still hear a lone guitar, playing softly behind her by the garden of stone statues. At the entrance was Venus de Milo sporting

Ray-Bans and a long red scarf that wagged like a tongue in the night breeze.

The guitar grew louder as she headed deeper into the garden. Tess recognized the song as the one she had been composing in her head on the bus earlier that evening. The statues she passed were posed as if a rampant Medusa froze them in place. In the center of the garden was a reflecting pool. Around it on the compass points, four colored glass globes reflected the stars and tortured faces of drowning victims.

She heard Kestrel's voice crooning from the pool. Kneeling by the edge, she peered in. Dressed in the suit they buried him in, his image was sitting on a stone bench strumming his Harmony acoustic guitar.

"I'm glad we didn't bury you with the Gibson," Tess said, letting tears run down her cheeks.

"Yeah, there aren't a lot of electrical outlets where I am."

"Where are you?" Tess asked, dipping her hand into the pool. The reflection shimmered and her hand got wet, but she wasn't any closer to touching him.

He shrugged.

"Why did you do it?"

"I didn't. I was murdered."

Tess's head snapped up. "But your wrists were slashed. You were drunk and stoned. You left a note."

"The note was some song lyrics I had scribbled down." Kestrel's fingers flew over the strings. "Leza did it. She found out I was cheating on her, with you." He stopped playing long enough to make sure Tess was looking at him.

Tess shook her head, tears spilling faster.

"I tried to stay away because I know you don't like to talk to us ghosts," he said. "I remember you telling me how you would try and help them and it took all of your energy, your life. That nothing good ever came out of helping a vengeful spirit."

TALK TO ME

"I wanted to see you." Tess admitted. "I didn't want to say goodbye."

"It doesn't have to be."

"Kes, I'm so sorry. I never thought she would find out about us. Or react like that."

"Hey, me neither," Kestrel said. "But your life is in danger." He played a spooky riff. "I think she's coming after you next."

"It's been almost three months. I don't think she's going to come after me. She's never said anything, never even hinted she knew."

"Has your audience been more violent? Has anyone offered you any drugs? She's tricky. You'd never see it coming." He gave a bitter laugh. "I sure as hell didn't."

"Do you want me to go to the police?"

Kestrel snorted. "Who would believe you? You said it yourself. I was a textbook suicide. I want you to kill her first."

"No," Tess said. "I'm not doing that. It was bad enough I was knocking boots with her man."

"So you think I deserved this?"

"No. No, of course not."

"She killed me, Tess. She killed me out of jealousy. She killed me because of us."

"He's lying," a disembodied voice came from the red gazing globe in the north side of the pool.

"He's telling the truth," the blue globe moaned from the southern side.

"Maybe if you were nice to us, we'd let you know for sure," the western green globe flashed.

"Yeah, can you kill my old lady too?" the yellow eastern globe pulsed.

The band started up again with a screech of dueling whammy pedals. Tess nearly fell into the pool.

"Don't go," Kestrel said.

"Don't go," the globes parroted.

Tess scrambled to her feet and backed away, hitting one of the flinching statues. She wanted to get lost in the music, into the driving beat of the drums. Tess slammed a martini holding socialite and started the mosh pit. She enjoyed the impact of the frenzied bodies. It felt good to be battered and bruised. Making her way towards the front of the stage, Tess lifted her shirt and jiggled at the lead singer. He eagerly helped her up on stage, but quickly lost his smile when Tess grabbed his mic and started singing the song better than he did.

In the end, it took two security guards to haul her off, but before they took the microphone away from her, Tess managed to yell out, "Thank you! I'm Tess James from Turn of the Screw. We're playing Down Low's on 3rd Street all week."

She was lying on the hood of the car when Nando and Myrna were rounded up and tossed out too.

"Remind me why I took you here?" Nando asked as he unlocked the car.

"I saw Kestrel."

Nando looked at Myrna and then back at Tess, shaking his head in warning. "Oh yeah?"

"But you knew I'd see him tonight, didn't you?"

"I suspected." Nando pulled onto the highway and tried to catch Tess' gaze in the rearview mirror. But Tess had her eyes closed.

Myrna chattered on and on and didn't seem too upset when Nando didn't invite her up. Tess saw her perch on the stairs again outside their apartment building.

When they were alone, Tess asked, "What else do you know about Kestrel?"

Nando shrugged. "Nothing."

"How did you know I would see him tonight at this party?"

Nando let them into the apartment. "Seems the boys that own that pad are into the occult. They have all this ghost hunting equipment. I heard they can trap ghosts like Ghostbusters."

Tess shook her head. "Why would they do that?"

"I dunno. Maybe they hope the ghosts can give them the winning lotto numbers."

"Didn't look like they needed it."

"Maybe they already got them from their ghosts."

"It doesn't work that way," Tess said. "If Kestrel didn't know which horse was going to win in the fifth while he was alive, he's not going to know when he's dead."

"Hey, all I know is that these boys are real good customers. They gave me this." Nando went into his room. Tess heard some fumbling around and he came out with a handheld scanner. "They called it an EMF. It detects ghosts." He turned it on, but nothing happened.

"Do these guys know Leza?"

"Leza?" Nando tossed the device on the couch. "Nah, she's not in their league. Why do you ask?"

"Kestrel said Leza killed him and that she was going to kill me too."

"Why?"

Tess looked down at her shoes. "He didn't say."

"Maybe it wasn't really Kestrel at all you saw."

Tess looked up at him in confusion.

"Yeah," Nando said. "Maybe it was like an evil spirit."

"I don't think there are evil spirits," Tess said.

"Why? There are evil people."

"I don't think so. It depends on your point of view."

"Child molesters are evil."

Tess thought about it. "Or are they just sick?"

"Same thing."

"Some people would think drug dealers are evil."

"Nah," Nando said. "I'm a business man. If it wasn't me, someone else would be selling it."

Tess' head was beginning to throb. "It's almost dawn. I'm going to bed. What about your girlfriend down there?"

"Myrna?" Nando shrugged. "She's a free spirit."

Tess shrugged back and went into her bedroom.

"Tess?"

She looked over her shoulder at him.

"You were great tonight." He flashed the horns and banged his head.

The next night, Tess was putting on her make-up, dodging the rocker chick in her "dressing room" mirror.

"You're a good girl," the woman said.

"Why is that?" Tess answered.

The woman gaped at her for a moment. "You can see me? You're talking to me?"

Tess finished up on her lipstick and grabbed her guitar to turn away.

"Wait!" The woman said frantically. "Because you stay away from alcohol and don't do drugs."

"I slept with my sister's boyfriend," Tess said and closed the janitor closet's door behind her.

Leza was standing there. "New lyrics to a song?" She arched an eyebrow.

"Yeah," Tess said. "And the next line is she killed him. She made it look like a suicide but I haven't figured out how that fits into the rhyme scheme."

"You're so creative. I'm sure you'll figure it out." Leza smiled.

Tess stared at her, trying to see if she was playing a game or if she was sincere. They always had a weird relationship. It wasn't love. It wasn't hate. There had always been competition. Tess was Mommy's favorite, Leza Daddy's. Tess wished she'd known when it started to get toxic, who dealt the first blow. Was it when Leza stole the money Tess had been saving up for a new guitar to buy a designer purse? Was it when Tess took Leza's Barbies and gave them all Mohawks?

"Have a nice set," Leza said and started to walk away.

Tess paused. Wasn't it time to stop all the nonsense? Leza was a lazy, mean, jerk. But Tess didn't think she would escalate their fights to murder. Maybe it was time to just grow up. "We should go out after the show. Maybe take in a late dinner? You haven't been around since Kestrel died."

Leza turned back. She was blinking away tears. "I wanted to be alone."

"OK," Tess said and shifted from side to side. "Let me know." She was glad to get on the stage and away from her sister. It was too awkward, although probably her own guilt was to blame for that. When she allowed herself to justify her actions, Tess comforted herself that Leza didn't really love Kestrel. She just slept with him first.

The curtains were still down, but Tess could hear the crowd, restless and wild like a caged beast waiting to break free.

"Don't stand there."

Tess looked around. Betty was just settling into her seat behind the drum set.

"Did you say anything?"

Betty frowned at her and shook her head. "No, you hearin' things?"

Mark came from the other side of the stage. The bandage was off his nose, but he still looked like a raccoon. "You all right Tess?"

Tess nodded and moved away from the amp. "Let's switch sides. It'll give the audience a different target to throw things at."

"I hear that," Mark said and began doing an instrument check.

"Ladies and Gentleman, Thugs and Hos, I give you the Taming of the Screw."

"Turn of the Screw," Tess sighed and exchanged eye rolls with Mark as the lights went out and they started their opening rift. The curtain lifted and the first cheap pyrotechnic went off—horizontally instead of vertically. But when Mark took the brunt of it in the chest, he staggered and caught on fire. The crowd was cheering as he started to flail. Tess froze for a moment before wildly looking for a fire extinguisher. A security guy beat her to it and was spraying white foam over Mark. Looking up, she caught Leza's eyes as she was standing over Mark. She didn't seem surprised. She seemed numb, blank.

Mark had third degree burns over three quarters of his body. He died on stage but was resuscitated in the ambulance, only to die again at the hospital later that night. Betty quit the band.

Which was a shame, since Turn of the Screw was getting serious press. Two band members were dead in less than six months. The offers were rolling in. Tess had a spot on the local news that brought two recording companies calling. This time she really would be in the studio all weekend long.

"This is why all rock and rollers get high," Nando told her. "It's too much stress."

"I tried it once," Tess said. "Pot," she clarified at his interested look. "It was OK, I guess. I got silly and hungry and then I couldn't sing or write or play well for about a week. No thanks."

"Pot's for kids. You need something good. Something designer. Like XTC or smack or acid."

"Why?"

"To enhance your mind."

"My mind is pretty much enhanced."

"How about to enhance my bottom line?"

"That I'll believe," Tess said. "Do you think Leza killed Mark?"

"No, I think that big firework that stuck in his chest killed him."

"She could have tampered with it. No one would have questioned her back stage."

"Anybody see her do it?"

"Nope."

"I think you need to have another talk with Kestrel," Nando said.

"He doesn't appear in any mirror or window I look into. I think he only exists in that dumb garden pool in Ghostbuster Central," Tess said.

"I can get you in," Nando said.

"Another party?"

"There's always another party. But you're going to have to dress like a girl so they don't recognize you from your last performance."

They took the Caddie again. Myrna was still in her pink party outfit. Tess was wearing her old prom dress. It still fit, even though she looked like a linebacker with the poofed shoulders. It was a shiny blue. She dyed her hair to match.

At the first chance, Tess slipped out into the stone garden. Venus was stripped of accessories and the statues seemed to stare at her when she made her way to the center. The pool was dark and silent.

"Where is he?" she asked the globes, but their faces stared silently back at her.

"They don't like you," Myrna said. She sat down on a stone bench and swung her feet.

"Kes?" Tess whispered and put her hand into the cold water of the pool. She felt something moving under her fingers and yanked her hand back.

"They don't like being ignored."

"You can see them?" Tess asked.

"You're not the only one who can. They're my friends."

"Ask them where Kestrel went."

"You have a gift and you're wasting it."

"I have a psychosis that kept me in a mental hospital most of my childhood." Tess said. She began to tap on the water, splashing it over the tiles and her sateen dress. "Kestrel. I'm here. I need to speak with you."

"Leza's not trying to kill you." Myrna said and joined her by the pool. She basked against the yellow globe, which pulsed a soft golden light over her face. She looked like the poster child for jaundice.

"I know that." Tess said. "At least, I think I do."

"Kestrel is."

"What? Kestrel is what?"

"He's lonely. He doesn't want to be a ghost. He wants to live. He thought that if you killed Leza then she'd be with him. But when that didn't happen, he thought he could jump into Mark's body when he died the first time. But it doesn't work that way. The body won't accept another spirit."

"You're crazy. You're a drugged up psycho. I don't know what Nando has told you, but you've warped it."

Myrna scowled at Tess. She bared her teeth which looked pointed and yellow in the globe's light. "You're a selfish, spoiled idiot. You've had another world open up to you and instead of trying to learn about it, you've shunned it."

"My music is the only world I want to know about."

"You're so stupid you're dangerous. And Kestrel is going to use that against you."

"Ghosts can't affect the real world. That's why they try to use patsies like me."

Mryna smacked her open palm across Tess's face.

"Oh, it's on. You crack whore." Tess dove for her, but her fingers clutched right through her. Driving back her fist, Tess tried to punch Myrna but only succeeded in falling off balance. She felt a hard shove and was pushed into the pool. Hands tangled in her hair and kept her face against the cement. Tess struggled. The pool was shallow enough that she could get leverage by kicking her feet against the bottom, but then they were grabbed too. When her lungs started to protest and bubbles of light motes swam in front of her eyes, Tess was released. Soft guitar music played and Tess saw a white light.

Hands lifted her out of the pool and threw her against the statue a few feet away. She took deep gasping breaths as the music jangled into discord and then stopped all together.

"Did you get that?" asked a man with an EMF scanner in his hands.

"Off the chart. I can't wait to see what the camera picked up," another said. "I saw orbs, and the heat sensors dipped really low."

Only Nando came over to her. "Are you all right?"

"Where's that bitch, Myrna?" Tess said between chattering teeth.

Nando shrugged. "Who knows? I told you she's a free spirit."

Tess gave a coughing laugh, which the orbs mimicked.

"Did you get that?" asked the man with the scanner as he darted around the pool.

"Take me home," Tess said.

That weekend, the studio was a little claustrophobic, but at least there wasn't anything exploding, and the sound technicians refrained from throwing their bottled waters at her during the session.

Kestrel sang at her side and Myrna, still in that awful pink dress, shook a tambourine. Mark showed up when the mood hit him and jammed for a bit. He seemed to have hard feelings for Kestrel, so he didn't stay for long.

If you play the track back at the right frequency, you can even hear them.

The Woman of Chitral
by Sarah Islam

I HAD TRAVELED ALL DAY to reach the cabin in Chitral. Tirich Mir stood towering over the Hindu Kush range and I was a tiny speck, an insignificant nothing. They say that its shadow was so great, so awe-inspiring, that the ancients believed it could blot out the entire universe. That's why they called it Tirich Mir, the King of Darkness. I craned my neck and looked at the proud peaks that had vanquished great armies, ill-fated soldiers of fortune and, in recent times, Islamic fundamentalists who had wanted to use it as their insurmountable fortress. Tirich Mir was not only unconquerable, it was also secretive. Hiding in his massive bulk were hundreds of secret valleys and unknown hamlets that, up until a few years ago, had been independent kingdoms.

Khuda Bukhsh, the caretaker of the cabin, bustled around me, instructing the porters and supervising the storing of dried food that I had brought from Peshawar. It had been a grueling fourteen-hour drive from Chirtal Mayoon, and we had bumped and jerked our way through the breath-taking Lowri pass, maneuvering through hairpin bends and slippery roads, staring down at the carcasses of trucks that had fallen into the valley below.

The Cabin was a solid little structure of wood and stone that had been built by a British adventurer sometime during the last days of British Raj in the subcontinent. Now it could be rented through the Pakistan Tourism Development Board for a pittance to tourists who wanted to experience life in the rugged frontier town of Chitral. Beyond the mountains was Afghanistan, and down here the locals believed that their Tirich Mir was the haunt of fairies, djinns and demons who would protect them from evil.

For almost six months of winter every year, the cabin was completely cut off from the rest of Pakistan. I stood at the simple wooden door of the cabin and thought of Ali. My brilliant, fast talking, introverted friend Ali Khan who had disappeared from this cabin about eight months ago. We had grown up together and we had both talked about 'chucking it all up' and writing a novel. He had beaten me to it when he suddenly quit his job at an advertising agency in Lahore, packed his bags and moved to Chitral, a second-hand typewriter under his arm. I had followed him halfway to Peshawar where I now worked at Radio Pakistan as a researcher. We talked on the phone occasionally whenever he descended into Chitral Town or when he stopped by in Peshawar on his way home to Lahore. I envied him his dreams and looked forward to his letters which he had promised to mail me soon.

Then one night in the middle of a beautiful spring, he disappeared. A massive search had been organized, but he could not be found. His family had pulled all the strings they could to keep the search going. After eight months, it looked like he was gone forever.

About a month ago, Khuda Bukhsh had come in to see me. I saw him sitting absolutely still on a stool outside my office one morning, his tribal wool cap in his hands. I recognized him from Ali's description, so I went and introduced myself.

He stood up respectfully. "Salam Sahib! I am Khuda Bukhsh of Chitral. I am the caretaker of the hunting lodge where Ali Khan Sahib was staying." He spoke as if he had rehearsed his speech many times. His voice sounded rusty, unused. I asked him to follow me into my office. "Please sit. Will you have tea?"

He seemed grateful, and we waited while his tea was brought in and we both drank the sticky sweet Pathan brew. Tea is serious business around here, and we honored the ritual with the gravity it deserves. He sat quietly after we had finished, his eyes focused on the threadbare rug on the floor. Like all tribal men from the mountains, his perfect stillness unnerved me.

"How can I help you, Khuda Bukhsh?" I said.

"Sahib! First allow me to tell you that I am very sorry that he is no more with us…May Allah keep his soul."

I nodded my head. "Amen."

He sat very still. I waited. "Sahib, I waited and prayed to Him that they would find him somewhere safe. I too joined the search parties, but Allah in His infinite wisdom chose to keep the whereabouts of Ali Sahib a secret from us. But now I know…" His eyes wandered out of the window. "The snow will cut off the roads in a few days and I thought it was my duty to come to you."

I was beginning to wonder if this would take long. Was the man perhaps asking me to pay him for serving my friend?

"Ali Sahib was a good man and he was young. So young…" He sighed. "I am an old man. I tried to warn him but he wouldn't listen…"

"Warned him about what?"

"About socializing with the Kaffirs, Sir!"

"Did he…? What did he do?"

He looked over his shoulder and leaned towards me. "Allah is my witness, Sahib! Many years ago when the British ruled over us, the cabin was built as a hunting lodge. A young white Sahib there fell in love with a Kafir woman and married her in their pagan ceremony. Then he was called away and she waited for him and waited but he never came back. She fell to her death…"

He was rambling and I was looking for a polite way to end this conversation. "What has this got to do with Ali?" I asked. He sat and stared at me. "Well?"

"I am afraid that you wouldn't believe me if I told you."

"Try me!" I said.

"Ali Sahib was very interested in the story and kept on waiting for her. She came!" He said.

"Listen, old man!" I was angry at him for wasting my time. "Are you saying he eloped with a ghost?"

He shook his head. "He did not elope, Sahib. He is still there. I am afraid for his soul!"

I had had enough. I began to laugh.

He waited patiently for me to finish and sat with his head bowed. "I am a village man, Sahib. My ancestors toiled in the mountains to make a decent living. I did not go to school like you or Ali Sahib, but what I am telling you is the truth." There was something in his tone that sobered me up. "Many years ago my elders were also members of the Kafir clan, Sahib. We converted to Islam, but most of our clan members did not. They still live there like pagans. Ali Khan was very interested in their rituals so he befriended them. There was a plague, Sahib…" He stopped and wiped his brow.

"Plague? Did you inform the authorities?" I was confused. What did he want me to do about that? "Maybe I can find a phone number and put you in touch with NGOs who might be able to help."

He shook his head. "Not that kind of a plague sir."

I raised my eyebrows. My patience with his slow manner was beginning to wear thin.

"There was an evil spirit, Sahib...who was killing off their young and causing panic amongst the Muslim villagers too..."

I smiled. "Look Khuda Bukhsh, I can understand that people up in the mountains would be superstitious and I am sure they believed in this...this plague or whatever it was and thought that some supernatural entity is involved but you are a God-fearing man and you should know that there is no such thing!"

He lowered his eyes. "If you don't believe me, come with me and you can see for yourself."

I shook my head. "I am sorry Khuda Bukhsh. I can not go with you and I do not believe in this superstitious mumbo jumbo. Now, if you will excuse me..." I turned to the computer and started to read through the morning's emails.

He stood up. "Ali Sahib left this for you." He brought out a packet of letters addressed to me from his breast pocket and handed them to me.

"When did he give these to you?" I asked, turning them over in my hands. "Why didn't you..." But he was gone.

I read those letters the same night, and what I read in them disturbed me so much that I applied for a month's leave and came out here. Khuda Bukhsh met me in town, arranged porters to bring my supplies up, and now, while I sat by the fire, he busied himself making tea in the other room. Darkness has a habit of creeping up on you very quickly in these mountains, and he was getting nervous. It would be a treacherous descent into town, but he was convinced that his peer or holy man would protect him against the dark forces of night.

Ali's belongings had been packed and sent to his mother in Lahore. The room where I would sleep was built of stone, and a large fireplace stood to my right. A moth-eaten deer head hung over it, and a rusty clock stood on the mantelpiece. On the floor lay a colourful Chitrali rug tattered with years of use, and a teak wood writing desk stood by the tiny stone window. I had brought my own sleeping bag and decided against using the filthy single string bed by the wall.

Khuda Bukhsh brought me salty black tea and left quickly. As I drank, I wandered to the window and looked out. The cabin was perched precariously on a small shaggy cliff. On one side, a deep ravine dropped hundreds of feet below. The only way to approach the hut was through a rough pathway cut into the stony ground. It was a tough climb, but once here the solitude was priceless. There were no neighbors for miles around, and the view was an undisturbed vista of the timeless mountains and cloud forests.

I finished my tea and decided to explore the cabin. The two other rooms had been built more recently. The first was no more than a small storeroom that was now filled with supplies for the winter: sacks of coal, sugar, dried chick peas and tins of wheat. Khuda Bukhsh had thoughtfully chopped up firewood and stacked it neatly by the wall.

At the farthest end of the cabin was a simple kitchen where hot coals burned in a stone hearth on the floor. A few paces away stood a wooden hut that served as bathroom, and I peered at it through a roughly hewn window. The door hung open and banged in the wind. "That door needs to be repaired," I thought.

I yawned and turned away. My back hurt and I wanted to sleep, but I decided to read the letters again. The first once was dated almost nine months ago.

```
Dear Bilal,

I am having absolutely no luck with the novel.
The travails of Lahore's elite have begun to grate
on my nerves and I no longer find it fulfilling to
write about them. On a stuffy afternoon when my
```

cabin was filled with the smoke of Khuda Bukhsh's culinary experiments, I went into the village below. You know how I have always been captivated by the pagan tribe of Kalash, right? Here I was closer to them than I had ever been, and I was struggling with a novel about my life in the plateaus of Punjab. I had promised myself that I would not be distracted while I am here, but the sight of them wearing their beautiful black dresses, carrying inhuman loads of firewood on their heads and their happy faces succeeded in breaking through my resolve. I had already begun to find my novel burdensome and started entertaining thoughts of a bigger, better, grittier book set amongst the lovable pagans of the Islamic Republic of Pakistan. I know you would smile when I say that. But I was fascinated by them and determined to learn more. A book that I found behind the shed in my cabin has further fuelled my interest in these people. They are supposed to be descendants of the Greeks and are said to have been left behind by Alexander the Great! I am not surprised, though, as some of them still have the golden hair and light eyes. As I delved deeper into the book, I realized that they still believe in the existence of fairies and mythical demons, blood sucking supernatural creatures and benevolent Djinns!

Imagine, my friend, an ancient people, almost God-like in their quest to cling to their pagan rites and way of life, fighting off invaders (of which there have been many starting from the Mongols to the Muslims and the British) and staking their right to live undisturbed in the land of their birth. It never ceases to amaze me that they exist. And exist with such passion and cheerfulness when all around them the world is changing. Only a few hundred miles west lies Taliban country, and here is a bastion of paganism that has refused to die! Sorry. I am ranting again, so let me go back to the story of how I managed to find to them.

I have made a habit of going into town every week and trying to get the locals to talk to me about supernatural beings. But most of them are Muslims and get uncomfortable, so they change the subject quickly. Two weeks ago my luck changed for the better. If you ever visit me, I will take you to the tea shop down in the village that is run by a little Pathan tyrant with henna-dyed hair and a face that looks like it was folded up and then smoothed out again. His name is Nasir Jan, but everyone refers to him as 'Chacha.' That afternoon I was sitting on his hard bench, drinking his milky brew when I heard the words "rituals' and 'hauntings.' I turned to see a wizened old Kalash man with a wide toothless grin. He was telling two captivated Punjabi truckers that his village had been haunted by mysterious cases of sudden deaths where the bodies would be left completely drained of blood. I sat perfectly still, my skin bristling and heart pounding. Could it be true? Vampires in the Hindu Kush Mountains in the midst of an Islamic revival? This was too delicious for me to ignore. I did not want to scare the old man away, so I casually sat beside him and weaseled my way into his attention by offering him more tea. As he loosened up, I even brought out the sachet of salty biscuits that I always carried with me to balance the sugar in Chacha's concoction. His name was Bashara Khan and like the other men of his tribe, he had a Muslim name but was a Kafir (I flinch when I say this word. We Pakistanis call them Kafirs or 'infidels' when all they are trying to do is live the way their ancestors have lived for thousands of years).

"Could they have been attacked by wild animals? I'm sure there are many..." I said gesturing towards the stark mountains.

Bashara shook his head. "No injuries, no injuries!" he said. "No blood left in them!"

We were conversing in halting Urdu but we helped each other out by gesturing profusely. "Did you notice any bite marks-here?" I pointed to the side of my neck.

He gave me a knowing look and nodded slowly. I could see he was uncomfortable in the presence of so many Muslims around him in the tea stall, for we tend to view these superstitions with revulsion. In these mountains one can never be sure how many locals are supportive of the Taliban and their brand of Islam. So I paid and we left together. We walked towards the general direction of Chitral village. His people live high up in narrow valleys above town, their houses literally clinging to the steep stone face of the mountain. I was feverish with excitement and could barely control myself from asking him more about the 'plague.'

"They have been bitten in the neck, like you say, but the betaan (Shamans) has read the omens in the sky and we will offer sacrifice to stem this evil." I must have looked shocked and he smiled. "Goat! Goat sacrifice!" he said. And for good measure he used his fingers to make horns on his head. We laughed.

I grabbed my courage with both hands. "Can I come?" I asked.

He stopped and turned to me, his brows furrowed. After what seemed like an eternity to me he nodded slowly. "You are a good man! You seem to be knowledgeable about the plague also." I was ashamed at leading him on but I forced myself to look him in the eye. "Tomorrow morning before the Sun is high we will go to Rumbur valley." He pointed into the distance. "I will come and get you from this spot after you hear the Muslim call to morning prayers."

I nodded happily and we shook hands. My heart was beating so fast, Bilal! I decided to get a good night's sleep to prepare for my day with the Kalash tribe. I am writing to you now in the dead of night in my cabin. Tomorrow morning I will meet with Bashara Khan and go to his village to see with my own eyes what supernatural being plagues them! My mind is whirling with thoughts of vampires, Count Dracula, wooden stakes through the heart and strings of garlic hung on doorways. I am curious to see what the Slavic tradition of vampires will be translated into here in this desolate land between Pakistan and Afghanistan. I will write to you soon.

Best, Ali

Evening had fallen and the fire in the grate was burning low. I yawned and stretched my back. I threw a few dry twigs into the flames and watched burn. It was already eight and I didn't know why I had come here. Ali's letters had unnerved me. To think that my educated, agnostic friend had been pursuing vampires in the secluded mountains of Pakistan had intrigued me enough to visit this cabin where he had been infected by such a fantastic idea. I wanted to walk in his shoes and experience his adventure. But most of all I wanted to find him. Khuda Bukhsh had refused to tell me why he thought Ali was still here in this cabin, and I was determined to find out. I dined on the food Khuda had left for me in the kitchen: a plate of rice accompanied by a thick curry of eggplant cooked with wild tomatoes and dried okra. It was frugal fare but delicious. Somewhere an owl hooted and I became aware of how perfectly quiet it was.

After dinner I went out into the night to smoke and stretch my legs. The cold grasped my face and made me dizzy. I stood by the door and lit a cigarette. In the distance I could see smoke rising and the dim light of lanterns moving about on a cliff. I was looking at the village of Sheikhanadey or literally "village of the converted infidels." The locals called the unconverted ones 'Siah Posh Kafirs' or black-clad Kafirs because of their preference for that colour. It was getting colder so I stubbed out my cigarette and went inside. I lay down in front of the fire and read the second letter. It was dated four days after the first one.

Dear Bilal,

I hope Peshawar is treating you well. You will remember that in my last letter I was waiting for Bashara Khan to come and take me to the Kalash village. Next morning, I dressed in my warmest clothes and hurried down to the village. It was still dark and I was carrying a rucksack full of thermal underwear, mosquito repellents, an extra pair of walking boots and of course my camera. I sat and waited on a flat rock just a few paces from the tea stall where we had met. It was deserted at that hour, and I entertained myself by listening to tribal songs that I had downloaded into my MP3 player in Lahore. I know! I know! Not a very 'rugged' thing to do, but you know me, I am addicted to music.

As the Muezzin cleared his throat and gave the first call to morning prayers, I saw Bashara Khan walking towards me, his thin chappals scraping the stony ground and his big woolen cap pulled down over his ears. I called out to him and he came towards me, his face grim.

"What's wrong?"

"Bad business, Sahib!" He shook his head. "Another one was found this morning by the river. A young child this time!"

I was stunned. "When was the last one found?"

"Six days ago. Come Sahib! Let's hurry. It is a long walk, and we need to bury the child before we can sacrifice the animal to stem this evil."

We walked fast. A couple of hours later I began to regret that I had not suggested hiring a jeep to take us to the village. We passed through picturesque valleys and climbed precarious rocks. By noon I had convinced Bashara Khan to hitch a ride on a jeep carrying a load of chattering Afghan traders on their way home. They dropped us off by the side of the roaring Rumbur river where I craned my neck to get my first glimpse of Bashara's village. It was a steep climb, and our shoes squished and squelched in the mud. Dusk was already falling.

The 'village' was a primitive cluster of dwellings, mud and stone houses built on top of each other, every single one of them struggling to hold on to its place and not tumble down into the valley. No one was there. All the houses were empty. Bashara Khan stopped to wash his hands at an outdoor trough, and I took the opportunity to peer inside some of the dwellings. Most were just one-roomed affairs with a hole in the ceiling to let out smoke and no trace of any modern gadgets anywhere. The village did not even have a telephone!

Bashara excused himself, popped into a small hut, and returned with a leather pouch around his neck. He had filled it with a pungent red wine. We both stood on the mud road and took swigs of the delicious and strong liquid that tasted of mulberry.

"Where is everybody?" I asked.

"They must be celebrating the death of the boy, Mahamurat."

I was surprised. "Celebrating? Did you say…"

He nodded and took my arm. "Come…I will show you!"

We walked to the end of the road or lane or whatever it was and started climbing a small hill above the village. The smell of juniper and mulberries filled my nose. But something more pungent also forced its presence on me, something rotting. I held my tongue and kept climbing. Then I heard the faint sound of clapping and singing in the distance.

"We Kalash do not mourn the death of our people." Bashara said looking over his shoulder at me. "It will be a little different this time because the boy was murdered."

We were almost at the top and I couldn't stand the smell of decay and rot that was now so strong that everything else was forced out of my mind.

"Bashara, I don't mean to be rude, but what is that horrible smell?" I tried to sound as casual as possible.

"You will see!" he said firmly, so I held my nose and followed him up the last stretch.

He got there before me and stood waiting patiently as I struggled up. When I got near him, he pointed to his left dramatically.

"See!" There on a scraggy ledge were three open coffins, their rotting remains exposed to the elements. Flies buzzed around them and vultures circled in the sky. "That's the Kalash way of death."

I was feeling dizzy and leant on a tree trunk. "Why...are they open?" I managed to speak without gagging.

He shrugged his shoulders. "We Kalashis think that it is better to let souls escape quickly so that the dead can re-unite with their loved ones and roam the pasture of afterlife with them. It is for the best."

From the rotting dead, I transferred my attention to the group of Kalashi men and women who stood in a circle just a few feet away from us. They were clapping and singing in low tones. Bashara Khan took my hand and led me to the group.

They parted and made way for us. Bilal, my dear friend, what I saw there made me almost fall to the ground in horror. I knew then that I had taken on an adventure that was probably too much for my frayed city nerves. In the clearing was the body of a small child, maybe eight or nine years old, lying on a simple string-cot. His mother and sisters sat on the ground near him, their hair completely covering their faces, moaning in a low voice. The boy lay on the bed, his eyes closed and his body shriveled. Whatever had attacked him had squeezed out every drop of blood from his frail body. His mouth was puckered and his eyes had fallen into their sockets. I covered my face and staggered back. The men and women slowly took their positions again and began to clap and chant.

Bashara led me to a flat rock and helped me sit. He gave me a sip of wine from the leather pouch and I drained it.

"He couldn't have...he can't have died this morning. He's...he's lost all his blood!"

Bashara patted my shoulder. "That is what I told you Sahib. The evil spirit has come back and our betaan has traveled a long way from another village to read the signs."

"What do you mean 'come back'? Has it been here before?"

He sat cross legged at my feet and sighed. "Yes. You see these mountains around us?" He pointed to the peaks rising in the distance and I couldn't help looking. "These mountains gave birth to us, they sustain us, and we respect them. But there are very dark things that live there too." He chewed on a piece of stick. "We do not have many betaans left anymore to guide us. There is one, Aksaam Khan who lives about two days walk from here. He arrived this morning and will read the omens." He threw away the stick and spat on the ground. "Perhaps we will know what to do then..."

I was sweating and the smell of putrefying flesh was still strong. I remember reading somewhere that smell is the weakest sense we have and after a while human beings can get used to even the foulest stink. I can tell you, Bilal, whoever wrote that, lied. The stench was almost alive and it seemed to be circling us and trying to touch us. I was probably lightheaded after the long journey, and the presence of those damned coffins probably triggered it, but I can tell you that I have never felt as abandoned as I felt then, even though I was surrounded by living people. I shook my head violently but couldn't shake the image of worms snuggling into the moist flesh falling away from bleached bones inside those open caskets just a few feet away. I got up and retched by the side of the rock.

Bashara Khan suggested that we go down into the village and rest in his house. I agreed wholeheartedly. The descent was easy, and soon we were in his one room hovel sitting on the cool mud floor. He put the kettle on to boil as I lay down with a wet handkerchief on my forehead.

I remember from the book that I found in my cabin that the Kalashis and even their Muslim neighbors have a very strong belief in the existence of supernatural entities. Even after so many years, legends about Djinns and fairies that guard the Tirich Mir mountain range persist among the locals. Mountaineers have been known to climb a certain distance and then die mysteriously. Local climbers refuse to climb further saying that the abode of the supernatural starts there.

Bashara brought me tea. I thanked him and drank quickly. He sat by me on the floor.

"Her name was Taigun, Sahib. Taigun Bibi." I turned my head and looked at him. Where had I heard that name before? I sat against the wall and he began to talk in a low voice. "She was one of our own. When the British arrived down in the valleys, they also discovered our beautiful land. It was so pristine, so bountiful that they became greedy. They thought we were primitive people and would not resist them. So they built roads and sent missionaries and tried to civilize us. But we had our own way of life so we fought them. The Great Spirit Mahadeo helped us and created such fierce snow storms that the British were afraid to fight us anymore. They abandoned their greed. But they still came. They still wanted to hunt big game, so they built hunting lodges and isolated cabins to keep an eye on us." He doodled in the soft floor of the hut as I watched him silently.

"One of the white Sahibs was called Timothy Harding. He was a bad one. He was shunned even by his own kind. He built a cabin down in the valley and brought up tubes and ointments from the plains. Through the night, smoke would be seen rising from his chimney. Mad laughter and blood curdling shrieks were heard, and locals also reported seeing a black figure flying through the night sky. Pretty soon tongues started wagging and everyone was convinced that he was a magician. Sometimes, in the early morning before the Sun came up, he would gather herbs from the meadows muttering to himself. You follow me?" I nodded.

"Now this Taigun Bibi met him on one of his morning walks and they began to talk. They met every day in the fairy meadow near the sacred lake. He bewitched her. Taigun decided that she would marry him and live up in his cabin." He was squatting on the floor, his hands dangling on his knees. "Our women are free Sahib and can choose to marry anyone. We are not as closed as those Muslims down in the valleys." He sighed again and shook his head. "Only after a month of the marriage, locals in the valley started complaining that their cattle were being drained of blood by the wicked white Sahib. Things got so bad that the police were called in. But when they reached the cabin, he had disappeared and with him Taigun had also vanished.

No one ever saw him again, but a few months later, she wandered into the village. At first no one could recognize her. She used to be so beautiful…." He stopped and his eyes had that far away look in them like he was imaging her beauty. Then he started talking again. "She had aged. Her mouth which was so ripe and full only a few months ago, was drawn into a thin line. She walked through the village with her hair flying, her headdress in tatters and her feet bleeding from sharp stones. The elders of the village were happy to see her and welcomed her back. But she was not the same Taigun anymore. She walked to the 'Baishali' and shut herself in. You know what a Baishali is, Sahib?" I nodded. (The Kalashis have special huts built for women when they menstruate or are going to give birth so that their impurity does not pollute the others.).

"So she shut herself up and in a few days everyone noticed that she never seemed to sleep at all! They would hear chanting and moaning at all hours of the day, and at night she would shriek and throw herself at the doors. The villagers were scared. At first everyone thought that she would give birth to Harding Sahib's child, but her screaming and shouting unnerved them. So a wise woman was selected to see what was wrong with Taigun. Taigun Bibi refused to see her or talk to her, but the woman tricked her into revealing herself. After that night, things were never the same in that village, Sahib!"

I was afraid to ask him what happened next, yet I was dying to know her fate. Bashara Khan took a sip from his leather pouch and grimaced. "She was not human anymore, Sahib! She had shriveled up like that child you saw up there...but she was still breathing!" He spat on the ground and the horror of his words was written large on his face.

Bilal, my dearest friend, you know that I can not be accused of having a weak constitution, nor am I prone to hysteria of any kind. Right? But sitting in that hut while darkness approached swiftly and listening to the story of the woman who had lived such a long time ago, I could literally feel my heart fleeing to the soles of my feet. I was aware of the thin hairs on the back of my neck standing stiff, and I was finding it hard to control my ragged breathing. I licked my dry lips. "So, she was a vampire?"

He did not understand that word. "Sahib, she had turned into a woman who could neither die nor live! That Timothy magician had turned her into a prêt soul." I nodded. The Kalashis do not have a word for the undead, but the concept was pretty clear. They classified anything evil under the generic name of 'pret' like the Hindus believe in 'prêt atmas' or evil souls.

He was looking at me sadly as the sweat flowed down my face and soaked my shirt. It had come to me suddenly. I knew where I had heard that name before. Please have patience, and I will tell you. A few months ago, I had been writing furiously back in my cabin when something made me stop. I can not remember what it was, but I stopped. Strange! I hadn't noticed how hard it was raining. I got up, made some tea and stood with the back door open, smoking. Something was about to happen, and I remember how stiff my body had been, waiting and watching. Then I heard it. Someone was knocking. I rushed through the house and opened the front door.

She was drenched from the rain and stood shivering in her bare feet. The light from the fire inside lit up her face and I couldn't help noticing how beautiful she was. I invited her in and gave her a towel. She dried herself by the fire as I stood watching her. She took off her headdress and unpinned her dark hair. I pretended to sit on the bed and smoke, but I couldn't take my eyes off her. Her face was like a Mughal painting, long eyelashes falling on her blushed cheeks, a single stone dazzling on her nose and a beautiful high forehead. She looked at me sideways, caught my eye and smiled.

We made love that night, the night after that and then another night. Three nights in all. I would not be exaggerating if I told you that if I had died then I would have been content; I would have wanted nothing more. She never spoke to me, but her eyes expressed her love and bewitched me totally. On the last night, she pointed to the wall above my head. Someone had scrawled something. I lit a lighter and leaned in to read. Taigun Bibi. Someone had scratched that name with a sharp object into the wooden beam on the wall. She smiled and pointed to herself and then at the wall.

"You are Taigun?" I asked, and she nodded playfully. "Who wrote that?"

But of course she didn't understand and never answered me. That night as I slept, she crept out and I never saw her again. My head was spinning. She had come to me, seduced me, and left me with bite marks all over my neck. I touched my neck now. The wounds had healed. They had made me smile before, but now I shuddered as I touched those bumps. Was I turning into one of them? I wanted to cry and bang my head on the walls but I couldn't move.

Bashara Khan coughed and I was shaken out of my nightmare. I willed myself to listen to him again. "She needed to drink blood to sustain her… her body, so she had shut herself up. She was confused and afraid, I think, but she was also in pain." His eyes softened. I marveled at his ability to show compassion for such a horrible affliction. But the Kalashis really are a marvelous race and can face even the most painful horrors with a quiet philosophical turn that we city folks can never muster.

It was almost dark in his hut now, so he got up to light a kerosene lantern. The mourners were beginning to return, and we watched them file past our hut in a procession, still singing and clapping their hands. I shuddered as I thought of that small boy shriveled and lifeless left on a measly cot exposed to the stars. Soon wild animals would attack his body. I was angry and wanted to face the fiend who had done so much harm to these simple people. I remembered the boy's mother, her face hidden behind her long hair crying for her beautiful son. I hated Taigun. She was no longer the romantic vampire I was hunting, but had become a living demon that needed to be vanquished.

I must have fallen asleep because the next thing I remember is Bashara shaking me. "Sahib, wake up! Mahamurat's father has thrown a celebratory feast for us. You must come, they are expecting you!" When Kalashis die, their families go into debt by throwing huge celebrations for the entire tribe. As I followed him out of his hut, I couldn't help wondering how much poor Mahamurat's family had spent that night.

The boy's family was as poor as the others in their village, and the modest mud hut was full with people. The boy's mother sat on a wall next to the house. Her hair still covered her head and she was still crying. An insane panic grabbed me at the sight of the poor woman and the laughing mass of people inside her hut. I wanted to run out and keep running until I reached my warm beautiful home in Lahore. I forced myself to calm down and began to look for a place to sit.

Bashara whispered in my ear, "Tonight after the feast, the betaan will read the omens in the entrails of a sacrificed goat and we will decide what to do next."

I was sitting outside on the road as the congregation had spilled out into the street. I closed my eyes. This is the year 2009. I was still in modern day Pakistan. But this hut, the singing by the people clad in black, the open coffins lying exposed under the stars on the cliff... these were a reality. I had fallen in love with Taigun, and Mahamurat's mother was wailing on a wall beside me. This was really happening. I was in the middle of it.

"What...what about the police?" I blurted out. "Have you thought of informing the police?"

Bashara Khan smiled for the first time that day. "Sahib! We are a fiercely independent community. We always settle our disputes amongst ourselves, and our ancient knowledge will take care of this horror, too." He looked at me and winked. "Don't worry, Sahib! You will see tonight. Besides, the police don't know how to deal with us or our traditions."

Dinner was being served. The boy's father had slaughtered ten goats and their blood was flowing in a narrow open drain under the cliff where we sat. The stench was overpowering, but I was too distraught to notice. Bread and goat curry was being passed around.

I turned my head and saw that Mahamurat's mother had stopped wailing. She was sitting very still, her head bowed and her black hair falling to the ground. I was oblivious to the chattering of the people around me. A cold sweat broke out on my brow and my spine was tingling. I could feel Taigun's presence here, but I was afraid to look around. Mahamurat's mother raised her hand to part her hair.

Bilal, I lost faith in God a very long time ago, and have never displayed any signs of a hysterical personality. I think you will agree with me. As I sit here writing this letter to you, my hands are shaking. I have surrounded myself with as many lanterns and torches as I could find. Believe me my friend I am not losing my mind! She parted her hair raised her head and looked me straight in the eyes. Taigun! It was her!

Here Ali's letter ends. I sit and stare at the paper, my mind whirling. Last night I was in Peshawar. The city bustled around me, my water pipes had burst again, the plumber was late, and my mother had decided to visit me even though we haven't spoken in months. Life was normal. My concerns had been trivial, human ones. Tonight I am in a secluded cabin staring Tirich Mir in the face and reading about a vampire in the hidden valleys high above Pakistan. I shuffle through the papers hoping to see something I might have missed before. There is nothing. This was the last thing he wrote before he vanished into the night. Khuda Bukhsh says that Ali returned from Rumbur nine days after he had left and never spoke a word. He gave him these letters addressed to me, and that's the last time anyone ever saw him. I am not concerned if Tai-gun Bibi lived or died. All I want to do is to find my friend. Tomorrow I must go into town, find Bashara Khan, and ask him about Ali. I will not be going alone. The Frontier Police will be coming with me...

The Angel in the Trees
by Dan O'Brien

I WALKED EVERYWHERE. I had to, I had no car. I never did, never trusted them. Never felt the need to, being a lifelong New Yorker, or thereabouts. And even here, down South, as they say, I worked not far from home through a walk in the woods to a small college campus where I wrote mostly fluff pieces really for the college alumni publication. They called it a magazine. I was new to this town if you called it a town, a postage-stamp-sized campus stuck with a cluster of homes, and then the more far flung houses, where I lived, in the woods, alone. I liked it this way. Even those walks at night that could sometimes get quite lonesome. I was often set upon by dogs, though strangely they'd never bite, but bark vociferously as if I were the one frightening them. A grey fox would slither like a shroud across the road through the high beam of my flashlight. The deer will wait perfectly still in the dark till you step blindly beside them, and then they snort obstreperously, and thunder off terrified into the woods. It was wonderful. Sometimes, from afar, across the occasional field, the retreating deer with their white tails bobbing looked more to me like ghost-riders approaching in the moonlight. It certainly could get strange. As it did that night, about nine-thirty, I believe, my usual time to walk home (I preferred to work late mornings into evening), the oval disk of my flashlight skimming across the surface of the dirt road. When suddenly I heard the sound of something falling, a crackling through branches and then a thud like I thought a body might sound, hitting the ground. Though I've never heard such a thing, have you? I threw my beam to where the sound came from: nothing there but trees. The tree branches grew loud as if suddenly tossed with wind, soughing, I believe is the word, though I couldn't feel a thing on my face or neck or hands. It swelled to a roar, and the night in front of my face grew black, my flashlight made no dint. Then everything went quiet again. Just as quickly as it had first grown loud. I turned round a bend in the road, climbing uphill, my flashlight swerved in the dark and lit upon, standing in the trees with his eyes upon me: an angel.

I did not know what it was. Never having seen one. Have you?

He looked like a man. His body had its own light, pale, as if passed through water. His hair was black and his skin white. He looked like a victim of drowning. I assumed it was a he because of the nature of his face, his features. But there was something sexless about him, not quite androgynous, but—. I could not see his clothes, the light obliterated all detail, he could have been naked for all I knew. And this light stretched not only out from him but up, like bright strings stretched into the canopy of trees above.

He looked at me like he'd known I was coming. As if he'd been waiting for me all my life.

He neither smiled at me nor glared. He held out his hand, as if he had something to give me. A dog barks close by in the trees, and when I look again he's gone.

You should know now that despite a lifelong atheism, or really was it simply a kind of lazy secular agnosticism? this was by no means the first time I'd seen an angel. Or a ghost. Or suffered hallucinations. You see, I still don't know what to call them! I was here in the woods for my health. Not that I ever considered myself truly mentally ill. On my bad days I felt gifted, and when I was healthy I knew I had been sick. I'd been sick in more ways than one.

I'd become divorced, lost my job. All in a few months, everything unraveled. I was sleeping all day, ordering my non-perishable groceries delivered past midnight. I'd have them left in my building at the bottom of the stairs, and late at night while everyone slept I'd slip out my door and spirit them away.

It's not a time I like to talk about much.

I'd been suicidal, without ever attempting. You could say I had simply wanted to die, in a vaguely hopeful sort of way, but that I was not interested in taking responsibility for it myself. And then, one day, out of the blue, as if someone were listening and answering my dark prayers, I discovered I was sick. I had all the popular treatments, recovery was considered doubtful.

Then this man moved in. A roommate. His name, he told me, was Rick. He was handsome in a filthy sort of way. He wore blue jeans, a leather jacket. He told me he rode a hog. (I think I had a crush on him.) He treated me well, listening to my problems, holding my hand while I threw up, or sobbing. He came with me to the hospital and sat beside me, stroking my face, and my neck, until I fell asleep.

Then one morning, sitting in our kitchen, over coffee, he reveals to me that his name is not Rick at all but Jesus Christ Son of Man.

Naturally, I was upset. I mean—wouldn't you—? I was terrified! This man was insane! I had to kick him out—it got ugly. The neighbors all complained when they heard the shouts and sounds of heavy things being thrown about. People called the cops on us. But when they broke down the door they found only me there, alone. Screaming, smashing things up. No one in the building had ever seen nor heard of Rick.

I couldn't call my parents, who were both alive still at the time (I had been an only child). They had not spoken to me, nor me them, in years. My marriage had been the reason. Or not the reason, the latest excuse. They did not want me marrying a non-Jew, they said. Can you imagine? in this day and age? We had stockings growing up at Christmastime! Though, to be fair, their colors had been blue and gold. Chanukah stockings. That's how it was.

And Elliot was Episcopalian like I was a Jew.

But what my parents really meant was they did not like him. Elliot. Did not trust him. They could see what I couldn't.

I married him without inviting them, and years later, after the divorce, after I'd gotten sick and suffered this apparent psychotic break, I found I couldn't call them. I wasn't working at the time. I had no savings left, no insurance. At the hospital I gave them Elliot's number.

Another thing happened at the hospital though, a wonderful, remarkable if somewhat problematic—. The doctors all assumed I was still delusional when I said I'd been suffering from cancer. They could not find a trace of it in me. And subsequent tests bore this out. Over the course of those last few months, roughly the time I'd lived with Rick, I'd been healed.

Now, before that, with Elliot, there'd been the incident in Vermont.

Elliot was a brilliant young Turk of an adjunct professor, so everyone told me, all the time, over and over again. Economic History or History of Economics, I never knew which. Or I knew but I've forgotten. Or I forgot because I never cared enough really. And one summer someone at Columbia loaned us their house in Vermont.

Elliot was to finish his first book up there, the book destined to make him a star in certain very small, very miniscule circles. I was between careers. I had been an intellectual, a neophyte with feminist ambitions, and Elliot and I had fallen in love, as they say, in grad school. But it took me five years to finish my dissertation on Neglected Female Poets of the Revolutionary War Era (it was just a working title), and when I finished I didn't care much for poets, of any gender, any era. I had grown to find academic pursuit inhuman somehow.

Something in that house in Vermont, in the woods surrounding, made my skin crawl. Literally. Sometimes the back of your neck will heat up as if someone were touching it with a very warm spoon, or their fingers, perhaps? Well, that was what it was like. Elliot didn't feel a thing. I was suburban bourgeois, he said. It was silence, the peace and the quiet—all that is anathema to the native New Yorker—that was what frightened me so! "You're scared of your self!" he'd say. "You're so afraid to be alone." And he'd laugh, and hold me. "Ghosts appear only to those who want to see them, Madeline." (I thought he was missing the point, and the definition, of a haunting.) "Do what I do," he'd say, "say it loud: I don't believe in you, ghosts!"

When I was scared of anything, he'd speak to me this way. (He'd made it clear, before we married, that he didn't want children.)

So I said, after him, I don't know why, "I don't believe in you, ghosts!" And he laughed, and let me go.

The problem, you see, as I saw it then, as I see it now, was that I at least a little bit believed in ghosts. I mean, don't you? Have you seen one? I'm not ashamed of it now. I often wondered at the time, inwardly, if I were just the smallest bit psychic. You know? I'd been so as a child. I'd seen people in my room, as I drifted off to sleep. Old folks, mainly, sitting in outdoor chairs, indoors, in my bedroom. It was funny. Or leaning up against my bureau checking his ghostly pocket watch. In the house, when we moved up from the city to the suburbs, this was when I was ten, for months I'd hear this accordion playing each night around bedtime. The same fractured tune, same misplaced breathing. Sometimes just the breath in the breathing box, I think that's what you call it, no melody, as if an extremely ungifted child, asthmatic probably, were laboring to learn it. As if he would be punished for not playing. My parents did not like music. They were book people.

That house in Vermont I remember was like a ship, or an ark really, left high on the mountainside. Four stories up with a cupola like a crow's nest on top of this really insanely steeply pitched roof. It was enormous for us, it swallowed us whole. It had been built, we had been told, by a painter named Galiel in the early 1800s. Galiel had been a merchant sailor, then a spice-trader in New York. Then after his wife died he found he liked to paint. His paintings were never of his wife but of the sea: shipwrecks, romantically imagined, beautiful shafts of light like ruined Doric columns set in tempestuous waves. He'd had a dozen children, Galiel, the thirteenth having died with that wife in labor. The family that lived there now, during summers and holidays (they were away on sabbatical, in Rome), left most everything they owned behind. So you could say the house was haunted by this family too.

We were sitting on the porch overhanging a precipitous ravine. The summer evening was almost preternaturally quiet. I was reading Renan's Life of Jesus—have you read it? It's good, it makes Jesus more of a man somehow. I'm no born-again but for some reason I'd always wanted to read this book, and now that I'd given up all academic pursuit I found I could read whatsoever my heart desireth, and my heart desired the Life of

Jesus. Anyway, just when I got to that point where Renan says, you know, that, "Miracles are what *never* happen" (emphasis mine), I paused to think about that. And when I paused I put the book aside, and I noticed how quiet it had become. I was about to remark to Elliot how peculiar this absence of wind or cricket or cicada—when we heard an infant cry. Inside our house, upstairs. An infant. (It would have been easy to go and find out which room if only we'd been brave.)

Elliot lifted his face from his book.

Ten seconds or so of crying... Then the crickets in the woods again.

He was quick to dismiss it as a kind of aural illusion: If life can play tricks on the eyes, then why not the ears? especially considering the ear is so impressionable an organ.

(He actually said that: "an organ.")

And besides, the architecture of the house was spooky.

Here we are, alone in the woods, tens of miles from any other human living beings—we were city folk! suburban-bred, and the wind (that old saw), or some dying animal in our innocence we could not name nor recognize—it was a sound of nature, he concluded straight away, caught in the echo chamber of our house. (Our house that was not ours.)

Or maybe the animal was in the house, in the walls perhaps, dying? He admitted there was a possibility of that.

But it was not like an infant's cry, it was an infant crying.

The other time I'd been alone: he'd gone down to New York for the day to give a paper, and because I'd begged he was driving home that night. I tried to wait up but fell asleep with the lights on (I always slept with the lights on, if I could help it).

And I woke up to what sounded like cannonballs—falling on the roof!

Or hail the size of bread loaves, large rocks falling from the sky—and falling on the roof!

Can you imagine—that sound—?

I felt—no, I knew, that our house was somehow under attack. As if a ship at sea, or in a storm, we were foundering on the rocky shoal.

I opened up the front door: no hail, no stones from the sky.

I ran to the stairs—I was not going to let this one get away, not this time—and still waking up I climbed to the second floor, the third—.

There were maid- and butler-quarters up there, long neglected into storage rooms, full of junk, memories, all wrapt in thick cauls of dust.

The crashing tumult continued above my head.

I imagined people up there now, like something out of Dante, very strange souls, very strong, like angels, or demons—beating their fists on the roof.

So up the stairs to the fourth and highest floor I ran, and switching on the hall lights as I flew, switching on every light in every room I passed—every door flung wide, the rooms staring back at me, furniture and crazy stacks of books and records, boxes, empty clothes and piles of damaged children's toys—"What are you looking for?" "There's no one here but you."

I stood in the hallway, as the roof and walls around me shook. Pummeled. I spoke from the bottom of myself in a voice I did not yet know I had: "I do not believe in you, ghosts!"

It's funny. It worked. The sound and shaking stopped.

You know I felt something surprising in that moment: they'd listened to me, whoever they were. Galiel the painter, his long-dead, long-birthing wife, their children. The sailors whose ghosts he'd entombed in those shipwreck-paintings. That thirteenth child, who'd cried that night for ten seconds long. "Thank you," I said, quietly, to all of them. I turned out all the lights.

Naturally Elliot didn't understand. I told him when he came home. I had to, because you see I met him at the front door and I burst right into tears. I cried, stupidly. I was happy, I insisted. ("Happy about what?") He brushed past me up the stairs, two at a time, inspected that fourth floor, even climbing up into the cupola and finding nothing there but one window pane diagonally split—he hadn't noticed that before—"There," I said—"that's your proof!" And he looked at me for the first time with fear in his eyes.

No, not fear...

It wasn't long after that he told me he was in love with someone else. He used that word, he thought it made it better somehow.

So you could say I had experience with ghosts. But I did not yet know what I believed.

It was my idea to move south, after the divorce, and Rick, my Hell's Angels Christ. I wasn't going to call what happened to my cancer a miracle. As Renan says, miracles are what never happen. It was the power of a desperate mind that had brought my Rick to me, in order to help me heal myself. (I was Jewish—how could I believe in Rick?)

The town I chose for myself is called Lowden. Which is an odd name, I'll grant you, considering how high atop a rocky plateau it sits: it catches the passing clouds like the head of a nail in a fence might snag a passing thread. And sometimes the clouds stick around for days, weeks even. A month of untempered grey is not unheard of. And really it isn't cloudy all the time but fog is the norm when the air is damp, and the air is always damp because, you see, Lowden is in the clouds.

The plateau looks like a mountain range that's been cut off at the waist, or knees. As if God shaped the landscape with a sword.

Sometimes, in a storm, lightning ripples synaptically through the fog and trees... silently: no thunder.

The town was founded in 1834 by a group of religious zealots from upstate New York (of course, you say). The Lowdenites, as they came to be rather ungracefully known, were Utopians who believed in free living, but not free love. In fact they abhorred the body so much so that, like so many Utopians before and after, they dribbled out unto extinction. Then Lowden became a copper mining town, and persisted in poverty for decades.

And then one day at the end of the previous century, an heiress to a copper mining magnate came up the mountain to visit this town where so many of her father's miners had lived and died. Guilt may have been her inspiration, or father-hatred, who knows? This woman was religious. Even at a young age her family and friends saw in her the violent light of zealotry. But she had not yet found her cause.

Until she came up to Lowden. And lo, the story, as I have heard it, as I have had cause to recycle it ceaselessly in the Lowden College Alumni Magazine, was that this woman fell in love with this place. She loved the clouds, the plateau in fog. And most of all she loved the trees. There is a spirit in the trees, I imagine her saying. And people would've simply laughed at her if she hadn't had the money to put where her mouth had been. She bought this town, built the college, raised twelve churches all of varied Christian faiths (which was roughly one church for every fifty souls in those days). She was absolutely, and unequivocally, insane. She said she did not care what one was, so long as one believed.

Now, it's true, that being Jewish by birth I felt sometimes somewhat out of place here. To say that I had not lived a religious life up until this point would not be entirely false modesty. My sins were many. I did not like old people, which I knew might become more and more problematic as I grew older. I'd never liked fat people very much, or babies, and yes I believe there's some overlap there. And you know already something of my problematic relationship to dogs, and in truth pets or wildlife in general (I am not an outdoorsy person, let us say).

And then there were the varying degrees of immoralities, sexual and otherwise, thank you very much, at any given time, at different points in my life, though not nearly enough points lately.

And also there was what happened with my parents, how they both died at once. Of mercy-killing, euthanasia, I guess you call it. Or suicide. They did it both together, which was so like them. And I didn't find out until they'd been buried two months.

In Dante, though I am no Dante scholar—English is my only language—American, I should say—in the fifth circle of Hell you will find the depressives buried in the marshy black waters of the River Styx. I remember reading that not too long ago, and it astounded me: I had not known you could go to Hell for that. For being "sullen," was I think the word used: Grim and sullen in the sunlit air, to paraphrase. And so these sullen souls are buried deep within the viscous mud, and their sighs are bubbles breaking the surface slime.

(I sigh all the time. It's often how I breathe.)

And above them, trapped in the very same mud, waist-deep like pigs or larvae, are the wrathful, those that lived a life of fury. As if anger towards others is slightly better than anger towards oneself.

I don't know how I feel about all that...

But Christian Lowden suited me fine. Like the copper mining magnate's daughter, I felt the spirit in the woods, too. I did, when I visited, years ago with Elliot on academic retreat. I'd hit it off well with a professor's wife named Nancy, and

Nancy edited the Lowden College Alumni Magazine. So after my divorce and illness and breakdown and so-called miraculous healing, without mentioning any of that, I picked up the phone and gave Nancy a ring.

"You don't look so hot," she said.

We'd been discussing a feature on this one-legged rock-climber, a student. We both said we found it inspiring.

I said I thought I should go home. I had this migraine.

"I didn't know you got migraines!" she said, as if I'd just told her I macraméd (good for you!).

The truth was I didn't get migraines anymore, not since Rick. I was scared, that's all, intrigued, let us say, by my vision of the angel. I'd passed that spot on the way in this morning where I'd seen him the night before: a weedy rise beside a dead or dormant tree. The grass where the angel had stood were not even downpressed: they flared up in a weedy thatch, shreds of leaves tangled in the brush.

On the way back home, it was hardly past noon, the fog was falling in. I was used to walking in it. I liked how it could open up your ears to things and help you hear the world as if peripherally, if not in three hundred and sixty degrees. The leftover raindrops rolling from a twig to the flat palm of a leaf below. The dogs as always barking behind that striated wall of trees (what were they saying to each other, across such great, blind distance?). A train whistles even farther off than that, one high pitched cliché sustained, not so much foreboding as nostalgic, elegiac. But mostly it was the raindrops I liked to listen to.

A car flashed round the bend—no headlights on. A student, I could tell, at the wheel of her white SUV. I slopped down into a ditch, and tried my best to glare up through the driver's side window. I was not noticed.

What is it about these girls and their SUVs? I assumed it was a girl, a student, I don't know why. And almost all of them drove these really very enormous cars purchased for their safety by their fathers. They sit high behind the wheel, like a princess on a stallion, or carried in a livery by slaves.

Someone stood now in the angel's place, through the fog he was just a shape:

"Tricky road," he called out to me.

The angel held a leash in his hand. The dog, this fat mud-colored spaniel, barked at my approach.

"I ought to carry a flashlight—like you." He chuckled: "When will I ever learn?"

This was Walter Tawwater. Say that name, you can't help but sound Southern. I'd met him a handful of times on the road these past months. We'd never stopped to speak really but pattered on instead like neighbors might, in passing, about the weather, the winter population of deer, a rabid raccoon rumored dead nearby.

He was a small man, old. And something in the bones of his face made him look half-demented: sharp cheeks and a jutting, delicate chin—a lecher, that was the word that sprang to mind. Or maybe he was ill. Have I mentioned how ancient he was? Harmless, I thought, as the dog barked, its eyes befuddled by cataracts, froth looping off its chin.

"You should get yourself a flashlight," I said as I passed, smiling, was I flirting?—"for safety's sake!"

He laughed again in that false fatherly way, and yanked the dog's bark up out of it. He took a step or two up from the road, into that grassy patch that was this morning pristine.

For this reason, I stopped.

"Everything fine?" asked Walter Tawwater. He smiled, his dentures were bright, a beacon in the fog.

I switched my flashlight off.

"You live around here, right?"

He nodded, "Up that way." And he pointed through an overhang of branches.

"Have you ever seen anyone out here?—alone, at night?"

"Besides you?" He laughed again. It was a nervous spasm, breathless. I thought he had emphysema, which is what my father had.

The dog barked again as if to mask his master's cough.

"What I mean is, do you ever see men out here?"

He looked at me, baffled, his fist before his mouth.

"Why? What've you seen?"

"I don't know."

"Well you'd best be careful. There's a pervert on the loose." (He said the word like pre-vert.) "There's some prevert going round, exposing himself to girls who go walking in the woods, alone, at night."

The way he smiled looked as though he thought these girls deserved it.

In the fall there had been a rape of a girl. They'd never caught the rapist. It caused a stir on campus, as it should, and in the community where there had been not one documented violent crime since before the time the churches were built. I wondered if I was a girl, from Walter Tawwater's point of view.

"Okay," I said. "Thanks for the warning!" And I switched back on my light. The fog was dropping now through the trees in soft, smoke-like folds.

Walter Tawwater jerked his dog's head up out of the grass: its nose had uncovered a dead snake like a small white stick.

"You'd best be careful!" he repeated his warning: "Otherwise you might find yourself exposed to!" and he laughed again, that wheezing spasm. I thought to myself, just for a moment, that clearly Walter Tawwater was the prevert of whom he spoke.

When I glanced behind me to see if he'd gone, he was still there, still watching me through the fog. His dog had turned his back on both of us, barking at something in the trees I couldn't see.

What was the angel holding in his hand?

That was what kept me up at night, or most of that first and second night. I had had to rely on sleeping pills, a drink or two, or three. Or four. And checking several times every window and every door was locked. And my brass fire poker in the bed beside me (sleeping with my poker), as had been my habit for some time now, as a woman, as a girl, living alone here in this dark woods full of angels and lechers. (The girl who'd been raped in the fall had been jogging not too far from here.) Because how did I know it was an angel I had seen at all and not a man? some flesh-and-blood prevert like Walter Tawwater?

And if not a man how did I know it was an angel? Why was I so sure? It could have been a devil, a demon of some kind. Or just your run of the mill ghost. A haunting, and nothing special about it at all.

What's the difference between a ghost-story and a God-story anyway?

Do you know?

What was he holding in that hand?

You see, because even when I was sick, I did not believe. I did not believe in God. As they say.

I wanted to, in foxholes and hospitals—it always felt some-how somewhat somewhere out there beyond me. Out beyond my powers. Of what? I did not have that gift. That's what I used to think. You have it or you do not. Children have it. Na-iveté? A friend of mine used to say all the time, "Either you're haunted, or you go to church."

What I had been haunted by, my whole life, if I'm honest with myself, and you, was: what if neither is the case, no God, no ghost. What if you reach a certain point in life, a certain age, as I had reached mine, and rather than finding oneself swept up in a desperate certitude of the facts of the things of the kingdom of the world to come—what if at this point you see what is truly horrific about life: that there is nothing there behind it all at all?

It's like you're walking in the woods alone at night. Your flashlight is your mind, forever casting out, fishing out into the black, piercing the caul of night with your one thin beam, your narrow mind, your narrow little subjective life, and seeing only maybe that step or two in front of you, as we all do, as all of us are guilty of... Maybe once in the odd while you cast your light out to the left or to the right, out into the wide landscape—you're ambitious, brave, you're desperate—and little bits of things appear, snatches of fragments of things—things that are true. But most of the time it's just the trees you see. But maybe, you think, maybe one day, your beam will light upon a face.

I lay awake in bed waiting for the fog of Nembutal to descend. This house I rented was only a few years old, no one had died here yet. Outside, wind chimes, rain gushed gently round the eaves and down through new copper gutter pipes. I was alone in the world. I felt somehow my plan was now almost complete. Not Elliot, nor what was left of my family—no one knew where I was, what had become of me. No one who had ever known me could be said to know me now. And no one who knew me now had any idea who I was.

I pulled the pillow over my face and fell asleep.

The next day Nancy drove me to The Piggly Wiggly (or The Pig, as we call it—the locals do) as she did every Friday before picking her kids up at school. We talked pleasantly about nothing: that one-legged rock-climber would have the cover this month, there'd been no unequivocal sun since Valentine's Day, Nancy's husband Don was experiencing an emergent hemorrhoid.

"Have you ever seen a ghost?" Maybe it was all this talk about the weather. I tried to make the question sound playful, daring.

"No!" she said, half-astonished (she was so cute). "Why do you ask? have you seen a ghost?" And she glanced at me.

I answered in all sincerity that "Yes, I've seen one or two in my day."

The windshield wipers clacked uselessly. The windshield was an almost perfect pane of water. Nancy swerved minutely in her lane.

"I've seen ghosts a lot," I said. "Or I should say I've seen some ghosts, and I've heard others."

(I didn't mean to sound defensive.)

"I think it's beautiful." And I left it there.

On the way home, Nancy's minivan full of food, for me but also for Nancy and her hemorrhoidal husband and their four darling kids, Nancy asked, "Have you ever heard of the Angel of Lowden?"

My God. I had not. Had I?

"It's a legend, a local kind: an angel guards the mountain."

"From what?"

"Sorry?"

"What does the angel guard the mountain from?"

"Oh, I don't know. Evil, I guess."

"And is this a Christian angel?"

"Now what do you mean by that?" she was laughing again, as if I were making some kind of red-state, blue-state joke. (I wondered if she knew I had been raised a kind of Jew?)

"Is it a Christian or a Jewish or a Muslim angel or what?"

She pressed down her turn signal, looked up into her mirror. We exited the interstate.

"Christian. It would have to be, down here, wouldn't it?"

On the side of the road we passed a tow truck with orange lights revolving. It maneuvered to lift a wrecked compact car that was black, burned out. There was no one inside I could see.

At the house Nancy insisted on helping me with the groceries, as she did every week. And every week I said No it's all right, I got it, Nancy. But this week I let her come in, I don't know why. I was slovenly these days. I'd yet to have anyone over on any very social terms. I hadn't decorated, per se. My laundry, clean and soiled and all shades in between, occupied two easy chairs and half of my new sofa. Boxes sat open-mouthed on the foyer floor. I had killed a spider with a dictionary, days ago, and the book lay on the carpet still, the spider dead beneath it.

"Are you all right, Madeline?" And I thought she meant my groceries.

She waited, frozen, deer-like, in the middle of my kitchen. She put her hand on mine, on the counter-top. I made a fist.

"I'm fine," I said. I laughed. No one had said my name in a very long time. It didn't sound like my name.

"I only ask because—"

"Do I seem not okay to you?"

"No, that's not it. I only meant if I was living out here, all alone, without Don..." She was shaking her head at me as if she admired me. Or maybe like I'd done something wrong.

After the silence, we laughed some more. All around us the week's groceries seemed to exhort us on to more practical concerns. We made some disparaging remarks about men, and Nancy said she'd love a month or two away from Don and this ubiquitous hemorrhoid of his ("all men are babies," she said—she actually said that! "Babies!"). And I walked her to the door and thanked her for the ride, for carrying my groceries in, "Good night, Nancy, have a nice weekend, I'll see you Monday morning."

That night I called Elliot. I would've thought our phone number would of course now be long defunct (we had not spoken in years), but a woman answered:

"Elliot?" she said, not to me but out behind herself, back into the apartment. (She sounded very sober, very cautious. Elegant.) Unless he'd kept this number, he still lived on Riverside. It had been his mother's, so in the split of course he'd kept it, along with all our friends, strangely. He taught at Columbia still, still walked to the same subway stop, unless there was sun and then he walked all the way up, through the park. He loved that park, along the river, the big trees. He loved to walk. It was the one hobby we shared, besides books. I remember that apartment perfectly. I often walk through it in my mind, like a ghost.

He picked up:

"Yeah."

This was how he answered: as if he were only slightly ticked to be interrupted in the midst of some profound yet workmanlike abstraction, rubbing the strain from his eyes with ink-stained fingertips (he preferred to write longhand, of course, the prick). I was shocked he could still sound so much the same.

"Elliot, it's Madeline Singer."

Isn't that hilarious? that I felt the need to give him my last name? (This would've been harder had I been sober.)

"Hi!" he said, as if excited to hear from me. It died out like that: "Hi...!"

"How are you?"

"Where are you calling me from?"

"The South."

The phone line hissed and crackled. Did he want me to be more specific?

"Wow," he said. Then, "Wow. Why?"

(Did he mean why the South? why call?)

"I moved here last year. In the fall. It's been great for me. Really great. I've always wanted to move down South."

"You have? Since when? I didn't know that."

"Yes."

"I did not know that."

"I know you didn't know that but it's true, Elliot. I like things better down here. Things are slower down here."

"I've heard that."

"Things are, I don't know, more real."

"Real? In what way real?" And there it was again: that old condescending cocksuredness.

I said, "People are kinder here, Elliot."

"Isn't that where they invented slavery, the South?"

"You know what I mean: people are honest. Unlike New York. They're giving, less judgmental. They're not snobs."

His silence meant he was insulted. Which was intended.

"I hate New York now," I added.

"You do?"

"Is that so hard to believe?"

"Are you alone?"

"Yes. Jealous?"

"What I mean is are you living down there by yourself?"

"So?"

It sounded like he was walking into another room.

"It's a spiritual place too," I added, "the South."

And against my better judgment I heard myself telling him the story of the Angel of Lowden. How it inhabited the air above this foggy plateau. How it protected the townspeople from evil.

"What kind of evil are we talking about here, Mad?"

(I'd always found that an unfeminine nickname, an unfortunate pun.)

"Mad?"

"I don't know, Elliot. Any kind of evil. You know, despair is a sin. I read that."

And because he didn't respond right away, I told him what I'd seen.

"An angel."

"Yes. Standing on the side of the road only two nights ago. I saw him with my own eyes. It was fantastic! I wasn't dreaming—he was looking right at me!"

I heard him whisper something: he was cupping the mouthpiece and speaking in very measured tones, trying for reassuring.

(Was that a child I heard crying in the other room? in the kitchen?)

"Madeline? Are you okay?" (That question again!)

"How do you mean?"

"Do you think you're healthy? Because if you don't mind me saying so I think you sound—. Have you been depressed?"

"Do you mean am I grim and sullen in the sunlit air? The answer's no, not really."

"What are you talking about?"

"I'm not ill, Elliot. I'm not depressed. I'm happy! Happier than I've ever been in my entire fucking life!"

I heard his breath. The rhythm of it shallow, repressed, like it always was. I closed my eyes and for a moment I could smell him.

"Don't call me again. Okay?"

"Ever?"

"Not when you're drinking."

"I'm not drinking—I'm not drinking now."

I heard myself cackle, like a witch, like an old hollowed out witch. He'd made love to me when I was a girl.

"Why didn't you believe me, Elliot?"

"Why didn't I believe you about what?"

"When you were gone and I heard those people on the roof of that house in Vermont. When I thought the house was like a ship at sea. Or before that, the baby crying. Why didn't you believe me when I told you I was scared?"

Behind his hand that woman spoke to him. I heard the word "soft," and her tone was critical.

He spoke again: "We should stop—"

I hung up.

That night I dreamed of the angel. He looked the same but he held a sword. He had no apparent wings, or wings like a hummingbird maybe, fluttering too fast to see as he hovered there, above me, above the naked trees. I saw him as if through branches, his bright body set out against starlight, and he walked as if upon the treetops, like pinpoints, from twig to twig his almost womanly feet brought no weight. The sword was liquid, like a lash of silver it dangled to the ground. And I climbed it, cutting my wrists and hands—I was with him in the trees. My hands and wrists and arms and legs were sliced like mouths. I balanced there on a high branch, sinking and just about to fall—he reached out his hand to me.

The next morning the sky was clear. Clear skies had been augured in my dream.

It was spring. Somehow. Suddenly. And despite all that bright sunshine, air warm and fat with pollen, what concerned me most this morning—for some reason I was worried—was what the angel might be protecting me from.

If he were protecting me at all.

What was out there, exactly, for me to be so frightened of?

Maybe Elliot and Nancy were right: I was not well. Maybe I was sick again.

Instead of the doctor I went to the library.

The Lowden College library is small and almost always infested with geriatrics. I couldn't find any books of local lore. I read some things about angels in general, of all kinds, all religions, but I found the topic multifarious to a fault. I asked the librarian, a thick, Amishy-looking young man. And he asked me back, as if I were joking, "What kind of lore?"

"Local. You know, ghost stories mainly." I smiled, coquettishly. "Maybe something about angels?"

"Angels?"

This old bitch at the paperback rack scowled in my direction. Other folks were listening now, too.

"Well what you ought to do is go talk to Walter Tawwater..."

I asked him to say that name again.

"Taw-water. He collects ghost stories and stuff. Legends. He used to work here. But he didn't have his certificate. He got fired, or retired. Who knows? You might call Walter an amateur folk-loricist—I know he would!"

The young man lowered his voice and leaned in across the countertop, and maybe he winked (it could have been a twitch): "But you best watch yourself around Walter. He's a real ladies' man. A dog."

Outside, students were jogging, biking, in shorts or with their shirts off though it couldn't have been more than fifty degrees. I was shocked by their young bodies. Where had they been all winter long? But here they are now, fresh from hiding, pale, reborn and red-cheeked, not all of them attractive or probably smart—some downright ill-equipped for the world, that much was clear—but all of them beautiful and sweet and sadder than they'll ever know in the simple fact of their youth. I wanted to cry for them. I wanted to speak, to give them some wisdom of some kind, but all I could think worth saying was, You are so fortunate. And I knew that was envy. The simple way some of them waved to me—. It broke your heart.

Along one stretch of road, sudden white flowers festooned the high bramble like a presentiment of marriage.

That car came racing down the hill, toward campus again.

I stumbled back down into the shallow ditch again, and again I could not see who was driving. It was the same car, or one just like it: a white SUV. I wondered who it was that lived out here who'd come barreling down along this blind curve on a regular basis like that.

After supper I went out again into the warm twilight and I waited, on the side of the road near the spot where I'd seen the angel only three nights before.

"Christ!" he said, when darkness had come, the fog had come back. "You scared me half to death, standing there like that. I thought you was some kind of pre-vert!"

He laughed feebly, he coughed. The dog would not bark: he looked drugged. I walked closer.

"I didn't mean to scare you, Mr. Tawwater."

"Walter."

"Okay."

"Why you standing out here all by your lonesome?"

"I was waiting for you."

He cocked his head like a hunting dog.

His house was neat, the furniture worn but clean. Knick-knacks and photographs in frames, nature-paintings and Nava-jo rugs—everything dustless and unsmudged. I was surprised to discover Walter was a vain man. A bachelor? There were no obvious photos of wife or children. The house smelled like potpourri and onions. The walls were of exposed wood, a log cabin feel.

The dog, whose name as it turned out was Webb, two B's, had free reign here. He sat on the sofa on some brocaded pillows as if waiting to be entertained.

Walter offered me a drink. With his coat off he'd shrunk, as if that were possible. He shuffled, his back round, and from time to time he'd adjust his teeth discreetly with his tongue. He dropped ice from tight hands into these brightly cleaned glasses. He poured gin and tonic without asking.

"The Lowden Angel is a fact. People been seeing her for ages." (Her, I thought, how can that be?) "Even before the Lowdenites came up the mountain, Native Americans known all about her."

"It lives here? On the mountain? Why?"

He brought the drinks to me. They rattled in his claws. I took my glass from him, as he lowered himself beside me, on the couch with effort, and pain, the dog named Webb between us. (Webb had found he liked me now: his head lolled wetly in my lap as I stroked.)

"Angels got to live somewhere," said Walter, and he chuckled, heavily, lifting his glass up: "To angels."

"Is this a holy place?"

His glass stuck to his lip. He looked at me, then the window. I could see my face reflected next to his.

"I don't know nothing bout holy." He shrugged and drank.

I drank quickly too, and deeply, and shivered at the numbness on my tongue, the bite in my throat.

He smiled at me, "Whoa there…"

"What's the angel look like?" I asked.

"You ever been in love?"

This shocked me.

"I have. Many times. It used to be hard on my wife, that

I could fall in love so much. I kept so many things from her. I feel bad bout all that. But I suppose I got this talent. For loving. You want another?"

I did.

"Where's your wife? Are you divorced?"

He was fixing me my drink. "We don't believe in all of that."

"I've never seen her."

"She's dead."

He sat down again, handed me my drink.

He looked a bit jealously at his dog in my lap. Then he grimaced like he tasted something bad.

"She died there." And he pointed without looking, near the TV. "I cared for her."

He was looking back at that black window again. Past his reflection. Webb was twitching in my lap like he was dreaming.

Walter's eyes, in the window, were wet. Was he crying?

"You've been in love before," he said, turning back to me, "I can tell."

Then when I didn't answer: "You got somebody now?"

I thought to explain to him about Elliot. To tell him about all those ghosts up there in Vermont. To mention how Elliot cheated on me because it was probably my fault. I wanted to touch his hand.

"You're nice. I like talking to you," he said.

"I've seen the angel, you know."

"Have you!" He laughed, then coughed into his fist terribly... He sat back on the couch, waiting.

"Three nights ago," I said.

"Three nights? Is that right?"

"On the side of the road. It was watching me."

Then, as if in confidence, he leaned in again:

"You know, I think I've seen her too."

The dog slithered out of my lap, onto the floor. It disappeared. The room was cold like a window had been opened.

"I've seen her many times, many nights, for many months now. Everyone sees her, walking through the woods, alone, at night."

He held out his hand to me. He was trying to open his fingers.

I let him kiss me. I don't know why. I was drunk. Not really. He tasted like gin. No one had wanted to kiss me in such a long time, I laughed all the way through.

"What's funny?" I shook my head as if to say, It's not your fault you're old.

When he touched my breast I stood.

"You're the angel!" he called out after me—"Don't you get it? Don't you see? You're the angel, baby!" as I walked down the trail from the house, stumbling in the dark on stones and leaves and dirt. I stepped in mud and thought of Dante. I lost both shoes and kept walking, barefoot. The dog was barking somewhere in the woods behind me. The light from Walter's house was like spears through the branches. I wondered if he'd follow me, if he were a pervert, a rapist. I could outrun him if I had to. I could kill him with my hands. It was sad! the way he talked about his wife. So sad! I was laughing through tears as I walked.

I turned on my light, but it was dead now.

The night was full of fog, no moon. I had a short walk home, I knew it now by feel. I had yet to climb the hill.

"You're the angel," he'd said to me. He'd held out his hand.

Headlights came soaring round the bend. Did I move toward it, or away? I felt it hit me. Crush through me like wind. It seemed to drive straight through me and then away.

When I got home my front door was open. I tried to turn on the lights in the house, but I couldn't. I walked all over. "You're the angel," he'd said to me.

Someone's here: I look in all the rooms. I hear nothing in my ears. I walk to the bedroom. There he is, waiting, beside my bed like a bridegroom. Like before in the woods except now he's in my house. He's not angry, or sad. Compassionate or disappointed. It's simply him, his presence, that makes me see that my clothes are torn, my flashlight's no longer in my hand, has been lost, thrown into the woods by the impact with the car. That I am wet now with blood. My arms and legs and head. That I have in fact stopped bleeding.

He holds his hand out to me: inside he holds that mysterious thing.

www.ingramcontent.com/pod-product-compliance
Lightning Source LLC
Chambersburg PA
CBHW030533270626
47155CB00024B/2804